The Killer Trees

David E. Manuel

Copyright © 2012 by David E. Manuel

All rights reserved

This is a work of fiction. All the characters and events portrayed in this book are either products of the author's imagination or are used fictitiously.

Cover design by David E. Manuel

Cover photograph by David E. Manuel

All statements of fact, opinion, or analysis expressed are those of the author and do not reflect the official positions or views of the CIA or any other U.S. Government agency. Nothing in the contents should be construed as asserting or implying U.S. Government authentication of information or Agency endorsement of the author's views. This material has been reviewed by the CIA to prevent disclosure of classified information.

ISBN-13: 978-1480266339
ISBN-10: 1480266337

The Killer Trees

Chapter I
Kindling

BEAUMONT, TEXAS is one hot, muggy, miserable town, even in November. I'd been there a week and was looking forward to being anyplace else. As far as I can tell, the whole Gulf Coast is just one long strip of refineries, chemical plants, and poisonous snakes. It's a tribute to human ingenuity that people have been able to carve out an existence in such an inhospitable place. Of course, it probably wasn't quite as inhospitable before they built the refineries and chemical plants. But the snakes have always been there.

Most people wouldn't be surprised that I'd been sent to the area by the Environmental Protection Agency. It might surprise them to know why, though. I wasn't there to make sure those refineries and chemical plants weren't spewing toxins into the ground water and atmosphere. There's about as much chance of a government agency stopping corporate pollution as there is of stopping the sun from daily turning Beaumont into one hot, muggy, miserable fucking place. Less, really. Corporate America has the resources to buy off enough elected officials to keep the government out of its hair: the sun doesn't have a lobby that I know of.

But even the deep pockets of big business in the USA aren't deep enough to buy off everyone. There's always somebody who wants to make trouble. Hell, there are even people who object to Christmas. You just can't please all the people, as they say. Although, I have to admit, I've always been a bit suspicious myself of guys who like to dress up in red suits so kids will sit in their lap.

I wasn't in Beaumont to fight pollution or save Christmas. My mission was more critical. I'd been dispatched to take care of a client who seemed to have a bug up his ass about what he described as the "despoiliance" of the water-moccasin infested swamplands surrounding Beaumont. At least, that's what he called it in the anonymous letters he kept mailing to every newspaper and posting to every environmental web forum he could find. He made the mistake of mailing several of them to the EPA. That got my department's attention.

Crackpots are usually harmless. Maybe one in a thousand might actually do something more than rant. People call in bomb scares to schools all the time. It's not like the police can run down every one. That's why they just sit around eating donuts until a bomb actually goes off in some school somewhere, then track down the perpetrator and throw him in jail. Most of the time, anyway.

But when you're talking about something important, like a refinery, something that generates millions of dollars and fuels the trucks and cars clogging America's highways, the government can't afford to sit on its hands and wait for the serious crackpots to act. We're paid to protect the environment, after all. At least, the important parts of the environment.

So I was in Beaumont tracking down a crackpot to determine if he was harmless or not. Well, actually, I was just there to kill him. The EPA doesn't like to take chances. But sometimes I take a personal interest in evaluating whether I'm eliminating a real threat or just putting another loony out of his misery. I've been in the business for a couple of years; best I can tell, maybe one out of four clients was an imminent threat, meaning I'm batting about .250. Hey, that's not all-star quality, but it's a respectable major-league average.

This client was easy to find and looked typically pathetic. It takes someone pretty dumb these days to believe letters and e-mails can truly be anonymous. Rudy Larson would have been just another redneck with stringy long hair lucky to graduate from high school and get a job unloading sacks of potting soil at Home Depot, except at some point he decided to become an environmentalist. There's a cell of these people in every town, kind of like the old days when communists were insinuating themselves into the USA, before Starbucks and WiFi turned the leftists on to lattes and Facebook. And Marx is no match for Oprah when it comes to influencing modern American teenagers. But there are always malcontents, and these days they tend to gravitate to tree-hugger groups. Not that Rudy was smart enough to understand environmental science. I suspect he was trying to impress some local woman who liked tofu and hemp clothing. It's not always the case that there's a woman responsible when a man goes bad, but it's pretty common.

Rudy wasn't just a harmless crackpot, though. I followed him for a few days—to his job at a local Jack in the Box (I guess Home Depot hadn't had any openings), to a community center where the Beaumont chapter of the South Texas Environmental Action Committee, all four of them, met—and wrote him off as a yokel. Then I let myself into the garage apartment behind his parent's house that he occupied, rent free of course.

Rudy Larson's apartment was packed with cartons of black powder, blasting caps, plumbing pipes, and a decent Black and Decker drill. Like everybody else these days, he had a computer connected to the Internet that he'd used to locate and print off instructions for making pipe bombs. That his impressive arsenal and Internet research into terrorism had not come to anyone's attention just underscored not only that he had lousy parents but also that the billions of dollars spent yearly on the Department of Homeland Security are wasted. Luckily for the taxpayers, Rudy was trying so hard to get noticed, he got noticed by me and my secret EPA program.

Lucky, too, that for the most part, terrorist wannabes aren't usually the brightest folk. Black powder is pretty volatile stuff. A couple of Rudy's cartons were sitting open. I spread a little of it around the messy work area where he had his bomb-making equipment sitting out in the open, then sprinkled some liberally on the threaded ends of all his pipe pieces. Galvanized metal heats up when friction is applied, especially the kind of friction you get when screwing on an end-cap. More than a few would-be pipe bombers have blown themselves up because they were a tad sloppy pouring the powder into the tube. I was just giving Rudy a leg up on being stupid.

I parked across the street from his parents' house where I had a nice view down the driveway to the garage. This particular evening he didn't get home until after eleven—probably pulled the evening shift taking burger orders. Admittedly, I was pursuing a long shot.

There was little reason to believe he'd do anything except go upstairs, pop open a brew, watch TV or surf the Internet for a half hour or so, and then hit the rack. I figured to give him a couple of hours before assuming he'd gone to sleep. The longer term plan was to watch him come and go for a couple of days. If he didn't blow himself up by then, I'd have to take more direct action.

Luck is generally with me, though, and it's a safe bet anyway that someone with Rudy's limited smarts wouldn't leave a terrorist toolkit lying about if he didn't like to tinker. After about fifteen minutes of waiting, I was rewarded by the telltale sound of a muffled but distinctively explosive THWUMP emanating from his apartment accompanied by a flash of light. Smoke poured out the kitchen exhaust pipe within half a minute, followed by a louder and brighter secondary explosion that blew out the glass in his front window. As I pulled away, flames were starting to shoot out where the window had been. People came running out of their houses, pointing to the now quite impressive bonfire that old garages tend to make when they get ignited. Certainly nobody paid any attention to me. If somebody had noticed my rented Chrysler Sebring pulling away, thought it curious I left my lights off, jotted down the license number and reported it--well, the police would have traced it to a rental agency in Houston and learned that it had been rented by an educational software salesman from Fort Worth named Grant Tombes. By the time anybody who cared figured out that Mr. Tombes had disappeared off the face of the earth, Richard Paladin would be back in his office near Union Station in Washington, DC.

Richard Paladin's me, of course. Sort of.

Not that I was worried about an extensive investigation into the death of Rudy Larson. Even the world's most incompetent arson inspector wouldn't be able to miss the remnants of Rudy's bomb-making laboratory. I doubt if Beaumont's finest would be allowed to put "dumb-fuckedness" down as an official cause of death, but they'd find something almost as descriptive. There's nothing cops like more than a case that closes as soon as it's opened.

I drove back to Houston early the next morning and caught a flight to Washington. After take-off, the plane banked over a collection of some fairly impressive chemical plants belching noxious emissions into the atmosphere. Looking down, I felt satisfied and, well, a little smug that the people sweating for a living below me had no idea that there was now one less loony-toon trying to take away their livelihood. It's a good feeling, knowing what you do does make a difference in this world.

I closed my eyes and contemplated ways I could pad my expense accounting. Making a difference is important. Making a decent living is even more important.

November typically brings a cold, wet, constant drizzle to Washington, and this year was no different. Slogging from the Fairfax Metro stop to my apartment was damp, dark, and frigid. I quite enjoyed it. Life should be a test of one's toughness, I say. And it made getting home to my tiny, moldy old rooms in one of Fairfax's few remaining World War II era apartment houses seem almost comforting. The place was empty, though, which still took some getting used to. Before the Beaumont job, I'd had a very entertaining two weeks mentoring a new hire into the program, a gorgeous former stripper named Yolanda who'd reciprocated my lessons about spotting a tail and working under assumed identities by showing me a few tricks of her own. She'd recently graduated to real work assigned by my boss, Frank. I had to admit, I missed the sex. But the constant companionship had been getting on my nerves. I prefer to work alone.

The solitary nature of my work continued to puzzle the other occupants of the old converted brownstone, halfway between Union Station and the Capitol Building, that housed my office and the offices of about a dozen other EPA employees. They were all paper-pushers of some sort, busily engaged in what they believed was the EPA's mission, fighting to keep America clean, verdant, and safe. Most of them spent their days toiling away in the office and their evenings watching television in the suburbs of the Washington metropolitan area. This at least allowed them the illusion that their efforts were having some effect. I travel a lot. It's pretty obvious to me that any tax money being spent on this aspect of the EPA's mission is a complete waste; my travels have convinced me to boil and filter drinking water whenever possible, for example. On the road, I usually just stick to beer. Breweries are about the cleanest industries I've come across.

Of course, those tax dollars aren't really wasted. Maintaining the illusion that the EPA is an environmental agency is important. It provides cover for people like me.

I slipped into the office at 9:45 on a Thursday morning. Usually I come and go pretty much unnoticed. My colleagues tend to stay in their offices most mornings, probably catching up on their newspaper reading or doing some Internet shopping. I have to walk right by the administrative assistant in the common area, of course, but she looks old enough to remember VJ day; most mornings she's sound asleep in her chair when I come in.

This day I ran right into Conrad Millpond getting himself a cup of coffee. Millpond had been with the EPA almost fifteen years. I still didn't know exactly what he did professionally for the agency; the previous administrative assistant told me once he was a chemist of some sort. He certainly didn't do lab work: there wasn't anything like a lab in our office area. Mostly he spent a large portion of every day doing laps around the Mall. Millpond was an avid runner.

"Paladin. Good to see you. Hadn't expected you to come in today." The administrative assistant almost jumped out of her chair, startled from her deep sleep. Millpond looked chagrined. My impression is that the office staff makes a sincere effort not to disturb her, probably afraid that a loud noise will shock her into cardiac arrest. He lowered his voice. "You missed my announcement last week."

"What, you get a promotion or something?" I try my best to miss every piece of news dealing with the rest of the office. The supervisor of this particular bastion of the Federal bureaucracy, a pudgy fellow named Tweegle, had staff meetings every Tuesday at nine-thirty. I hadn't attended one yet. It's not like I actually work for the guy.

"Oh, nothing like that. I meant my MCM time. Made it in under four hours."

It took me a moment. Government wonks love acronyms. There are so many of them, just figuring out what bureaucrats are saying to each other can be a real challenge. I'd worked in the office months, for example, before finding out that the constant carping about CRABs didn't mean my office-mates weren't practicing safe sex; they were upset that the Common Resource Allocation Budget had been cut, so they had to bring in their own coffee supplies. But I finally remembered Millpond saying something to me months ago about "training for the MCM"—Marine Corps Marathon.

"Congratulations. Anything under four hours is impressive." I doubted I could do it, as a matter of fact. Sure, I run. I like to do a ten-mile training run at least three times a week, usually as a warm-up to weight training. And I'm pretty fast in a sprint, too. I've never had to chase down a client, but I figure it can't hurt to be ready if the occasion ever arises. But I'm not looking to win any races, marathons or otherwise. I'm satisfied knowing I can take on the goons and thugs I run into in my line of work.

"Next year I'm hoping to beat three and a half hours."

"I'll be pulling for you, Conrad." I don't interact with my office colleagues often. When I do, I try to act sympathetic. Telling him I didn't give a shit if he ran in front of a bus during one of his training sessions would have been more honest, but it wouldn't have contributed much to my office cover. My office mates have been told I'm a 'chronic poor performer' assigned there while the EPA tries to figure out what to do with me.

"You should think about entering next year, Paladin. You look pretty fit. I'd give you some pointers on training. It's a real confidence booster."

"Hey, I'll give it some thought." Fat fucking chance. Yeah, I'm fit. And Millpond was doubtless in great shape and had a heart that would beat forever. But like most serious distance runners, he was skinny as shit and looked like he'd have to struggle to unscrew the top of a jar of peanut butter. I could have broken him in half like so much kindling. Not to mention, lacking confidence is not really an issue with me.

"Well, let me know if you're interested." He took his coffee and walked back into his office. I glanced over at the administrative assistant. She'd gone back to dreamland. The smile on her face and rapid eye movement told me she was well into it. Probably dreaming about Rudolph Valentino.

I slipped by silently into my office and opened the little two-drawer safe. I always check first for a computer disk with information on new clients—my outfit still uses the little 3 1/2 inch plastic ones that fit in the slot on the ancient stand-alone computer that somebody obviously pulled out of a dusty warehouse when I was hired. There wasn't one; not a good sign, because usually two or three had stacked up when I'd been out of the office for a week or more. That meant more than likely there was an unusual assignment coming my way. My new boss—not Tweegle, but my real boss, a guy I call Frank who's obviously been in the spook business for awhile but who has a bit too much bureaucrat in him for my liking—had a penchant for springing big jobs on me in person. I'd rather just get the information on disk and take care of the client without a lot of useless conversation. Government people love their meetings, though, and spooks get a special thrill meeting you in some lousy restaurant and whispering instructions. I suspect they get training that the personal touch keeps guys like me motivated and under control. Training for bureaucrats probably isn't much different than the training I'd had forced on me in the Army, full of useless crap and utter bullshit.

I plucked a new disk from the box in the safe to start writing up my report and expenses on the timely demise of Rudy Larson and noticed an envelope lying in the bottom drawer. Fresh envelopes show up in the safe routinely, too. They contain driver's licenses and credit cards for the aliases I need in the field. But those are always in the top drawer. This one was special. Someone had typed 'Richard' on the front in neat, small print.

Doubtless there was a note inside with instructions from Frank. Call me paranoid, but I'm sure a lot of people have had a few fingers blown off opening envelopes they were absolutely sure had a note from someone they know. I laid it on the desk, looked it over carefully, ran my hand slowly over the surface to see if I could feel anything lumpy or wiry inside, then took a pair of scissors and snipped off a corner of one end to take a peek. It contained a piece of paper. Not surprising, really, since the only other person with the combination to the safe was Frank's personal goon. Like I trust him.

I tore open the envelope and extracted the note. It was hand-printed in Frank's childish block letters. Either he never mastered hand-writing or, more likely, he thinks I'm not smart enough to read cursive. The note was short.

Casa Tapas, Annandale. Noon. Day after you get this.

That was pretty clear, I had to admit. It left me with one question, though. How would Frank know when I got the note? He didn't usually send his goon—the guy's name is Bruce, by the way, although I continue to think of him as Joe Clean—to check my safe every day. And I doubt he'd go to the trouble—or had a sufficient budget—to have a large team watching the airport for my return or surveying me on the street; I'd have noticed pretty fast if he had anyone tailing me. The obvious answer, of course, was that someone in the office, one of my EPA colleagues, was watching my comings and goings and keeping Frank informed. Spooks love keeping tabs on each other. I made a note to look for signs that one of my colleagues was showing more interest in me than normal. Millpond came to mind.

I got to the business at hand. If Frank was sending me off on a complicated job, I'd want to have my paperwork in order before I left. Getting over-reimbursed for my expenses is one of my priorities. Keeps the cash I've got stashed in my freezer growing. My momma always told me it's important to save for a rainy day: I doubt if she was thinking of the contingency that you have to lam it if your government suddenly decides its pool of licensed killers is an embarrassment.

The cold drizzle turned heavier Friday, making my hours-long exploration of the Northern Virginia area prior to my meeting a bone-chillingly soggy experience. Rain drives most pedestrians indoors, though, and that makes it pretty easy to spot a tail. I didn't. Sometimes bad weather gets me thinking I'm wasting time and effort looking for surveillance. I work for the government, after all. In a logical world, I wouldn't have to worry about cops or FBI agents following me since we're all on the same team ... theoretically. But

I'd been with the government long enough to know that turf wars between agencies are almost as deadly as the war against terrorists. And, of course, there was always the chance some terrorist outfit had gotten wind of me and was tracking my movements to take a shot at killing me. There are a lot of dangerous crazies out there, including the few jihadists that most Americans think are our most dangerous foes. If guys named Abdul were all I had to worry about, my life would be pretty simple.

I approached the restaurant on foot, having parked a few miles away. Usually I don't use my car when going to meet Frank, but Annandale is one of the least pedestrian friendly places in the world. Washington's train system doesn't service it at all, and trying to get there by bus on a rainy day risks getting stuck in traffic as accidents start to congest all the roads, Washington drivers being some of the worst in rain I've ever seen. I trust myself to dodge traffic better than a bus driver, and, like I said, I do the last hour or so on foot anyway. I avoid the area whenever possible, but Frank likes to "employ the entire operating theater," as he told me once. Mostly I think he's on a quest to find the cheapest, dirtiest restaurant in the region.

He might have found it this time. Casa Tapas was in a decrepit strip mall that had somehow been overlooked by the rampant development that has been turning Annandale and most of the Washington area into endless rows of McMansions, mega-townhomes, and cookie-cutter shopping complexes where Washingtonians can pay too much for a cup of coffee in between shopping for overpriced shoes, clothes, kitchen gadgets, and electronic appliances to fill up their McMansions and mega-townhomes. From what I read, this has all been financed by huge mortgages and mounting credit card debt. We'll be in for a world of hurt if anyone ever pops the credit balloon the country's sitting on. But that's not my problem.

This day my problem was finding a place to sit once I'd gone inside. Casa Tapas wasn't much to look at, but it was packed with *Latinos*. Maybe Frank had finally found a place with decent food. Not that he'd care. Frank just likes to eat. Quality's not an issue with him.

Waiting just inside the door at the hostess' station, I looked over an impressive array of framed photographs hanging on the wall. They were all pictures of the same short, swarthy-looking guy in combat fatigues showing off various US-issued assault rifles and other military ordinance. But the fatigues didn't look like any military dress I was familiar with. More like something you'd get at an Army surplus store.

"May I help you?" I looked down to find the swarthy little guy standing at the hostess' station. I made a bet with myself that this was the owner and that he'd relocated here after the right-wing junta he'd served in his youth had been sent packing in one of the interminable Central American civil wars of the 1980s. They should carve an addition to that 'huddled masses' script on the Statue of Liberty: *Contras Welcome!*

"Got a table for two? I'm meeting someone."

"There will be a short wait for a table. There is room at the bar if you want to wait."

"What do you figure is short?"

"Fifteen minutes? Perhaps twenty."

"That'll be fine."

"What name?" He had a pen poised over his reservation book. I noticed there were no names on the list. He probably knew most of his customers.

"Richard." I'd thought about getting cute, telling him 'Oliver North.' But Frank frowns on shenanigans during clandestine meetings. I brushed past him to take a seat at the bar.

The barmaid was a taller, sleeker edition of the owner, probably a daughter or niece or other relation. She was pretty. Any other time I might have hit on her just to see if it got a rise out of her old man. Frank frowns on that sort of thing too, though.

"May I get you something to drink while you wait? A margarita?"

"How about a beer? Got any Mexican beer?"

"We are Salvadorans."

"Okay. Got any Mexican beer?"

"We have a Salvadoran beer. It is quite good."

"Sure. I'll have one of those." Every country seems to have a beer the expatriates are proud of. I was in a Texas-style barbecue place in Ohio once that made a big deal about having something called Lone Star. I typically enjoy a good, cheap blue-collar brew, but that stuff tasted like horse piss. Still, when in Rome . . .

The bottle of *Pilsener* she brought me wasn't half bad. She'd shoved a lime wedge into the top of the bottle. I had to admit, the combination of beer and bitter citrus was good. I wouldn't be making a habit of it, though. The rubes I grew up with in North Carolina wouldn't be caught dead shoving a lime wedge into a can of Bud.

Bruce followed me in exactly ten minutes after I'd arrived. He'd been waiting outside, watching I guess for signs of hostile Indians or Sandinistas. Frank always tells me he brings Bruce along to provide security. Anyway, he sends Bruce in to make sure the coast is clear before putting in an appearance himself. Who knows, maybe Frank pissed off a short-order cook or waitress once and he's afraid of running into them. More likely he's just been playing spy games so long he doesn't know how to be normal.

Bruce obviously had the same conversation with the swarthy ex-counterrevolutionary I'd had. I saw the guy jot down his name. Then Bruce walked over to the bar and sat down on the stool beside mine. This was a first.

"I told Frank places like this are usually pretty busy at noon." He sounded irritated.

"It's a booming business, feeding the dispossessed armies of CIA-sponsored ex-Latin-American dictators."

"You noticed the photos, too. Guess this guy fought with Pancho Villa or something."

The barmaid was back. "May I get you something to drink while you wait . . ."

"Got any Mexican beers?"

This time I noticed her roll her eyes. I'm betting she got that question a lot. "We are Salvadorans."

"Get him one of these *Pilseners*, hon. They're good." She shot us both a glare and left.

"Gee, she's kinda touchy."

"Hell, Bruce. How would you like it if everybody just assumed you're from Missouri 'cause you've got a red neck?"

He glared at me. We're not really friends. "I am from Missouri."

"Oops. Sorry about that." Today was not going to be the day I started developing a warm and fuzzy relationship with him. "We may be waiting awhile. Want to give Frank the all-clear signal so he can join us at the bar?"

"Let him stand out in the rain." The barmaid brought his beer. He took a long swig.

"You don't seem to be your normal, chipper self today, Bruce."

"Guess I don't like November weather in Washington."

We sat drinking and not talking for ten minutes. Whatever was bugging him, I decided to let it fester in silence.

"I have a table for you, sir." The owner seemed to appear out of nowhere. He'd probably had plenty of practice sneaking up on people in the jungles of El Salvador. "You two are together?"

"No." Bruce said it pretty adamantly. If I were the sensitive type, my feelings might have been hurt. "In fact, I'll just eat at the bar, if that's okay."

"Certainly, sir."

"I think I left my lights on. Be right back." Bruce hopped off the stool and headed out the door. Jose Contra looked alarmed, like Bruce was walking the tab. I got in his way just as he was starting to bolt out the door after him.

"Whoa, there. No need to get excited. I'm sure he's coming back."

"But he said he does not know you." He was looking real suspicious by this point. I couldn't tell him Bruce was just going out to signal our spook boss to come on in. But I couldn't let him try to run Bruce down, either. Given the mood my colleague had been displaying, I figured there was a good chance he'd snap the little Salvadoran's neck.

"I'm a pretty good judge of character. He seems like the honest type. If I'm wrong, put his beer on my tab."

"You are sure you two are not together?"

"Never seen him before. Honest. I'd just hate to witness a misunderstanding over a single beer."

Just at that moment Bruce came back, returning to his stool while the owner glared. Jose Contra obviously had a pretty short fuse. Frank's policy of never meeting at the same restaurant twice was looking pretty smart.

"You said you had a table for me?"

"Yes. This way." He kept his eye on Bruce while he walked me to a rickety wooden table in a corner. "Enjoy your lunch, *senor*."

"Grass-yas." That's all the Spanish I know.

Frank came in five minutes later, spied me in the corner, waved off the owner trying to intercept him at the hostess' stand and came right over, oblivious to the dagger eyes the guy was shooting his way. One thing was certain; everybody in this place was going to remember us vividly. This was beginning to shape up to be the worst clandestine meeting in history.

"Glad you could make it, Paladin. Hope you are well."

"I'm just swell, Frank, and I'll be even better if we get out of here without getting knifed by a gang of Bay of Pigs veterans."

"Whatever are you talking about?" He'd settled in and was perusing the menu. Frank has to know food is on the way before he can focus on anything else.

"Your goon has managed to piss off Jose Contra over there, and I think he's decided the only three *gringos* in the place are in cahoots."

"Jose who? You know that fellow?"

"No, Frank. I'm being sarcastic. That short guy over there is the owner."

"His name's Jose? You introduced yourself?"

"Again, I'm being sarcastic. Jose Contra, get it?"

"He was with the Contras? I thought this was a Mexican restaurant."

"It's Salvadoran."

"Oh." He went back to the menu, then looked up. "The Contras were Nicaraguan."

"Never mind, Frank. Just try not to attract any more attention."

The swarthy Salvadoran came over to take Frank's drink order, still looking pretty unhappy. I short-circuited further questions about Mexican beers, pointed to the bottle of *Pilsener* in front of me. "Two more of these." He headed back to the bar.

"Something bothering you today, Paladin?" Frank looked slightly alarmed. I guess the thought of a professional killer developing emotional problems disturbed him.

"No, Frank. It's your boy Bruce. He's acting erratic."

"Oh." He glanced over at the bar. Bruce was staring into his bottle of beer. Very unprofessional. "I think he's having problems at home. Don't ever get married. Wives are a real pain in the ass, especially in our line of work."

"I'll keep that in mind." I wondered if Frank had ever considered the possibility that wives married to husbands who are always out playing spy games might have a few legitimate gripes of their own. But I wasn't in any position to lecture. I had an ex-wife bouncing around somewhere. She'd walked out on me ten years earlier, and it wasn't because she objected to my line of work. Her objection at the time had been that I didn't have a job and didn't seem inspired to get one. I've matured some since then.

Frank was back to perusing the menu, looking concerned. "Don't they have an enchilada platter? I don't see any tacos, either."

The owner had brought our beers just in time to hear Frank's complaint. "The menu is all Salvadoran dishes. No enchiladas or tacos."

"Do you have something like a taco?"

Now the owner rolled his eyes. "*Carne Asada* comes on a tortilla. You want the platter?"

"Sure, I guess." Frank sounded hesitant. The owner turned his attention to me. His glare could have melted butter.

"*Bistec encebollado*." I know nothing about Salvadoran food. I just picked something off the menu.

"Rice and beans?"

"Sure."

Frank took a swig of his *Pilsener*. "Is this a Mexican beer? It's not bad."

So much for my efforts. The owner spun around and stalked off. I don't know Spanish for "spit in the *gringos'* food," but I'm betting that's what he said to the chef.

"Christ, Paladin, what is it about you and restaurants? Try not to antagonize the guy any more than you already have." Frank was even more oblivious than usual. I decided to let the matter drop.

"Okay, Frank, obviously you've got another off-the-wall assignment for me. I assume that's why I found your little note instead of new client information when I got back. Unless we've run out of clients."

"Not likely. How was Beaumont, by the way?"

"Hot and miserable."

"I checked the local news. Was it really necessary to burn down half a block?"

That took me by surprise. "If more than one garage burned down, blame the city for having an incompetent fire department."

"I'm not blaming you. That's what they get for letting someone set up a bomb-making factory in their neighborhood. I'm assuming, of course, that you didn't just get lucky by the guy blowing himself up while you twiddled your thumbs."

"He'd have gotten around to it eventually. I expedited the process."

"Anyway, nice work."

"Thanks." Alarms were going off in my head. Compliments from Frank could only mean I was going to get a doozy for my next job. "I'll sleep better tonight, knowing you're pleased."

"Always with the sarcasm. There's just no point being nice to you." He went quiet while the owner brought our food. Frank's *carne asada* and my *bistec encebollado* looked almost identical, strips of beef grilled in peppers served on a tortilla. Frank picked up his knife and fork and sat staring at the plate for a moment, like he was having trouble figuring out how to approach eating it.

"Frank." He looked up at me. I folded the tortilla on my plate around the meat and peppers, picked it up and took a bite. "Like this."

"Oh, I see." He followed suit, took a big bite, and smiled. "Hey, this is pretty good. Better than a taco."

"You might want to keep that compliment to yourself. In case you missed it, they're kinda sensitive about being compared to Mexicans." No big surprise that Frank liked his lunch. But I had to admit, mine was damned tasty. This place would be worth coming back to, as long as I waited long enough that the owner didn't remember me and my idiot companions. But Jose Contra didn't look like the kind of guy who forgets a face.

"So I have a somewhat unusual assignment I'd like you to take."

"What a surprise."

"How much do you know about forestry?" Typically, he took a big bite before dropping his off-the-wall question.

"Forestry?"

"Yes. The study and management of forests." He spit out a significant morsel of beef when he said 'forests.' I've got a strong stomach. Lunching with Frank, it's a necessity.

"I know forests are made of trees and lots of people can't see them. The forests, that is. For the trees."

He ignored me. "The logging division of the Santomo Corporation has been having problems with a new leasehold on a stretch of national forest in Oregon."

"Okay. I'll go kill the CEO of Santomo. Shouldn't be a problem."

"What?" He looked around, alarmed. "Are you crazy, blurting something like that out in a public restaurant?"

"Gee, sorry, Frank. Guess I got carried away."

"Besides, that's not your assignment."

"Really? Too bad. And here I thought you were sending me to stop somebody cutting down another forest."

He looked pretty worried for a minute. Then it finally hit him I was joking. "Try to be serious, Paladin."

"I will, as soon as you start making sense and stop talking about logging companies and forests. What the fuck has that got to do with us? Last time I checked, the national forests were the responsibility of the Department of Agriculture."

"They are. But Ag isn't really set up to manage a clandestine operation."

"They don't have a goon squad? What's the government coming to?"

He raised an eyebrow. I think he was trying to decide if I wanted him to answer my questions. Finally he decided to ignore them. "The CEO of Santomo is a personal friend of the President."

"I assume by that you mean he's a big campaign donor."

"Exactly. He asked the President to take care of their problem. Quietly."

"Then what's the big deal?" Frank had a way of not getting to the point that drove me nuts sometimes. "So there are some tree-huggers blocking logging roads or something and you want me to take care of them. Just tell me who and where. But I'm still not sure why Agriculture needs us to do their dirty work."

"It's not that simple." He swallowed his food and took a swig of beer. At least I'd be spared the barrage of food spittle momentarily. "Three officers of the logging company have been killed in the last three months, and the chief finance officer for the subsidiary committed suicide two weeks ago."

"Three killed?" Well, at least his story was getting interesting. "You mean murdered?"

"One died in a car crash, one was killed by a falling branch from a tree, and the most recent one got lost hiking around the leasehold and died of hypothermia. Actually, not the most recent. That was the suicide."

"How'd the guy kill himself? Sleeping pills? Slit wrists?"

"Seems he hanged himself. Left a suicide note saying he felt guilty about all the trees Santomo has destroyed."

Obviously the deaths weren't accidents and a suicide. Otherwise, Frank wouldn't be telling to me about them. "So you've got yourself a very clever serial killer who doesn't like logging companies and knows how to cover his tracks. Why not let the local authorities investigate? Or bring in the FBI? Isn't that what they do for a living?"

"Santomo would like to get started cutting down some trees. A high-profile investigation of some eco-loony trying to stop them by killing their employees won't help them do that."

"Right. Not to mention getting a lot of press and the attention of other people who think forests are a good thing. I'm guessing this lease has been done on the quiet."

"It's classified, as a matter of fact. Hasn't leaked to the press at all." He smiled smugly. Spies love secrets, especially secrets they get to share with other spies at clandestine meetings.

"I didn't know you could classify leasing national forests to logging companies."

"Still haven't read the Patriot Act, I see."

"Christ, it covers this sort of thing? I had no idea."

"It's in the classified part of the bill, of course."

"Of course." In my experience, most government secrets have little to do with protecting the country and a lot to do with making sure the public doesn't get enraged about what its government really does.

"Anyway, we've arranged a cover job for you as a forest ranger. That's why I wanted to know if you've ever read up on forestry."

"Great. So I get to wear a stupid hat and tell kids about Smokey the Bear."

"You also get to carry a gun. It's a federal law enforcement position, you know."

"Okay. I'll try to act stupid as well as look it."

"You're to report next week to the ranger station in Ogloskie, Oregon. Right now there's one ranger there."

"So I get a partner again." I didn't consider that good news. "Hopefully he won't be as big an idiot as the last one. Is he a goon, too?"

"She's really a forest ranger. She knows nothing about any of this. She's been told you're a real forest ranger, too."

"What reason was she given for an extra ranger suddenly being assigned?"

"Actually, she's been requesting an additional ranger for years. The service is simply informing her that her request has finally been granted. She'll be happy to have a subordinate, so I doubt she'll question it." Maybe he really believed that.

"Subordinate? This job just keeps getting better. And how do you expect me to do my job with Ranger Rita ordering me around?"

"Oh, you'll find a way, Paladin. You always do."

"I guess the last piece of bad news you have is that you haven't got a clue who the client is."

"Afraid not. I'm relying on you to figure that out."

"You know, we've had this conversation before. Do I really need to remind you that I'm not a detective?"

"You don't give yourself enough credit." He downed his last morsel. At least I wouldn't get any more food particles on my shirt. "And this job should be easy. You just need to find whoever it is that shares your unique skill for arranging fatal accidents."

"Apparently it's not such a unique skill." I'd only eaten about half my lunch. It was good, but I'd lost my appetite.

"One more thing."

"I can't wait."

"Whoever is killing Santomo employees, they're obviously pretty adept at this sort of work. I wouldn't be surprised if they'd had some training somewhere."

"You think someone like me has gone rogue, started to take the EPA's credo seriously?"

"It's a possibility." He really did look concerned. I wondered what he wasn't telling me. "Just be careful."

"I'll try not to get killed. I know how embarrassing that would be for you."

"The director has assured the President personally that we'll take care of this. Failure is not an option. The President takes a very dim view of failure."

"Funny. Thought he'd have gotten accustomed to it by now, with all the experience he's racked up."

"Very amusing. I suggest you keep your politics to yourself and concentrate on the job at hand."

"I don't have any politics, Frank."

He gave me a look, like he was noticing something about me for the first time. "I guess that's right, isn't it, Paladin. That's the closest thing to a political comment I've ever heard you make. Did you even vote in the last election?"

"Sure I did."

"Who for?"

"Bo Bice. He lost to Carrie Underwood."

He shook his head. "That's crap, too. Even if you watched TV, you wouldn't watch *American Idol.*"

"You got someone reporting on me from home as well as from my office?"

He stared for a minute, like he was considering saying something. Then he signaled for the check. "Speaking of your office, if you stop by, you'll find Bruce has left all the information you'll need in your safe. If you catch a flight Sunday, you can report to your new job Monday morning."

"You said I get to carry a gun. Is there a permit in the files Bruce left to let me carry it on a plane?"

"There's an address in Portland. Take a cab there from the airport. They'll issue you everything you need."

"Convenient."

"We had a few days to get things set up while you were screwing off in Texas."

The owner brought the check and stood over it while Frank counted out some bills from his wallet. He didn't leave much of a tip. Jose or whatever his name was picked up the cash, snorted, and stormed off.

"One more thing, Frank. What if I draw a blank on this one or run into complications?"

"Then you'll handle them like always." He'd picked up a toothpick from a little jar on the table and started cleaning his teeth. Frank's lousy table manners were plumbing new depths. "But if you feel the need to contact me, I've included instructions in the information packet. It's an e-mail address for an encrypted server. Just find a computer, log on and leave a message in draft. Somebody will check it periodically at this end."

"Great. I'm sure there are dozens of Internet cafes in Ogloskie."

"Ranger stations have computers these days. Just make sure your new boss isn't looking over your shoulder."

"I'll try to be careful." I noticed there were now several people waiting at the bar and the hostess' station for tables. The place was still packed. Out of the corner of my eye I could see the owner glaring at us, wondering how much longer we were going to occupy our seats now that we'd paid. "I think I'll leave first today, Frank. Give me fifteen minutes, if you don't mind."

"Of course. Glad to see you're finally taking tradecraft seriously, Paladin."

"You're my model." I got up and walked out, hoping fifteen minutes was long enough for the owner's patience to run out. With any luck, he had enough of the old guard sitting in the restaurant to get a gang together and throw Frank and Bruce out on their ears.

The files I retrieved from my safe were pretty thick. I spent a rainy Saturday in my apartment reading about the Santomo Corporation and its logging division, Conifer Company. Conifer supplied raw product to a host of other Santomo subsidiaries that made everything from two-by-fours to paper. Apparently it's pretty hard to get through the day without consuming something produced by Santomo. There was even a little brochure titled *Going Green with Santomo* that touted the company's environmental record. I recognize bullshit when I see it. I'm sure dollars were the only "green" Santomo was concerned about. That was pretty obvious from the business plan the corporation had filed with Agriculture for the leasehold on the half-million acre tract of the Oquala National Forest that was currently such a headache. Wading through pages of legal jargon and high-minded sounding euphemisms, even I was able to tell that Santomo's management planned to cut every mature tree they could find.

First, they needed me to stop whoever was culling Conifer Company's managers. There were files on the four deaths. Frank's summary at Casa Tapas hadn't done the killer justice; he was an artist. Conifer's operations manager, Fritz Langford, had been driving about 90 mph on the one two-lane road into the Oquala when he'd lost control of his car and crashed into a tree. Two weeks later, Langford's boss, Conifer's Vice-President for Forest Industry, was standing under the very tree Langford had collided with—I was betting Ed Walker was suspicious and decided to have a look at the accident scene personally—when a large branch that had apparently been weakened by the crash fell on him, snapping his neck. Things quieted down for a month after that, until Garth Riefenthal, Conifer's senior forestry expert, decided to do a survey of the Oquala and categorize just how much money his company was going to make. A search of the woods after he didn't come back found him sitting peacefully—under a tree, of course—stark naked and stone dead. The local coroner waxed eloquent in his report about how dangerous it can be in Oregon's forests if you get lost—apparently the last stages of hypothermia often lead people to do erratic things, like take off all their clothes. Needless to say, all three deaths had been listed as accidental. I figure the motto of most local law enforcement agencies should be "Why look for trouble?"

Then came the suicide. Bob Roper hadn't given anyone the impression he was depressed before his wife got up and found him hanging peacefully with a suicide note in the pocket of his pajama top. She didn't find him hanging in the basement or attic, either. Again, the coroner concluded that he'd gotten up in the middle of the night and walked out into his back yard in a pricey suburb of Portland where he made himself a noose and hanged himself from . . . wait for it . . . a tree.

When I tracked down this client, I hoped I'd get a chance to ask him a few questions before getting rid of him. I was damned curious how he'd pulled off these four murders, especially the hypothermia one. I'm good at what I do, but this guy was a fucking impresario.

Chapter II
Welcome to the Web-foot State

IT WAS RAINING IN PORTLAND when I arrived. I get the impression it's always raining in Portland. DC had been cold and wet when I left, but this felt different, rawer. The wind off the Pacific was a steady reminder that you'd reached the edge of the continent and there was nothing but cold, blue ocean waiting for you out there. I thought about Riefenthal shivering in the cold until his mind went. The American Northwest is no place for weekend car campers. Or even experienced backpackers, apparently. Riefenthal's file indicated he was an accomplished backwoodsman; he'd taken off one summer in college and traversed Tibet on foot. Before the Oquala, I doubt he'd been lost in the woods for even a brief moment of his life.

The address Frank had provided was a motel on the outskirts of town. I had a room number and a series of paroles—stupid sounding phrases for me and my contact to repeat so we'd know we were really who we were supposed to be. Usually they read like something a very bored spook who's been deskbound for too long came up with to amuse himself. I dragged my duffle up the stairs to 217 and rapped on the door.

"Yeah?" I wondered if whoever was inside had a gun trained on the door. As silly as all this spy-craft can be, if it had been me in there, I'd have been aiming something that could punch out the door and through the visitor on the other side, like a pump-action twelve gauge with double-ought buckshot.

"I'm here to fix your plumbing."

"Plumbing ain't broke. TV's not working, though."

"Let me in and I'll take a look."

"You repair TVs, too?"

"I'm a Jack of all trades."

The door opened, revealing a wiry guy about my age in jeans and a flannel shirt. "Where do they come up with this crap? 'Jack of all trades,' for Christ's sake."

"Probably figure no one else uses the phrase anymore."

"Great, so it's either the agent I'm expecting or a complete dork."

"Yeah." I winced when he said 'agent.' I really don't think of myself as a spy.

"Anyway, welcome to Oregon. Hope you like mud." A .45 automatic was sitting on the nightstand by the bed. I'd been right about him pointing a gun at the door. Other than that and a little suitcase sitting open next to the TV, the room was empty.

"You're supposed to have some gear for me."

"It's in one of those storage-rentals about a mile from here. I've been here five days waiting. What the hell took you so long?"

"I had other business to attend to. Sorry if you've been bored."

"I don't like sitting in a motel every day for almost a week waiting for somebody to show up."

"Maybe you should consider another line of work. Wal-Mart's usually looking for guys to unload trucks."

"Funny." He grabbed a rain jacket from the back of a chair, picked up the .45 and put it in one of the pockets. "Frank said you're a real comedian. Bring your duffle. You won't be coming back here."

I followed him to a beat-up old Jeep Cherokee in the parking lot. It had California plates. He wasn't a local. "So you talked to Frank about this job?"

"I talked to him about meeting you and showing you where your stuff is stashed. I don't even know what's in the storage locker. A guy driving a flat-bed showed up five days ago and gave me the address and a key. The locker rental's paid up for a month. You just pick the stuff up and drop the key in the slot by the office on your way out."

"Too bad. Guess we won't get the chance to become best buds, swap stories about working for the government."

"What are you talking about?" We were bouncing along in his Jeep now, splashing through big puddles on the road. The road wasn't all that bad, but the suspension on his Jeep was crap. I grabbed the handrail to hold on. "I don't work for the government."

"Oh. Who do you work for?"

"Western Express. Delivery company."

"I see." I was surprised Frank would trust even a small part of this kind of job to a private company. And the guy had mentioned Frank like he knew him pretty well. "Frank does a lot of business with you, I guess."

"You been smoking something? Frank's the chief operating officer of the company."

"Sure. I was just jerking your chain." So the EPA was running a front company, a delivery service. That must come in handy, I realized. And my boss Frank was posing as a senior company executive. Interesting. Interesting, too, that the employees had been kept in the dark who they really worked for. Of course, it would have made sense for Frank to let me know what

I was walking into so I wouldn't say something stupid about working for the government. But I get the impression that Frank likes to set me up to look stupid. "So do you get a lot of jobs like this, arranging deliveries of stuff you don't ever see to people you've never met?"

"Sure. That's mostly what we do."

"The cloak and dagger stuff doesn't make you curious?"

"Nope. I mean, it's obvious this company is a front for the CIA or the Mafia or something. But as long as I get paid, they can deliver whatever they want to whoever they want."

"Still, I'd think you'd be a little curious about a job that requires you to carry a gun."

"I'm not required to carry a gun."

"What's that in your pocket?"

"I got a right to defend myself. It's in the Constitution."

"Okay." He had a point. And if the EPA wanted to contract out some of its western operations to a few militant gun-toters; well, the government's all about diversity in hiring these days.

"You can find your own way from here." He'd pulled up in front of a fenced-in collection of storage vaults with garage doors. The sign in front read *U-Lock-It-Up*. Imagination is not a requirement in the storage business, I guess. "Here's your key. It's number 371B."

"You're sure it's not gonna explode when I open it?"

"Like I said, I just arrange pick-up. Whatever's in there ain't my concern."

"Got it." I took the key, grabbed my duffel and went searching for 371B. Fortunately there was a map just inside the gate. I found it without much trouble; 371B was a full-size garage. I let myself in.

Inside was a Ford F-150 pickup with a fairly large shipping trunk sitting in the bed. I looked inside the cab; keys were in the ignition, and a thick legal-size envelope was lying on the seat. I picked it up and ripped it open without bothering with my usual inspection to make sure it wasn't explosive—if somebody wanted to go to this much trouble to blow me up, more power to them.

It was a complete dossier on Clayton Everett Stillbridge, 10-year veteran of the USDA Forest Service. Paper-clipped to the dossier were a driver's license and USDA ID card, both sporting my picture. There was a forest ranger's badge, too.

I pulled the set of keys out of the ignition and found one that looked like it would open the shipping trunk. I could have waited until I'd gotten to Ogloskie and checked into a motel somewhere to look inside, but curiosity got the better of me. I hopped up into the bed and opened it. Right on top was one of those stupid Ranger hats with the wide brim. I put it on; a perfect fit. Looking at my reflection in the rear windshield, I could tell I looked about as idiotic as I'd expected.

"Hi, kids. I'm Ranger Clayton." A little practice couldn't hurt. I adjusted the hat to a nice jaunty angle. "Remember, you can start forest fires just by playing with matches. Try it sometime."

I dug around a little more in the trunk and came up with a large revolver in a nice leather holster attached to a Sam Brown belt. I unholstered it. It was an impressive piece, a Ruger Super Redhawk .44 magnum with a 7.5 inch barrel. I hefted it. It had a nice balance.

"Hi, kids. I'm Ranger Clayton. I can blow a really big hole all the way through you if you don't listen to Smokey the Bear."

The one motel in Ogloskie looked like the Bates Motel from *Psycho*. That didn't worry me too much. If a lunatic dressed as his mother decided to come after me in the shower with a knife, he was going to be in for a rude shock. Anyway, the manager didn't look anything like Norman Bates. After I'd rung the little bell at the desk for maybe fifteen minutes, a large, muscled black guy who looked to be in his late fifties appeared. He sized me up, obviously wondering what the hell I was doing ringing his bell after ten on a rainy Sunday night.

"Man, you must be as lost as it gets."

"What makes you say that?"

"Because you're about as far from anyplace as you can be. You got any idea where you are?"

"Well, if this isn't Ogloskie, then I guess I am lost."

Now he looked surprised. "You're in Ogloskie, all right."

"So I'm not lost."

"Not if Ogloskie's where you want to be." He grinned. "But you must be a lost soul to come looking for this place."

"I was hoping to get a room."

"Sure. Let me check." He looked up at the rack of keys on the wall. A key was hanging from every hook. "Seems to me we have a few rooms available. You just passing through or will you be with us for a few days?"

"Got a job here. Don't know where I'll be staying. I might need the room for a few days."

"A job in Ogloskie?"

"Yeah. You sound surprised."

"There are exactly three businesses in Ogloskie. There's a general store, a restaurant, and this place. I ain't hired anyone in ages, and you don't look like a short-order cook or a store clerk."

"Forest ranger."

"Forest ranger?" He laughed. "Hell, that's right. Ruby said they might be sending somebody new."

"Ruby?"

"Yeah. Ruby Dockerty." He gave me a funny look. "Ranger Ruby, your new boss."

"Oh, yeah. It's been a long drive. I'm tired." Her file was sitting in the envelope in the cab of the F-150. I'd planned to read it after I got checked in. "I'd like to get some sleep, get an early start finding the ranger station tomorrow."

"You won't have to look very hard. Just stay on the road you came in on straight through town—all twelve buildings—and you'll find it at the end of the pavement where the Oquala forest begins."

"Thanks." I picked up the key he'd removed from the rack and dropped on the counter. He hadn't asked me to sign in or give him a credit card. I guess he figured he could find me if he needed me to pay the bill. "Hope you don't mind my asking, but how do you stay in business?"

"Don't mind at all. I got low overhead; own the place outright. And in the summer there's usually a fairly steady stream of hikers looking to see the Oquala. After they've camped out for a few days, most of them like to take a shower and spend the night in a bed."

"Makes sense. There something special about the Oquala forest that attracts more hikers than other national forests?"

"Yup." He grinned again. "It's haunted."
"I see."
"Nah, but you will." He turned and headed back out the door to wherever he'd come from. I hadn't even caught his name. In fact, I realized, I could have just come in, grabbed a key, and made myself at home. Maybe that's the way he preferred to do business.

I drove the pickup along the row of rooms to number 23, the very last one. It was one of those single story motels laid out in an L; my room had a great view of the parking lot and the road in front of the place. Inside was clean; bed, bathroom, a small armchair, a lamp. There was no TV. I wondered if they'd heard of TV out here. Lifting the curtain on the window in the back revealed pitch black. I dragged in my stuff, turned on the lamp, and sat down in the chair with Ruby Dockerty's file. Time to figure out who I was going to be pretending to work for.

Ranger Ruby had been in the Forest Service a remarkable twenty years, having joined right after she graduated from the University of Wyoming with a degree in forestry. She was forty-three years old and had been manning—womanning? personning?—the Oquala station for the last five. I wondered if she'd committed some transgression that had gotten her exiled to a singleton station in the middle of nowhere. There was no mention of anything negative in her file. There weren't many positives, either. It was pretty much a bare summary. The bogus Clayton Stillbridge file was much more detailed. I knew nothing about USDA personnel records. Apparently, neither did whoever pulled together my cover. I got the funny feeling that my overly-detailed file was going to mark me as a plant.

Maybe I wouldn't be around long enough to worry about it. The way the motel owner described it, Ogloskie was one of the least populated places on Earth. Not having to cull through a long list of suspects would make finding the client pretty easy, I figured.

I'd planned to go through the Stillbridge file before hitting the rack, but I was tired. There'd be time to look at it later. Or not. I was there to kill somebody, not try to win an Oscar.

Lying in the dark before I dropped off, I thought about the motel owner's comment that the Oquala was haunted. Hopefully my client wouldn't turn out to be a ghost. I've heard you can't kill a ghost.

Monday morning I got up early, donned my brand new ranger uniform—it would have been smarter for Frank to give me one with a little wear on it—hooked on my Sam Brown with the .44, plopped the stupid hat on my head and headed out the door at six-thirty. I wanted to be early, have a chance to look around the place where I'd be hanging the idiot hat before having to confront the woman who thought she was my new boss.

Finding the station was as easy as the motel-owner had suggested; I pulled around back and parked next to a dusty green Chevy Blazer with a Forest Service emblem on the side. Not seeing another personal vehicle, I figured I'd succeeded in arriving before Ranger Ruby. I climbed out of my Ford to explore a bit.

"Glad to see they sent someone else who likes to get an early start." It was a woman's voice booming from the station window. Ranger Ruby obviously liked to get up at the crack of dawn. So I'd have to pretend to be a morning person for awhile. "Come on in. I got a pot of coffee going."

I stepped onto the landing and through the screen door into the cabin. The sun was trying to break through the clouds, but I could tell it was going to lose that battle. It looked to be a cold, wet day. Coffee couldn't hurt.

"Ranger Dockerty? Pleased to meet you. Clayton Stillbridge." I stuck out my hand. She gripped it firmly while she gave me the once-over. I studied her, too. She was attractive; brown hair with streaks of gray pulled back in a ponytail, healthy figure that bespoke plenty of exercise and filled her ranger uniform nicely, blue eyes that looked more stern than inviting.

"Welcome to Ogloskie. Mind if we dispense with the formalities? I prefer Ruby."

"Call me Clayton."

"You expecting trouble today, Clayton?" She glanced at the .44 in its holster.

"Never know what the situation is at a new post until you report. Besides, I didn't want to leave it at the motel."

"You staying at Wilson's place up the road?"

"Unless there are two motels in town, I guess I am."

She laughed. "Wilson's place is all there is. The service maintains a residence here. It's a duplex. I only take up half. The other side's yours if you want it."

"Great. The motel is pretty Spartan."

"The residence isn't much better, but it'll give you more space than the motel and a kitchen, too. You take anything in your coffee?" She produced a mug from a cupboard and poured.

"Black is fine."

"Just the way I like it. Why sugar-coat life, I say." She handed me the cup.

"Couldn't agree more." It was strong and bitter. Maybe we were kindred spirits.

"Pull up a chair and let's get to know each other a bit. Then I'll show you the town's restaurant. I assume you haven't had breakfast already."

"As a matter of fact, I haven't. I was hoping you'd steer me someplace good." There was a little wooden chair across from the one desk in the office. The .44 Redhawk felt a bit cumbersome. I unclasped the Sam Brown and set the rig on the desk.

"Like I said, there's not much choice around here. Closest town of any size is Prestonville, forty miles south on 18. They've got a couple of decent restaurants and a McDonald's." She sat in the chair behind the desk, eying the .44. "Damn, that's a big cannon you're lugging around."

"Eight-inch barrel makes it more accurate." Her interest in the piece Frank had sent was making me wonder if she one of the granola-munchers who think guns are the root of all evil. "Guess you don't find a sidearm all that necessary out here."

"Other than the occasional group of drunken lumberjacks, the only real worries around here are mountain lions and grizzlies. The Department prefers we don't kill the mountain lions. They get too close to populated areas, we're supposed to tranq 'em and move 'em back into the hinterland."

"Tranq?"

"Yeah. There's a tranquilizer gun in the gun cabinet over there." She pointed. I'd already noticed the cabinet with what I'd recognized as a dart gun next to a .30-.30 deer rifle.

"What about the grizzlies?"

"If possible, we're supposed to tranq them, too."

"Better have a pretty strong tranquilizer."

"In my experience, a grizzly that gets close to people is on a rampage. Nothing short of a bullet'll stop one then."

"That what the .30-30's for?"

"That popgun? That's just for show." She opened the top drawer of her desk, shuffled some papers aside, extracted a set of keys, unlocked the lower right drawer, and took out a revolver that I could see had a slightly bigger bore than my .44. She laid it gently on the desk in front of me, a big grin on her face. "That's for grizzlies."

I picked it up to have a closer look, impressed. It was a brand new Smith & Wesson 500. I'd read about them. S&W had only been manufacturing them for a couple of years. "The Department issued you a .50 caliber handgun?"

"Nah. I bought it all on my own, special-ordered it as soon as they came out."

"Well, it'll damn sure stop a grizzly. This thing could punch a hole through an armored Humvee." I sat it back down reverently.

"Okay, Clayton. Now that we've established my gun's bigger than yours, what do you say we get some breakfast?"

"Sounds like a great idea." I'd decided I liked Ruby Dockerty.

"I'll lock the artillery up in my drawer, unless you want to carry yours around all day."

"Happy to leave it here, if you don't think I'll be needing it."

She drove the Blazer hard, spitting gravel as she accelerated out of the parking lot. I found myself holding the handrail on the passenger side just like in the Jeep a day earlier. Four-wheel-drive makes some people pretty aggressive when they get behind the wheel, determined, I guess, to see just how far they can push things before skidding out of control. I had the feeling riding with her would be quite an experience once the first snows hit.

We made it into town without sideswiping any parked cars or flipping over, though. Actually, she seemed to know how to handle the Blazer pretty well, whipping into the parking lot of a large wooden building with smoke bellowing out of a stove-pipe and a sign out front that just said *Ogloskie's*.

"Here we are, Clayton. Finest restaurant in town." She jumped out and headed inside. I followed a pace behind, still self-conscious in my uniform. Inside the place was warm, rustic, and welcoming. The floor was unvarnished wood planking, as were the walls which were adorned with photographs that seemed mostly to document men with large-bore rifles next to dead trophy animals; grizzlies, stags, mountain lions. I figured they were all decades old, from the time Americans believed bringing civilization to the West meant killing off wildlife. There were maybe a dozen tables and chairs and a few stools at the counter. It had been a long time since I'd been in a small town that seemed content to stay that way.

Ruby went straight to a table. There were four other customers: the motel owner I now knew was named Wilson was digging into a platter piled with pancakes, fried eggs and bacon; a couple that looked to be in their late fifties sat in a corner sipping coffee, reading newspapers, and ignoring each other; a younger, scruffy, ponytailed guy in jeans and a flannel shirt was eating oatmeal at the counter. None of them paid us any attention. We'd been seated less than a minute when a barrel-chested man with a thick mane of blond hair came out of the kitchen carrying a coffee pot and two cups. He sat the cups in front of us and poured coffee without asking.

"Morning, Sven." Ruby smiled at him, but it was perfunctory. I'd been wondering if she had a beau in town. It pretty clearly wasn't Sven. "Meet my new partner, Clayton Stillbridge."

"Nice to meet you, Mr. Stillbridge. Welcome to Ogloskie." He didn't sound all that welcoming.

"It's a pleasure, Sven. And call me Clayton , please."

"Sven here is the owner." She winked. "Right now it looks like he's the waiter and chief bottle washer, too."

"I'm the cook, too, when Fred back there is sleeping one off."

"What happened to that waitress you had working for you?" I could tell Ruby was needling him for my benefit. She clearly knew the answer already.

"Young people these days ain't very reliable."

"Sven's waitress ran off with a lumberjack last week." She was enjoying herself, filling me in on local gossip. It was actually making me feel at home. Keeping my guard up around her was going to be a challenge. "She gave Sven a whole day's notice and asked for two week's severance."

"No great loss. She was a lousy waitress. Anyway, hiking season's over. Figure I'll wait 'til spring to hire somebody. What can I get you?"

"How's the oatmeal today?" She grinned again. I got the impression I was witnessing a daily routine.

"Same as always. Best bowl of oatmeal in Oregon."

The scruffy guy at the counter spun around on his stool. Obviously he'd been listening. "And I keep telling you, Sven, that oatmeal is supposed to be a sweet, creamy porridge with a somewhat neutral flavor to serve as a base for raisins or cinnamon or even maple syrup. And you keep serving this lumpy, bitter concoction that's chewy and sticks to my teeth."

"Then order somethin' else." Sven didn't even turn around to look at him. "Even better, go eat someplace else."

"You ever hear that the customer's always right?" Scruffy was back eating his bitter, chewy oatmeal as soon as he finished offering this piece of wisdom.

"Only from you." Sven turned his attention back to us. "You want oatmeal today, Ruby?"

"No, Sven." She was having trouble not laughing. "I'll have my usual."

"Eggs, toast, and bacon. Right. What about you?" He gave me a look that said I'd better keep any oatmeal comments to myself.

"I'll just have pancakes, fried eggs and bacon."

"Buckwheat, buttermilk, or blueberry?"

"Uh, buckwheat, I guess."

"How many eggs?"

"Two."

He raised an eyebrow. "You on a diet?"

"Okay, three then."

"How you want 'em cooked?"

"Like I said, fried."

"No shit." He was losing patience. "You want 'em over easy, sunny side up, turned into slabs of rubber?"

"I like the yolks runny."

"Okay. Fred should be able to handle that. Assuming the aspirin's kicked in by now." He turned and went back to the kitchen.

"Don't mind Sven. He's not a bad guy. Just hates dealing with customers."

"Not a recommendation for running a restaurant. He inherit the place or something?"

"He's owned the place as long as I've been here; moved here ten years ago. Told me he saw an ad for this place and bought it because he wanted to get out of Montana."

"I'm sure a lot of people have wanted to get away from there over the years. But most of them move to large cities."

"He said Montana was getting too crowded."

"Oh." That explained his lack of people skills. "Too bad. I was hoping he was descended from the founding Ogloskie family."

"Sorry to disappoint, but there were no founding Ogloskie's, either. Just a Russian named Vladimir Ogloskie who came here in the 1870s or something. Built a trading post and ran it for a few years. Oquala Indians hacked him into little pieces."

"What for? He sell them bad whiskey or something?"

"Ask Dewaldo. He's the expert on local history." She turned back to the scruffy guy. "Dewaldo, get over here and meet Ranger Stillbridge."

On command he picked up his oatmeal and coffee and joined us. I got a better look at him. He was wearing round wire-rim glasses that gave him a bookish appearance, but he was lean and tanned, too, like he spent most of his time outdoors. Rather than make him look like a hippie, the ponytail gave him a sort of Ninja air.

"Nice to meet you, Stillbridge."

"It's Clayton." It struck me that he didn't look up from his oatmeal, just ate it methodically. "Dewaldo. That's an unusual name."

"Tell me about it."

"Is it Dutch or something?"

"No idea. My mom apparently had a great uncle named Dewaldo and she just liked the name. Thought it made Davis a little less ordinary. That's my last name. Davis."

"So, Dewaldo, I'm curious. If the oatmeal here is so bad, why don't you eat something else?"

He looked up, pondering. I wondered if the question had never occurred to him. "Dunno. Been eatin' oatmeal every morning since I was a kid."

"I'll tell you right off, Clayton," Ruby interjected, "that you can give up trying to figure out Dewaldo."

"Don't know what you mean by that, Ruby." He'd gone back to his bowl.

"Anyway, Clayton was just wondering what the original Ogloskie did that pissed off the Oqualas."

"Oh." He put down his spoon, looked up at me like he was trying to gauge whether I was really interested. "There're a couple of theories."

"I'd love to hear them." I was being honest. I'm always interested in a good murder story.

"He was Russian orthodox. Not surprising, since he was Russian. According to some trappers who told the authorities in Salem what happened, his trading post had a bunch of religious icons, a pretty odd-looking crucifix, and some contraption for burning incense.

They speculated that the Oquala thought he was some kind of demon."

"You sound skeptical."

"Personally, I think a bunch of the Oquala bucks were pissed off that he was messing around with their women. That's what the Oquala chief says, anyway."

"The tribe's still around? I didn't know there's a reservation around here."

"Tribe's long gone." He'd gone back to his oatmeal. "Chief's the last one left, far as I know."

Ruby rolled her eyes. "He's talking about a crazy man who lives in a shack out in the Oquala forest. That old man is no more an Indian chief than me, Dewaldo."

"You should show more respect, Ruby. You've been in those woods. That old Indian knows a lot more than you give him credit for."

"You gonna tell my new partner that old wive's tale about the woods being haunted, now?"

He kept eating, didn't say anything.

"Wilson said something like that last night." I grew up in small-town North Carolina. There are always stories like this when you get far enough into the sticks. "So what's the story with that? People believe the ghosts of the Oquala are still out there, angry at their mistreatment by the white man?"

"Not quite." Ruby nudged Dewaldo. "Go on, tell him. You know you're dying to."

"They say Ogloskie cursed them before he died, said his spirit would never rest while a single Oquala walked the earth."

"So his ghost is haunting the forest, stalking Indians?"

"That's what Blue Feather says."

"That'd be Delbert Blue Feather." Ruby was making it pretty clear she thought Dewaldo was a bit cracked. "He used to go by Delbert Sandesty, before he started claiming to be about one-twelfth Oquala and became a medicine man. Found himself an old beat-up cabin deep in the forest. He's been out there about 10 years, living illegally in a national forest. The Department's tried to evict him several times, but he's so far off the beaten track, it's impossible to get a bulldozer up there to flatten his shack."

"He's not bothering anybody." Dewaldo seemed to have a very personal interest.

"How do you know so much about what he says, anyway?" It was more than idle curiosity on my part. A crazy Indian living in the woods might feel threatened if he heard a logging company was about to start deforesting his home. He was beginning to sound like my number one suspect.

"Dewaldo hikes out to visit him once a month or so. During the summer, he guides a few groups all the way up to Chalker Mountain.so they can sit at the feet of a real live holy man. Isn't that right, Dewaldo?"

"I like to get up into the back country. It's quiet up there." He gave Ruby a sad-dog look. "It's public land. He's got as much right to be there as anyone. More, maybe."

"Oh, don't get defensive." Ruby was apparently getting tired of needling him. "The Department lost interest years ago. No one is going to force your personal Indian to leave."

"One thing I still don't get." There was a lot I didn't get, but I figured it was best to take things one at a time. "How'd Vladimir Ogloskie come to have this town named after him? Sounds like all he did was build a trading post and get himself killed. I'm not sure that's all that memorable."

"It just sorta happened." Dewaldo scraped the last bit of oatmeal from his bowl and swallowed it. No doubt he had a healthy colon. "Trading post was the only thing here for years, abandoned after Ogloskie got himself killed. Became sort of a landmark. *Ogloskie's place*. That got shortened to *Ogloskie's*. In the 1890s, the Army finally got around to the Oquala and built a fort up here, Fort Destiny or something like that. But everybody just kept calling it the 'fort up at *Olgoskie's*.' Somebody always builds a town next to a fort. That became *Ogloskie's* and then *Ogloskie*."

"And here we are today, living in beautiful downtown Ogloskie." Ruby sounded downright proud of the place.

"Any remains of the fort still around?" Hearing mention of the Army always gets me curious. And ruins sometimes attract preservationists and other do-gooders, the kind of people who get mad when companies want to start cutting down trees and bulldozing places.

"Nah, the Army tore the fort down after they killed off all the Oquala." Dewaldo said this matter-of-factly, like it was common knowledge.

"Say again?"

"After they killed the last of the Oquala, they tore the fort down."

I gave him a minute to put the rest of his comments into context with that last remark. He didn't. Amazing how often we overlook obvious inconsistencies in what we believe. "You don't see the contradiction?"

"What?" He looked truly puzzled.

"Two, really. If the Army killed all the Oquala, then why's Ogloskie's ghost still roaming the woods out there?"

"Huh." He got a pensive look. "What's the other one?"

"The other what?" I was beginning to see that talking to Dewaldo could give me a headache.

"Contradiction."

"Oh, sure. If the Army wiped out the Oquala, how is it your friend Blue Feather is an Oquala chief?"

"Oh, I see." He grinned. "I don't mean they really wiped out the tribe. They just killed the adults. Took some kids—boys and girls—and shipped 'em back east. I think a lot of them got adopted by well-meaning white families intent on civilizing savages, that sort of thing. In fact, the garrison commander packed some little Oquala girl off to his wife in Virginia to raise as their own daughter."

"Now how could you possible know all this, Dewaldo?" I was getting suspicious that he was spinning a very tall tale, testing to see how gullible the new guy in town was.

"Captain Lowry, the garrison commander, was so proud of his work here saving Oregonians from the savage red man, he wrote a book about it. There's a copy over in the library in Prestonville. I read it when I first moved here. Local history makes for great campfire stories with a group of hikers. It's part of being a good guide, just like in a museum."

"Okay, I see your point." I could imagine some of the back-to-nature types sitting mesmerized by stories of ghosts and brutal Army commanders killing Indians and kidnapping young Indian princesses. "But, if the tribe was pretty much wiped out and the children scattered, how did Blue Feather find out he's an Oquala chief?"

"He had an epiphany."

"Huh?"

"A revelation."

"Oh." I've known a few people who've had those. Usually it traced back to a bad bottle of booze.

"And, of course, I'd say there's confirmation in the fact that Ogloskie's ghost is still out there. Pretty compelling evidence that Blue Feather is what he claims."

"Right." I saw no reason to poke holes in Dewaldo's obvious delusions. If he really believed in ghosts and Indian chiefs revealed by the Great Spirit, it probably just made him more entertaining to his customers.

Sven appeared with two large platters piled with food. It looked great. My pancakes and eggs glistened with bacon fat from the grill, and the bacon was four thick-sliced slabs. This is the kind of food that's supposed to have us all dying of heart disease before we're fifty, but looking around the place, everybody seemed fairly robust and healthy.

Dewaldo was still staring in his bowl like he'd missed an oat. "So what do I owe you, Sven?"

"Same thing you owe me every morning." Sven was not a guy I would irritate for no good reason. But Dewaldo seemed to take no notice. "Four dollars for the oatmeal. One dollar for the coffee. Twenty-five cents for the county sales tax. That comes to five dollars and twenty-five cents."

"Okay." Dewaldo produced a wallet—one of those zippered-nylon ones you get in hiking equipment stores—and slowly counted out six one-dollar bills, placing them meticulously on the table. Sven swiped up the bills, wadded them up and shoved them in his pocket.

"You want change?"

"Keep it."

The big restaurant owner snorted and walked off.

"He always acts like I'm stiffing him or something." Dewaldo shot an annoyed look to Ruby and me. "I give him a fifteen percent tip, which is more than reasonable, I think, given that he owns the place and doesn't even make a very good bowl of oatmeal."

"Actually, Dewaldo, seventy-five cents isn't quite fifteen percent of five twenty-five."

"Really, Ruby. You don't expect me to include the sales tax when figuring the tip?" He shoved his wallet back in his jeans and stood up. "Anyway, I've got to get going. Nice to meet you, Ranger Stillbridge."

"Please, call me Clayton."

"Oh, yes. Clayton. Right." He didn't seem in a hurry to get someplace, but his mind was definitely on something else as he walked out.

"Odd guy." I wanted to know a little more about him. I'd need to find out as much as I could about everyone in Ogloskie, and Dewaldo and his Indian guru seemed like a good place to start.

"He sure is." Ruby was digging into her breakfast. "He knows his way around the Oquala forest better than anybody else in these parts, though. This is one of the last large expanses of virgin wilderness; two, sometimes three groups a year get Dewaldo to guide them out to Chalker."

"Hunters?"

"Oh, no. We get hunters during deer season, but they don't venture so far off the beaten track. Dewaldo's clients tend to be city people who think spending a week in the woods being dirty and miserable will change their lives or something. Plus they get to meet a real-live Indian chief. Blue Feather's his big draw. Besides, I don't think Dewaldo approves of hunters."

"Environmentalist? Vegetarian?"

"No. I've seen him eat meat. He loves hiking, so it wouldn't surprise me if he's into environmental causes. Mostly I think he likes being out in the wilds. Hunters make too much noise. He's the contemplative type."

"Like some of the old mountain men, I guess."

"Maybe." She stopped eating, thinking. "You know, I think he has a divinity degree from Harvard."

"You're kidding."

"Nope. Sven said something about that once. But he doesn't seem all that religious."

"Maybe he couldn't find a job and got disillusioned. I doubt there's a lot of work for people with degrees in religion."

"I'm pretty sure he never looked for a job. One thing I do know; his family's loaded."

"Really? He doesn't look like he's rolling in dough. How'd you come by that piece of information."

"I asked him how he made enough money to keep from starving, just by guiding a couple of hiking expeditions a year. For awhile I was wondering if he was growing marijuana out there somewhere. He was pretty embarrassed, actually. Told me his family runs a big mining conglomerate on the East Coast. Davis industries."

"I've heard of them. They're big in strip mining. So his family just sends him money and lets him bum around out here?"

"That's my impression."

"Interesting."

"They may be paying him to stay away." She was finishing up her breakfast. She ate fast. "I ran into him up by Indiola Creek a couple of years back. He was scribbling in a big looseleaf notebook he carries around, really caught up in what he was writing. I got right on top of him before he even noticed me. Got a good look. It was poetry. From the look of the notebook, he's written a ton of it. Maybe the Davises aren't comfortable having their own personal Walt Whitman in the family."

"He let you read any of it?"

"He slammed the notebook shut as soon as he saw me. I think he's kinda shy."

"Well, you've got quite a collection of characters here."

"Still a pretty boring place most of the time. But not recently."

"What, you mean the waitress running off with a lumberjack?"

"No." She was watching me closely. "I mean the sudden increase in accidental deaths."

"Oh?" I tried to look as dumb as possible. Actually, I'm pretty good at looking dumb when I need to. I'm not sure that's a talent I should be proud of. "I know lumberjacking can be dangerous. You have a rash of chain-saw accidents or something?"

"You really don't know?" She was looking for any sign I was familiar with the cases.

"Know what?"

"The rash of Conifer Company employees winding up dead in the Oquala."

"Oh, that's right. There was some hiker who got lost and died. Did he work for this Conifer Company?"

"Yeah, he did." She looked suspicious. Maybe I don't have as good a dumb-shit look as I think. "He was Conifer's forestry expert."

"Guess I'd better be careful. Obviously anyone can get lost in these woods. What was he doing there, do you know? Conifer have some interest in the Oquala?"

"Not that I know of." She sat back in her chair, watching me finish my pancakes. "Of course, there's rampant rumors that the government is handing the entire Oquala over to Conifer to clear-cut."

"That's crazy. Something like that, I'm sure you'd have been informed already."

"Don't know what part of the forest service you've been working for, Clayton. The part I've been in, the ranger on site would be the last person to know." She smiled. "Just what made you decide to take reassignment from Georgia, anyway?"

I'd glanced at enough of the Stillbridge file that I wasn't caught by surprise. According to my legend, I'd been assigned to someplace in the northern part of Georgia for the previous three years. "Decided I could use a change of scenery. It's pretty bureaucratic back east. When I saw this position listed, seemed like it might be a nice change working in a small station."

"Yeah. Funny thing, the Department suddenly deciding I need a deputy."

"Hadn't you been asking for one?"

"Sure. For five years. Then this Conifer fellow turns up dead and all of a sudden my request is answered."

"Well, forestry experts who turn up looking like stark-naked blue popsicles will get peoples' attention. But what are you implying?"

"Nothing at all." She waved to Sven for the check. "I was a little suspicious at first that you were gonna turn out to be some kind of undercover cop."

I laughed, believably, I think. "Take my word for it. I'm no cop."

"You don't look like FBI or anything. Guess I've been living next to the haunted woods too long. Starting to see spooks and goblins. Still, it's funny."

"What is?"

"You knowing about that Conifer guy being naked when we found him."

"Guess I read it in the newspaper."

"Sure." Sven had arrived with the check. "This one's on me. Consider it your welcome to Ogloskie."

"Thanks. Next time I'll buy you breakfast."

"I never say no to free eats." She laid out some bills. "Oh, and Clayton. Just an FYI. Nobody else around here knows we found that guy stark naked."

"Oh? Okay. I'll keep that in mind."

"Except Dewaldo. He found him. Radioed me. When I got there, we wrapped him up in a blanket before the rest of the search party showed up. I told the State Police about it, but not anybody else. Figured we'd save his family some embarrassment."

"That was thoughtful of you."

"So it wasn't in the papers." Her stare was like ice.

There's not much you can do when you stumble over yourself trying to act like something you're not. Whatever her suspicions, she was stuck with me. I decided to ignore my slip-up and move on. "Interesting."

"Very." She stood up. "Well, come along and I'll show you around your new territory, Ranger."

Chapter III
Suspects

A COUPLE OF DAYS WITH RUBY and I learned that being a forest ranger mostly means sitting around the ranger station with not a lot to do, at least at this particular ranger station in November. There wasn't even much paperwork. She assured me things were busier in the summer.

There wasn't much chance of a forest fire, either.

"We've had a lot of rain recently. It's pretty soggy out there."

So mostly I just got settled in. And showing me around my new territory turned out to be office work, too. After breakfast the first day, Ruby brought me back to the station and handed me a pile of maps.

"Study those before you go exploring. You'll see there aren't a lot of fire service roads in the Oquala. A lot of the place is only accessible by foot. You need to be pretty good with a compass and map if you don't want to get lost."

"I haven't gotten lost in the woods yet." It was true. I could have added that I hadn't spent much time in any forests outside North Carolina. But I wasn't ready to completely abandon my cover. Besides, I'd done enough compass and map work growing up and in the Army, I wasn't particularly worried.

The Oquala was impressive, though. It stretched across a significant stretch of south-central Oregon. The terrain was fairly flat except for the eastern section running up against the Rockies. That's where Chalker

Mountain was, and also where Delbert Blue Feather could be found. I wanted to know a lot more about him. He certainly seemed to have the best motive to keep Conifer out; preventing his hide-away from becoming a moonscape. His and Dewaldo's were the first names on my list of suspects.

I found out pretty fast that the list was short, at least if it was limited to residents of Ogloskie. I've been to my share of small towns: hell, I grew up in a backwater North Carolina collection of falling down shacks with exactly three brick buildings—the church, the post office, and the barber shop—population two-hundred ten. It was a metropolis compared to Ogloskie. The place had exactly ten residents. With my arrival, the population had exploded ten percent to eleven.

Prester Wilson owned and ran the motel. He'd bought it ten years earlier after retiring from the Air Force—Ruby thought he'd been a maintenance technician—did a few repairs, and opened for business. He didn't seem to make a lot of money, but he had his pension and apparently enjoyed himself. I figured he was just happy to be his own boss after years of taking orders from officers. A career in the military might have sent me into isolation, too, if I'd stayed in the Army long enough.

Sven Marsten, the refugee from overcrowded Montana, had been a real estate agent in Helena looking for a change when he'd spotted the for sale listing for Ogloskie's—the previous owner had run the place for 40 years and decided to get what he could and find a retirement home somewhere. I'm guessing he didn't get a lot of offers.

Sven's cook, Fred Walderman, had quite literally appeared out of nowhere, passed out drunk in the cab of his pickup, a few years after Sven bought the place. According to Ruby, he'd been extremely vague about where he'd come from and what he did before. After his fellow Ogloskians had observed him for awhile, they decided he wasn't hiding anything; he drank so much, he probably really didn't remember where he'd been before. But he could cook.

Arthur and Myrna Fey, the older couple I'd seen in the restaurant my first morning, owned and operated the general store. They stocked a variety of camping gear, freeze-dried foods, and assorted sodas and snacks popular with hikers returning from their adventures.

The only other residents were the Alvarez family. John and Lucinda lived on a small farm outside of town, just along the main road into Ogloskie, with their four-year-old daughter, Becky. John grew tomatoes, peppers, and snap peas in not too great quantities. Lucinda spent the summer months decked out in native-American garb selling blankets, beads, artifacts and handcrafts out of a small shack on the highway. Mostly they stayed to themselves. I'd asked Ruby if they were local.

"What, you think they're Oquala Indians? Lucinda just dresses up like that for the tourists."

"They come up from Mexico, then?"

"Christ, Clayton, you think they're illegals because they're Hispanic? In case you hadn't noticed, the entire West Coast is filled with Hispanics. They were here before us *gringos*."

"Sure, I know that. I just wonder how they make a living on such a small farm."

"John Alvarez has a law degree. From what he told Sven when he first showed up, he made a lot of money practicing water-rights law and moved up here because his doctor told him his blood-pressure was going to kill him if he didn't start taking it easy."

"Oh. I just figured his wife sold artifacts because they need the money."

"She sells that stuff because she likes to make more money. They buy it for nothing off the Internet and sell it to the rubes who come through here and think it's really hand-crafted by Indians. As if there were any Indians left around here."

"Blue Feather's an Indian."

"So he tells Dewaldo."

"I'm just surprised I haven't seen the Alvarezes around town." I'd had breakfast three mornings in a row at Sven's and spent the better part of a couple of mornings checking out what little of Ogloskie there was, all without an Alvarez sighting. "Don't they feel welcome? Nobody around here seems that prejudiced to me."

"John Alvarez is. He thinks we're all a bunch of ignorant, uneducated yahoos."

"I see."

Nothing about any of Ogloskie's other residents seemed suspicious, leaving Dewaldo and Blue Feather the most likely suspects. Of course, it was possible, maybe even likely, that whoever was taking an interest in stopping Conifer wasn't a local. I hadn't had much chance those first few days to find out about other visitors to the area. With hikers coming and going most of the summer, my client could have been operating below the radar for months posing as a backpacker. But they'd have a base of operations somewhere in the vicinity. Well-crafted murders require a lot of area familiarization, target casing and operational planning. Plus, a dedicated environmentalist willing to kill to protect trees would no doubt still be hanging around somewhere to see if his efforts were having an effect. Or her efforts, I reminded myself; just a month ago I'd gotten a blunt object lesson that male chauvinists who believe the fairer sex are incapable of violence can wind up with big lumps on their heads.

Thursday afternoon I was sitting in the station staring at maps, trying to decide how best to proceed. Tires kicking up gravel outside caught my attention. The station door swung open; I expected to see Ruby, back from her excursion to check the trail logs up the road. Instead, I found myself staring at a short guy— maybe 5 foot 5—staring back at me. He had an amused look on his face, like the sight of me in a ranger uniform was pretty damned funny.

"Can I help you?"

He looked around and took off his sunglasses. I'm not sure sunglasses were necessary, since it was still raining.

"Ruby not around?"

"She'll be back in awhile. Anything I can do for you?"

He furrowed his eyebrows, considering the question. "Doubt it." He looked through a stack of magazines Ruby had on a stand by the door, picked up one called *Outdoorsman*, sat down in the wooden chair across from the desk and started reading. I stared at him reading for a good five minutes. He ignored me.

"You're sure there's nothing I can help you with?"

His eyes peered out over the magazine, then went back to scanning the text. "Positive."

"Maybe I can get you a cup of coffee . . ."

"No, thanks."

". . . or pick you up and throw you out of here to teach you some manners."

He looked up again, raised an eyebrow. "Am I botherin' you? Here I thought I was waitin' nice and quiet."

"This is a ranger station, not a public library." He was a cool customer, I had to admit. Usually people take my threats seriously. I've got the muscle and body mass to back them up. Of course, I'm not usually sitting in an office wearing a dork uniform.

"Yeah, I know. It's Ruby's station. I'm waiting for her. Who're you?"

"I'm her deputy."

"Deputy?" He snorted. "When did she get a deputy?"

"Monday."

"You're here permanent?"

"Yup."

"Oh. I just figured you were some regional supervisor in for a visit. Sorry."

"And you would be . . ."

"Sorry, Mr. Ranger. You're right. I'm being rude." He stood up and put out his hand. I shook it. His grip was firm. "Walker Treadman."

"Clayton Stillbridge. Nice to meet you."

"Likewise." He sat back down and resumed reading. I got the distinct impression he was needling me, seeing how far he had to push before I got really pissed. I get this behavior a lot, usually from goons sizing me up to see if they can take me. Every time guys with too much muscle and not enough brains meet, they start trying to figure out how to establish themselves as top gorilla. I figure it's the strongest evidence that we really are cousins of jungle primates.

Walker Treadman didn't look like a goon. He was short, and his close-cropped hair was flecked with gray, a lot of gray. He looked fit, but not gorilla fit. This wasn't a guy who spent hours in a gym building muscle so he could bend steel bars, but he obviously spent some time and effort staying in shape. He was wearing a western-style dress shirt tucked into clean, pressed jeans, and he had on an expensive looking pair of cowboy boots. The outfit was a little dandyish, in fact. But he didn't look like a dandy, either. In fact, I was having trouble making him out. He'd have passed as ordinary except for that air of self-confidence; that's an air that sets off alarms in my head.

I decided to ignore him and go back to my maps of the Oquala. If he wanted to get a rise out of me, he was going to have to do more than sit there.

"You plannin' an expedition?" His eyes peered over the magazine, showing slight interest.

"Just want to be familiar with my new territory."

"Takes more than map knowledge to understand the Oquala."

"Are you going to tell me it's haunted, too?" I leaned back in my chair and gave him my undivided attention. If he was ready to talk, all the better.

"Haunted." He snorted again. "I've never seen any ghosts out there. But it's dense forest in places. So dense you can lose your sense of direction."

"In my experience, that's where a compass comes in handy."

"Compasses have been known to go haywire in there. Some iron pyrite up near Chalker Mountain."

"I'll keep than in mind." It would have to be a hell of a deposit to screw up a compass at any distance. "Sounds like you know these woods pretty good."

"I've hiked around 'em some, but I can't claim any real expertise." He was still scanning the magazine. "I'm a city boy."

He didn't look all that citifed. There was something familiar about him. But I was sure I'd never met him before.

Wheels spitting gravel outside interrupted my assessment. We both looked at the door just as Ruby came in.

"Hello, Walker. You're early." So she did know him.

"Just wanted to make sure you remembered to get gussied up for our date, darlin'." He'd stood up, quite the gentleman, revealing that Ruby had a couple of inches on him. I'd been wondering if she had a local beau. Maybe this was him.

"Walker's taking me dancing tonight, Clayton." She gave me a wink. I wasn't too sure what to make of it. "There's a dance hall down in Prestonville. Western swing. You should come."

"I'm no dancer." I could read the relief in Walker's eyes. He clearly didn't want a chaperone. "Besides, I figured I'd move out of Wilson's this evening, drop my stuff in the empty half of that duplex."

"Suit yourself." She turned her attention back to Walker. "You'll miss us cutting a rug. Walker's pretty light on his feet."

"That I am." He took her hand and made a little spin around her. I decided his earlier behavior had just been for the sake of marking territory. I could have assured him I didn't have any designs on Ruby, if he'd asked. Not that she wasn't a handsome woman. But when I'm on a job, I like to focus my predator skills on the client. Chasing tail is too distracting.

"So what has Walker been telling you about me, Clayton?"

"Nothing. We were talking about the Oquala. He says compasses go screwy there."

"Walker." She gave him a mildly disapproving look. "Trying to sell one of those GPS contraptions to my new deputy since I keep telling you no?"

"I'm tellin' you, Ruby, they're marvels of technology. Tell you your exact location within ten square feet every time. And they work everywhere."

"Until the battery gives out." She shook her head. "Walker sells outdoor equipment."

"You don't say." He didn't look like a salesman to me, either. "You got a store in Prestonville, or is it catalog sales?"

"Neither. Strictly wholesale. I'm the south Oregon rep for Trailhead Sports." He pulled out his wallet and extracted a business card, handing it to me. "Been trying to convince the Fey's to carry Trailhead merchandise. I can get you a wholesale price on a GPS, if you're interested."

"I'm old-fashioned. I'll stick with a map and compass. And if that fails, I just check to see which side of the trees has the thickest moss."

"What'll that tell you?"

"Which direction is South. Or North. I never can keep it straight."

"Well, don't worry." He grinned mischievously. "You get lost out there, I'm sure Ruby will come find you. Can't leave somebody lying dead in the Oquala. Might scare the backpackers."

"There aren't any backpackers out there today, at least none who logged in. This weather makes for pretty miserable hiking." She was looking over the maps I had spread out on her desk, surprised that I had dived into them so seriously, I guess. "So what do you think, Clayton? Considering making a personal exploration?"

"I was thinking I might take a few days to have a look around, maybe hike up to Chalker. Looks like I could get there and back in four or five days. If that's okay with you."

"Five, maybe. Tough going in places. You interested in meeting Blue Feather?"

"Well, if I make it that far, might as well pay him a visit. Unless you've got stuff you want me to do around here. You're the boss."

"Right." I'm not sure she believed that any more than me. "You want to hike over to Chalker, you'll need to get going pretty soon. Weather'll start to turn cold in a couple of weeks. We get an early snow, you won't want to be wandering around out there."

"So you don't have any objections?"

"Of course not. What else is a forest ranger to do if not explore the forest." She smiled, then got that stern look back in her eyes. "See if you can talk Dewaldo into going along, though."

"Yeah, I was thinking that." I could find out a lot about him on an expedition to meet up with Blue Feather; kill two birds, so to speak. Maybe literally. "You think he'd be interested?"

"Sometimes it's hard keeping him out of that damned forest. And I'm betting he'll be thrilled you want to meet his personal medicine man. Just make sure he knows you're not going to try and serve an eviction notice or anything. Wouldn't want to spook him."

"Not in a haunted wood, anyway."

"Don't laugh. I think he believes that crap."

"Hell, I never laugh at a good spook story. Besides, maybe Dewaldo will introduce me to Ogloskie's ghost."

"Well, if you do meet him, tell him for me that he's wasting his time. The last Oquala died ages ago. Blue Feather's no more an Oquala Indian than Walker here."

"Now, Ruby." Walker feigned a hurt expression. "I'll have you know I have native American blood coursing through these veins. Some of it could well be Oquala."

"So you claiming to be an Indian now, too?"

"Not pure blood." He smiled. "I am one-hundred percent mongrel, product of generations of drifters breeding with whoever they met."

"Now that I believe." She gave him a look that said there was more to their relationship than dancing. But I'd have been surprised to learn otherwise. The smaller the community, the more impulse there is to find someone to hop into bed with, in my experience. Probably some sort of biological imperative; either that, or succumbing to boredom. "Well, Mr. Treadman, if you'll follow me back to my place and wait patiently while I change, I'll let you take me to dinner before we go dancing."

"You got a deal, ma'am."

They didn't exactly look like two excited high school kids off on a hot date when they left, but they were obviously looking forward to having a good time. And with them out of my hair, it gave me a chance to check the e-mail site Frank had provided.

Frank had been right about even a remote station like Ruby's having a computer plugged into the Internet. It even had a high-speed connection, although the DSL line wasn't as fast as I'd become accustomed to at public libraries around the country. I opened the browser and checked the history tab. I've gotten in the habit of checking the history when I use someone else's machine. Most of the time I expect to find porno sites. Ruby's was pretty clean, though. All that was there was the Department of Agriculture, her personal e-mail site, a few online retailers like Amazon and REI, and a whole lot of links to web pages and articles on get-rich schemes, those "make millions with no initial investment" scams that are blatantly aimed at obvious suckers. Maybe she was worried about making a living once she got too old to rescue lost hikers and locate frozen corpses; government pensions aren't what they're cracked up to be.

I navigated to the e-mail site Frank had provided and logged into the encrypted account. Surprisingly, there was already a message in the drafts folder. I opened it. It was short and sweet.

Expecting results soonest. Stop screwing around.

Typical that Frank would start badgering me immediately now that he'd found a new way to send his spook messages. I wondered if he'd really care if I just threw a random client off Chalker Mountain and declared the case closed. Probably he wouldn't, but then the real killer might take out another Conifer supervisor and he'd get pissed. Besides, I take pride in doing my job well. He'd just have to develop some patience. I entered edit mode and added a few lines for him.

Having a great time. Lovely weather, wonderful scenery. Thinking about marrying my ranger boss and settling down. Meanwhile, send whatever info you can find on:

Delbert Blue Feather; aka Delbert Sandesty; self-styled Oquala Indian chief; squatter on Chalker Mountain.

Dewaldo Davis; related to Davis family owners east coast coal mining conglomerate; currently resides Ogloskie; hiking guide; possibly has divinity degree from Harvard.

Walker Treadman; sales representative, Trailhead Sports Inc.

I didn't have much reason to add Treadman to the list, other than my funny feeling there was something familiar about him. My instinct said he wasn't the client—I like to think I've got enough experience to smell out a tree-hugger, and he wasn't one—but he might turn out to be a spook for a rival outfit or even a federal agent on an undercover investigation looking into the same Conifer matter I was investigating. Government agencies are falling all over each other unawares all the time; the right-wing whackos who whine constantly that the government is too big are actually correct—but when they bitch about the "nanny" state, it's pretty clear they don't really know what they're talking about. Nobody I know in government is trying to be a nanny. Last time I checked, nannies don't go around killing people. At least, not that I've heard.

But if Treadman was another spook, I'd want to find out. Frank doesn't like running down leads for me, but he usually comes through. It was worth a shot.

I saved the message back into the draft folder and purged the history file in the browser. I've gotten pretty Internet savvy over the years, primarily from breaking into clients' homes and offices and finding out a shitload about what they've been up to because they aren't smart enough to stop leaving trails of cookie crumbs. I try not to be as dumb as most of my clients. That way I figure I may continue to outlive them.

It didn't take me long to pack up my gear, pay my bill and check out of Wilson's. He wasn't particularly anxious to get my money.

"So what do I owe you?"

"Let's see, you got here Sunday. That's four nights. I usually charge twenty-five a night. And there's a hotel tax. You gonna use a credit card?"

"I've got cash if you want it."

"Just call it a hundred, then. Pay me whenever you get a chance. No rush."

"How about I just pay you now and we get it over with?"

"If you prefer."

I handed him five twenties and he shoved them absent-mindedly in his pocket. He wasn't going to get rich running his motel the way he did. I don't think he cared. I was curious, though. His business would die fast once the Oquala was gutted.

"Ruby said you were in the Air Force. Must have been quite a change for you, moving out here. I haven't heard a plane all week."

"That's a good thing." He squinted, like he wasn't happy people were talking about him. "What else Ruby tell you about me?"

"She just said you used to be a maintenance tech or something."

"Didn't know Rangers were so inquisitive." I wondered if I'd touched a nerve. "Bit early for the census, ain't it?"

"Maybe I'm moonlighting for *Lonely Planet* and wanted to get some details so I could write up your place."

"Don't bother. I'm already listed in their Oregon guide."

"Really? What's it say?"

He laughed. "It says this is the only motel within forty miles of the Oquala National Forest. I guess they didn't think it was necessary to add I could pull maintenance on your A-10 Warthog if you decide to fly in."

"That was smart, though, buying the only motel close to a popular hiking area." I was fishing.

"You think?" He didn't look convinced. "Man, I thought this would be a breeze after all those years covered in lubricating oil listening to fucking pilots bitch. *Something just doesn't feel right.* Pilots are prima donnas."

"I guess this is a lot less stressful."

"Yeah, if you like fixing plumbing fixtures and hanging drywall when some drunk hiker just back from a week-long backpacking expedition decides to kick holes in the walls of his room." He shook his head wearily. "But I don't expect I'll be dealing with this crap too much longer."

"Business so good you're getting ready to retire again?"

"Got a feeler from a real estate agent recently. Somebody's thinking about buying me out."

"Lucky you." I couldn't see much to interest anybody. "Maybe the Marriott's have decided there's gonna be a backpacking craze sweeping the West coast."

"Nah, nothing like that. More likely some company's looking for housing for logging crews."

Obviously he'd heard the same rumors as Ruby. "This is national forest. It's protected."

"Well, that's right, ain't it." He grinned. "All these customers I've had the last year putting their room on their Conifer Corporation credit cards were no doubt just vacationing in the area."

"You think they've cut some deal with the Department of Agriculture?" I realized he'd probably have been in a good position to know the comings and goings of the Conifer victims, maybe get the drop on them himself. "Be a shame to see anything happen to a national treasure like the Oquala."

"You Rangers love your trees." He shook his head slowly, like he'd seen more than enough of trees for a lifetime. "Somebody makes me an offer on this place, I already decided I'm relocating someplace where the closest bit of nature is a golf course."

"You play golf?"

"Nah, but I'm sure I could learn. Officers in the Air Force play it all the time. Can't be too challenging."

"I know what you mean." Army officers I'd known loved playing golf, too. I suspect that means any idiot can figure it out.

After dumping my stuff at the duplex, I headed over to Ogloskie's. Really, there just weren't many places to go. The whole town—minus the Alvarezes—was there as I'd come to expect. Wilson looked up at me from a large platter of steak and fries, smiled. Maybe he was already contemplating his putter.

I sat down next to Dewaldo at the counter and ordered a beer when Sven came out.

"Don't have anything on draft. Just bottles."

"That's okay. Got Bud or Miller?"

"Not around here. Nobody orders that stuff in Oregon."

"Why not? People here don't like real American beer?"

"Oregonians prefer local brews. There are more than a thousand micro-breweries in this state. Whatever kind of beer you like, I can bring you. IPA, Porter, Stout "

"Got anything that tastes like Bud or Miller?"

He made a face and brought me a bottle of something called *Portland's Prize Pils*. It was okay.

"So what have you been up to, Dewaldo?" I didn't really need to ask. I'd seen him every evening, sitting in Ogloskie's, looking like he didn't know what to do with himself.

"Waiting for this weather to clear."

"Does it? Ever clear, that is?"

"Sure. Summers it gets downright hot. And in a couple of weeks it'll start to get cold and then we'll get snow. I prefer both to this rain."

"I agree with you there. Been thinking about getting out and exploring a little, but there's nothing worse than camping out in the rain."

"Hold off until middle of next week. We're supposed to get a shift in the weather that'll bring a last blast of dry air off the Great Plains."

"Didn't know you were an expert on weather as well as local history."

"You have to get to know the local weather patterns if you want to hike in the Oquala. I don't like lugging in more than I have to, but I also don't like getting caught in a snow storm without winter gear."

"Spoken like a real Boy Scout." He didn't say anything. Getting him to open up about himself was proving to be difficult. "Actually, I was thinking of hiking up to Chalker Mountain. Been studying the terrain. Figure I can make it there and back in four, maybe five days."

"I always allow a full week."

"Really? Is the terrain really that much tougher than it looks on the map?"

"No." He looked over at me, like he was considering just how much he should reveal about his back-country expeditions. "But why go to all the trouble to kit up for a multiple day excursion and then try to turn it into some kind of racing challenge? You want to see the Oquala, take your time and have a good look around."

"That's good advice." I didn't point out that most of my expedition experience involved getting to a location, killing somebody, and then getting the hell out of there as fast as possible. Given that I considered it likely my Oquala hike would be along the same lines, it was only natural I'd been thinking in terms of how fast I could pull it off. Taking Dewaldo with me would require adapting to a completely different philosophy than I'm used to. "You interested?"

"In what?"

"Coming along."

He looked back at me again. The question didn't surprise him. "You want me to take you to Blue Feather."

"Seems to me like he's as much a part of the Oquala as the trees. I'd like to meet him."

"You sure that's all you're interested in?"

"What else?"

"Maybe the government's tired of Ruby ignoring him out there. Maybe they sent you to kick him out."

"Then I'd be pretty stupid to invite you along."

"How you figure?"

"You'd be the one guy who could find a way to get me lost." I was watching him to gauge his response, see if something in his eyes indicated he'd done that before. He'd been the one who found Riefenthal, after all. Maybe he'd known where to look.

"You don't look like the type who gets lost." His expression didn't change. Maybe he just had a good poker face. He'd been sipping on a soda of some sort, something red and fizzy. I wondered if he was a teetotaler. He gulped down the rest in a big swig. "Why not? I need to take some supplies to Blue Feather before winter sets in. You can help me lug in some stuff."

"I thought real Indians live off the land."

"Some stuff he can't get up in the mountains. You don't mind some extra weight in your pack, do you?"

"Not at all. It'll be worth it to have some company."

"You got a pack?"

"Actually, my hiking gear is still in Georgia." Along with the rest of my phony cover story. "I was gonna see if the Fey's would rent me a backpack."

"I've got an extra one. Got a spare sleeping bag, too. I'll loan 'em to you." He glanced down at my feet. "Looks like you've already got a decent pair of boots. I'll pick up supplies for us. Just make sure you bring some extra underwear and rain gear, in case the weather doesn't hold."

"Appreciate it. Sounds like you know what you're doing."

"I wouldn't get many repeat customers if I didn't." It made sense. He wanted his clients to be happy. I just want mine dead. "I'll drop off your gear early next week so you can get packed up. Assuming the weather breaks, plan on swinging by my place Wednesday morning early and we'll get started."

"How early?"

"Four's good. We'll drive up the forest service road to where it ends and kick off from there."

"Man, that's an early start. When does the sun come up this time of year?"

"About six-thirty. I like being in the woods at first light. It's really inspiring."

"Yeah." I guess it was the poet in him. It was going to be a real test, hiking with this modern-day Thoreau. I wondered if I'd have to endure countless lectures about the awesome beauty of nature. I tend to think of wilderness as someplace you survive, not celebrate.

"You've got a gun, right?" His question caught me by surprise.

"Of course. Comes with the job."

"Be sure you bring it."

"I didn't think you were the hunting type, Dewaldo."

"I'm not. But grizzlies and pumas haven't yet learned the advantages of a vegetarian diet. Like the song says, I don't eat animals, and I like to make sure they don't eat me."

"You really a vegetarian?"

He grinned. "Occasionally."

"You surprise me, Dewaldo. From what Ruby told me, I figured you hiked barefoot, ate bean sprouts, and talked to the animals. Now I find out you eat the occasional piece of flesh, value good shoes, and go armed in the wilds."

"Guess Ruby doesn't know me as well as she thinks."

"What do you carry, anyway. Deer rifle of some kind?"

"Like I said, I'm not into hunting. I'm not going to shoot anything unless it gets close enough to threaten me. A rifle's not necessary for that."

"Just don't tell me you rely on a Bowie knife."

"Got a Colt .45 Peacemaker."

"Very traditional." I really was in the land of large calibers. It was a good thing I'd left my untraceable .22 Bersa Thunder automatic back in Virginia. Obviously, real men in Oregon—women, too—would laugh at such a toy, even though in the right hands and with a magazine of hollow-points it's as effective as any of the heavy artillery everybody in Ogloskie was sporting, in my opinion. "Anything else I should know about you before we spend a week together getting back to nature, Dewaldo?"

"Just that I'm not afraid of ghosts."

"That's good. Neither am I."

"We'll see."

One thing about living in a duplex next to your boss, you soon learn a few personal details that don't tend to come up in the office. My first night I learned that Ruby makes one hell of a lot of noise when she's getting banged by a short sales rep who's light on his feet. I'd been asleep when they got back around midnight, and they were actually very considerate, trying to be quiet when they pulled up out front and came in. It didn't make any difference. In my line of work, you have to be a light sleeper. I was wide awake before Treadman's tires stopped spitting gravel. They stayed quiet for about an hour; lying in bed I could barely make out their voices. Then the noise picked up.

Ooooooh, sweeeeet mother of Jeeeeeeesus! told me Ruby had something of a religious upbringing and also that Walker knew how to please a woman. Things finally got quiet around two. Walker left a half-hour later. Maybe he had an early sales call in Prestonville.

I figured I'd sleep in since Ruby obviously wouldn't be up at the crack of dawn. I figured wrong. She was banging on my door at six-thirty.

"You gonna sleep all day, Clayton?"

I crawled out of bed and went to the door in my skivvies. "Sorry, Ruby. Guess the alarm didn't go off."

"Saw your truck and figured you'd moved in like you said." She eyed me standing there in my boxers. I swear she licked her lips. "I made coffee. Come on over after you get decent."

"Okay, boss."

"Hope we didn't wake you up last night."

"I'm a pretty sound sleeper." It's a lie I've practiced a lot.

"That's good. I was afraid you might have thought Ogloskie's ghost was outside howling at the moon." She grinned.

"Well, I did hear something like that."

"I'm sure you did." At least I wasn't going to have to tiptoe around the subject all day. Ruby was obviously a woman who wasn't ashamed of her appetites. It was refreshing in a way. "Well, see you in a minute."

I showered and pulled on the idiot outfit. Honestly, I don't know what kind of person signs on for a career that involves dressing like a fool. Letting myself into Ruby's and seeing her sitting at her breakfast table looking damned fine in her uniform, I realized there were some people for whom the job was a perfect fit.

"Your boyfriend didn't stick around for breakfast?" I'd decided there was no reason to avoid the subject, especially since she didn't seem particularly embarrassed.

"I told him to go home. In my experience, people don't look good when they crawl out of bed. I prefer ending a date on a high note."

"Yeah, I know what you mean."

"There are exceptions, though." She arched an eyebrow. "You don't look so bad stumbling around in your shorts."

"If you don't really have coffee, you're going to find out just how sad I am when I'm still half asleep."

"It's right over there on the stove. Help yourself."

I poured myself a cup and sat down across from her. She didn't look like someone who'd gotten less than four hours of sleep. "So how was the dancing?"

"We had ourselves a mighty fine time. Walker's a lot of fun."

"He lives over in Prestonville?"

"Yeah. Nice little apartment."

"So he grow up around here?"

"Nope. Showed up about a year ago."

"Any idea where he was before that?"

"Don't I at least have the right to an attorney?" The stern look came back to her eyes.

"What do you mean?"

"Before you continue with the interrogation."

"Aw, Ruby, I'm just curious."

"Sure, Clayton." She stared at her coffee cup. "You got a funny feeling about him or something?"

"I'm sure he's a nice guy."

"He knows how to show a lady a good time. I don't mind that at all." She frowned. "But, honestly, I'm not so sure he's been asking me out because of my good looks and charm."

"Now why would you say that? You're the best-looking woman in these parts."

She laughed out loud. "Damn straight, Clayton. I'm the finest, sexiest dame in Ogloskie, Oregon. Got Lucinda Alvarez beat."

"Come on, Ruby, you know what I mean."

"Sure. Next you'll be telling me you'd be interested . . ."

"Well . . ."

"If I were just a few years younger." She gave me a look that said she could show me a few things. I didn't doubt it. "But all I'm saying is, I think Walker's here nosing around."

"So you think he's a cop, too?"

"No, not exactly. And I already told you, I've decided you're not a cop, either."

"So what have you decided I am?"

"I haven't. I'll let you know when I do."

"Let me know if you figure out what Walker is."

"Likewise."

"Listen, not to get too personal . . ." I realized I was asking too many questions, but Frank had instructed me to stop screwing around, after all. "But if you're not sure he's exactly what he says he is . . ."

"Why am I baying at the moon with him?"

"Well, yeah."

"Gee, Clayton, you only have sex with women you trust? What a boring life you must lead."

"Point taken."

"So what did you do with yourself last night while I was out tripping the light fantastic?"

"Actually, I persuaded Dewaldo to guide me up to Chalker Mountain. We'll be heading out next Wednesday. He says the weather's gonna clear."

"Didn't figure you'd have to twist his arm. He's been looking restless in all this rain." She was back to staring into her coffee. "You think Blue Feather might know something?"

"About what?"

"Trees falling on people. Naked corpses in the middle of the woods. That sort of thing."

"Why would I ask him about a rash of accidental deaths?"

"Why, indeed?" She didn't expect an answer. "Well, finish your coffee and let's go open up. Never know when some crazy hiker might show up wanting a map."

It was another uneventful day at the station. Ruby went off to check the hiking logs while I sat around at her desk, bored. Monotony's obviously a serious problem in the forest service. Not as bad as the occasions when I'd found myself stuck in my office back in Washington, I had to admit. I wasn't getting daily updates about the Combined Federal Campaign, anyway. That was a relief.

Walker Treadman stopped by at noon. Certainly there wasn't enough business in Ogloskie this time of year to keep bringing him to the area. If Ruby was right that he wasn't really love-smitten, then he obviously was nosing around for some reason he wasn't being upfront about.

"Ruby's out of the office again, Walker. You're welcome to wait."

"I was just in the neighborhood." That was such an obvious lie I didn't even bother to look up. "I'm takin' her to the movies tonight."

"You stopped by to finish that magazine you were reading?"

"Well, to be honest, I wanted to apologize if we woke you up last night." He broke into a lecherous grin.

"Hey, when I'm asleep, an atomic bomb couldn't wake me." Occasionally I find myself wishing this were true. A solid night's sleep might be nice sometime. "I wouldn't notice a car pulling up or anything like that."

"We were making a lot more noise than tires spittin' gravel, if you know what I mean." He winked. Obviously he wanted me to know about their boisterous sex as much as Ruby had. In his case I figured it was just more marking territory. I wondered if he had any inkling that no-trespassing signs make me curious to find out what's so special.

"That's great, Walker. You two make a nice couple. Seriously, don't worry about waking me up."

"I tried to quiet Ruby down, but honestly, when she starts moanin', well . . ."

So Walker wasn't much of a gentleman. Not that his lack of class added much to the profile of him I was building in my head. Most guys are louts when it comes to women. Not that I'm much better, but at least I've never felt the need to brag about noises I made a woman make. I guess I don't think of it as a major accomplishment.

"Like I said, you two make a nice couple." I went back to looking at the maps on the desk, hoping he'd get the point that I really didn't want to hear any more details.

"So what made the forest service decide Ruby needs an assistant? She's been doing this job solo for years."

"Ask her." Curiosity's natural. Still, I get suspicious when people ask me questions. "She's been requesting one since the day she got here."

"Sure." He didn't sit. He didn't look at me, either. He was staring at a photo on the wall of some large boulder that I assumed was sitting somewhere in the Oquala. People believe if they don't look at you when they ask questions, you'll assume they're just making casual conversation. It's a good trick. I use it myself. "But, well, the timing . . . "

"What about the timing?"

"You know, the rash of accidents."

"Maybe it occurred to somebody that the Oquala can be pretty dangerous, so having an extra ranger around might make it easier to rescue lost hikers before they expire."

"Makes sense. I know Ruby's happy to have you. With you sharing the load, she'll have more time to enjoy my company." He sat down, smiling. This was meant to make me believe he'd accepted my explanation and now wanted to be friendly. Actually, I was very aware what he really wanted was to watch my face while I answered his next question. "So how long you been with the forest service?"

"Not long enough to get a pension. How about you? How long you been in the sporting goods business? Must be pretty lucrative." I was watching him closely, too. His eyes darkened ever so slightly. Spooks love to turn questions around, get their inquisitors to start talking about themselves. Most people never notice, just mindlessly start telling you their life's story. Other spooks pick up on it fast, though.

"It's a living." We sat staring at each other for a minute, stares that said neither of us believed the other was what he claimed. "Well, I'd love to sit and chat all day, but I'm afraid I got to make a living."

"Thanks for stopping by, Walker." We both stood up, unfinished business hanging in the air. "I'd love to hear more about your line of work. Who knows. Maybe I'll decide to try something besides rangering someday."

He'd stopped smiling. "There are always opportunities out there for guys with skills."

I watched him leave and stared at the door for awhile, thinking. *Just what skills would those be, I wonder?* It was a rhetorical question.

I decided to check Frank's message site. He hadn't had much time to dig up anything. Then again, with all the Federal and state databases storing information about everybody and their mother in this world, there was a good chance a records search would turn up something fast.

There wasn't much, but there was something.

Preliminary check of criminal and official records shows:

Delbert Sandesty, aka Delbert Blue Feather, born Delbert Hardesty; conviction for bunco, 1983, Arizona, served two years Arizona State Penitentiary, paroled; charged with wire fraud, 1991, Nevada, charges dropped; arrested for disorderly conduct, Salem, Oregon, 1994, charges dropped; changed name legally to Delbert Blue Feather, 1995; no further information.

Dewaldo Davis; convicted, assault and battery, Cambridge, Massachusetts, October, 2000, sentence suspended; no further information.

Walker Treadman; no records.

Marry the Ranger and settle down if you want, but find the client and handle him first. Or her.

Of course, the assault and battery conviction leapt off the page at me. Dewaldo just got more and more interesting.

Chapter IV
Crunchy Granola Munchers

A WEEK IN RAINY OGLOSKIE left me feeling restless. I got up early Saturday and headed to Prestonville in search of a gym. It's a safe bet these days that any decent-sized town will have one, although the fitness craze hasn't put a dent in the obesity that's obvious when you drive around any of these decent-sized towns.

There wasn't all that much to Prestonville, despite Ruby's build-up. It took me all of twenty minutes to find a place just outside the main part of town, a one-story frame building with a sign in front announcing *Ore-Fit*. The name didn't immediately register with me as a gym. Fortunately, *Fitness Studio* was blazoned underneath. I pulled the F-150 into the parking lot—it was fairly full with maybe fifteen other vehicles—grabbed my work-out gear, and headed inside.

The front desk was manned by a fit-looking, tanned dude wearing wire-rimmed glasses and sporting a ponytail. At first glance I thought he was Dewaldo, but when I got closer I realized he was a few years younger and not quite as scruffy. He was wearing baggy black shorts and a tight-fitting black t-shirt with a little *Ore-Fit* emblem silk-screened on the left breast. I couldn't help wondering how he maintained such a perfect tan; my week in Oregon had been nothing but rain.

"Be right with you." He'd noted my presence but didn't look up, head buried in a stack of papers. From what I could make out reading upside down, they were sign-up forms for an advanced yoga class. He was checking signatures against a master list. "Sorry to make you wait, but I've got to confirm that everybody's signed the injury waiver."

"Injury waiver? For a yoga class?"

"We live in a litigious society, friend." He still hadn't looked up. "If you're here to join the class, I've still got room, but you'll have to sign the waiver form."

"Who gets injured doing yoga?"

"Happens all the time. People who've been sedentary their whole lives read an article that yoga can work miracles, sign up and wind up tearing or straining something. Then they want to sue. If you're just starting out, I'll warn you this is an advanced class . . . " He finally looked up at me, stopped in mid-sentence, and ran his eyes up and down in a fresh appraisal. I guess I don't look like the sedentary type. "Sorry. Today's the first day of yoga class. I just assumed you were here to sign up. What can I do for you?"

"Just moved to the area. Looking for a place to work out. Wondered if you've got any weights."

"We've got a weight area in the back, bench press, Smith machine, dumbbells. A few regulars use it. Most of our clients come for the yoga and aerobics. You say you just moved to the area? I can give you a pretty good deal on a year's membership."

"I was hoping you have a day pass or trial membership so I can decide if you'll suit my needs."

"I can sell you a two-week trial membership for fifty bucks." He was still eying me. Apparently working in a yoga-oriented club hadn't completely stifled the inner barbarian who was wondering if the new male was a threat to his local status as top tight-tee-shirted muscleman. "If you just want to try our weight area, I can comp you for the day. You're not one of those guys who spreads talc everywhere and drops the bar on the floor to impress everybody with how much weight you can lift, I hope. This is a family gym."

I looked over the crowd waiting for the yoga class. Other than two middle-aged guys with modest guts and gray ponytails, it looked to be a collection of fairly fit women in their early thirties. Quite a few of them were sporting form-fitting leotards to show off their impressively emaciated bodies. It reminded me of the yoga studio/fitness facility I work out in back in Fairfax, Virginia. The proprietor there, Pris, made it clear to me years ago that any cruising of the lonely housewives was her prerogative. I was betting that the guy behind the counter of Ore-Fit was doing the same thing, sizing me up to see if I might be a threat to his personal harem.

"I strength-train in conjunction with flexibility and endurance training. I'm not a body-builder."

"Yeah, I've got a couple of clients who are skiers who train like that. You don't look like a skier." He was getting a defensive look. He'd have preferred finding out I was training to be a gorilla. Muscle freaks are too caught up in their own physiques to waste time on women. But an all-around athlete ... "What brings you to Prestonville, anyway? You got a job with Conifer or something?"

"Actually, I'm living in Ogloskie."

"Ogloskie? You're kidding."

"Afraid not. Just arrived last week."

"What would get you to move there?"

"I'm the new forest ranger."

His eyes relaxed. He almost smirked. So I wasn't the only one who thinks of forest rangers as nonthreatening dorks. I kicked myself for not wearing the idiot uniform. He'd have been put at ease immediately. "Hey, welcome. You guys do a heckuva job out there, protecting nature and all that. Tell you what, I'll comp you the two week trial. Just fill this out."

He slid a form across the counter. I picked up a ballpoint and started writing down all the Clayton Stillbridge bullshit.

"If you like the place, I'll cut you a good deal on a year's membership. Honest."

"Thanks. I appreciate it." I didn't add that in my experience, whenever someone feels the need to say "honest" to convince you of their sincerity, they're usually thinking of screwing you royally.

"Nothing too good for our boys in uniform."

I also didn't bother to point out that the forest service isn't a branch of the military. "Got a locker room where I can change?"

"Just behind the weight area. Enjoy your work-out."

"Thanks." I grabbed my gear and headed toward the back, through the jumble of yoga students. I'd tossed some sweatpants and a tattered gray cotton t-shirt in my bag, pretty bland compared to all the brightly colored leotards and technical-fabric garments getting ready to start yoga-ing. Whatever people in Prestonville did for a living, it obviously paid well enough that they could afford expensive gym clothes.

Despite what the guy at the desk had said, I didn't have the weights to myself. When I came out of the locker room, a man in shorts, sweatshirt, and sandals was sitting at the bench press reading a newspaper. He was thickset; not exactly fat but certainly someone who could lose ten pounds and not be skinny. I made him out to be mid-forties, mostly from the streaks of gray in his otherwise jet-black hair that hung down over the cowl of his sweatshirt in the ponytail that was clearly *de rigueur* for the region.

He didn't look up when I came in, just continued reading. I wondered at first if he had retreated from the noisy yoga class to find a quiet place to read. But the bar on the bench was loaded with 230 pounds in free weights. Adding the weight of the bar, assuming it was a normal Olympic one, would mean he was benching more than 270. Nothing spectacular—that's what I lift and I'm not trying to be Charles Atlas—but nothing to sneeze at, either. Of course, a previous client might have been too lazy to remove the weights after finishing up. I watched the guy read as I started my pre-workout regimen of stretching and martial arts moves to get my muscles warm and limber, curious if he was working out at all.

It was maybe two minutes before he stopped reading. He kind of nodded, like he was agreeing silently with some point he'd read, folded the paper in half, set it under the bench, lay back, took a couple of deep breaths, then did four reps slowly with the bar. After he'd finished his last rep, he stood up, removed the collars from the bar ends, methodically added another ten pound weight to each side, reattached the collars, sat back down, retrieved the paper and started reading again. He repeated this procedure throughout my fifteen minute warm-up and had the bar nearing 400 pounds. I was impressed.

"You mind giving me a spot?" He glanced up at me from his paper. Obviously, he knew I'd been watching him.

"Not at all. That's a lot of weight."

"I'll just do a couple of reps."

"You training to failure?" I'd read about this method of lifting, low reps and add weight until your muscles give out.

"Maybe. We'll see."

He stored the paper under the bench again and lay down under the bar. I got into position to spot him. He lifted the bar, performed the first rep without any difficulty and managed the second one with concentrated effort.

"One more." He was whispering under the strain. I had to give him credit for being strong. He lowered the bar and got it about half-way back up, but the strength went out of his arms. I grabbed the bar quickly and helped him get it back on the rack. "Thanks."

"Don't mention it. That's more than I can bench."

He sat up and looked me over. "Don't know about that. You look like you've got some serious muscle."

"Not like that. Honestly, I never bench more than 300. And that's only when I'm feeling masochistic."

"You new around here?" He was giving me a serious once-over. "Haven't seen you here before."

"Just got into town a week ago. First chance I've had to try this place."

"It's a decent enough gym. Not a lot of weight-lifters. Most of the customers come for Gus's yoga and aerobics classes."

Gus was the guy I'd met behind the counter. He was working with the yoga students now, walking around them as they assumed various positions, correcting their form, bending over and helping them into proper positions. I could hear some of the women giggling as he bent their legs into position and straightened their backs. He didn't spend a lot of time with the two older men in the class.

"He seems to have a lot of satisfied customers."

"Sure. He's sort of a local celebrity. All-around athlete at the local high school, played basketball at Oregon State—not NBA caliber, but good for Oregon standards—then moved back here and opened this gym. He actually got a degree in physical fitness and nutrition, so he knows his stuff."

"Really. Maybe I should sign up for one of his classes. I've done a little yoga. It's good for maintaining flexibility."

"That important to you, staying flexible?"

"It's good to be strong. It's better if you're strong and agile."

"Yeah." He was still studying me. "I don't think you're the kind of student Gus is trying to attract."

"You don't say." Watching the class, I understood. "Maybe if I die and come back as a bored young housewife . . ."

"Bingo." He stood up. "You gonna do any bench? I'll be happy to spot you, return the favor."

"Thanks. But I don't lift to failure. Just do reps at a weight within my limits." I was curious, though. "You building muscle mass for competition or something?"

"Nah. Just the way I've always worked out. I got a bum knee, so I don't do a lot of running or anything. But I like to keep my upper body strong."

"Sure."

"So you just got into town a week ago? You work for Conifer or something?"

This was the second time I'd been asked. Conifer apparently had a large operation headquartered in Prestonville. That made sense, given all the forest in the vicinity and their secret lease on the Oquala. With a large number of workers positioned to start clear-cutting, I could understand their haste to resolve their recent difficulties. "Nope, I'm not with Conifer."

"I just assumed. They've brought in a lot of workers over the last six months. I'm not sure why. I guess they have a big contract in the works."

"Could be. I wouldn't know. I'm with the forest service."

"Oh? I didn't know there was a forest service office in Prestonville."

"Ogloskie."

"Ogloskie?" He grinned. "You're not replacing Ranger Ruby, I hope."

"Nope. I'm her new assistant."

"Interesting."

"What about you? Obviously, you don't work for Conifer."

"No, I don't. I'm semi-retired."

"You from Prestonville? I mean, it doesn't look like the kind of place people move to when they retire."

"Oh, I don't live here." He picked up his newspaper. I guess he was ready to move on. "I live in Ogloskie, too."

That caught me off guard.

"I thought I'd met the entire town already." Actually, I knew exactly who I hadn't met.

"Apparently not." He stuck out his hand. "John Alvarez."

"Pleasure to meet you, Mr. Alvarez. Clayton Stillbridge." His grip was like a vice. I had to strain not to grimace. "I heard you had a small farm outside town, but nobody mentioned your incredible strength or any other super powers."

"I just grow a few vegetables as a hobby."

"Ruby said you're an attorney."

"She did?" He looked amused. "Well, that's right. Practiced for a few years in California."

"What made you move out here to the middle of nowhere?"

"She didn't fill you in on that, too?" He wasn't defensive, just curious. "Moved here for my health."

"She mentioned something like that." I guess I'd expected he'd look frail. I don't usually think of muscle-men as suffering poor health. "You don't look sick to me."

"High blood pressure." His expression went serious. Either his health was a topic that worried him, or he was worried I didn't believe him. "Probably genetic. Exercise helps."

"Yeah, I'm sure it does." I doubt doctors who recommend a little exercise to their high-blood-pressure patients are thinking about having them bench press 400 pounds. But I'm not a doctor. "And I guess you can always bend a few steel bars to relieve stress."

He laughed. "You sound skeptical, Mr. Stillbridge, like you think I made up this whole moved-to-Ogloskie-for-my-health story."

"Sorry. Didn't mean to give you that impression. And call me Clayton."

"Sure, thing, Clayton. And call me John. I'm not offended or anything. I don't tend to take things at face value, either."

"Guess that comes from years of practicing law?"

He raised an eyebrow. "Yeah. Guess so. Must be something you learn in the forest service, too."

"Sure. It's all those wily coyotes."

"Well, I'll let you get on with your work-out, Clayton." He started to leave, then stopped and turned around. "You got plans tomorrow night?"

"Not really."

"Stop by around six and I'll have the wife cook us up something for dinner. You know where our farm is, right?"

"Sure, I can find it. Appreciate it. I've been getting tired of eating at Ogloskie's all the time."

"Understandable. The cook there's not bad for a drunk, but he's not exactly a world class chef. See you tomorrow."

"Looking forward to it." I was, mostly to find out why Mr. Antisocial suddenly wanted to be my best friend. Of course, maybe Ruby was wrong about him being a snob.

One other thing Prestonville had that Ogloskie lacked was a grocery store. On my way out of town, I stopped off at someplace called *Nature's Freshest* in hopes of finding beer. The refrigerator in my new home was empty. I also figured I could stock a few other essentials like cereal, milk, frozen pizzas. I entered the place with trepidation, though, unsure whether a place that sounded like a health food store would suit my needs.

I needn't have worried. The beer aisle would have made Carrie Nation weep. Sven had already warned me that Oregon leads the country in breweries, all of them trying to outdo each other in crafting the hoppiest pale ales, meatiest stouts, darkest porters, fruitiest wheat beers and snootiest lagers. I was hoping to score a case of Budweiser or Miller Genuine Draft, but I was out of luck; apparently I'd be forced to consume craft beer until I finished my assignment and escaped the rain-drenched state. I grabbed a few six packs of something called Beavertail Pale Ale. At least it came in cans.

The cereal aisle was an eye-opener, too. I'd had no idea there was such a variety of mueslis, bran flakes, and granola mixes. Ordinarily, I eat a light breakfast—cereal, maybe some whole wheat toast, juice and coffee—splurging on a plate of pancakes and eggs like Sven served when I was on a job or meeting my spook boss. That's because I figure staying fit requires not gorging yourself as soon as the day begins. But the residents of this part of Oregon seemed to be going me one better, starting their day by purging their colons with the highest fiber content they could find. After searching in vain for fifteen minutes, I abandoned my quest to find Kellogg's Corn Flakes and grabbed a couple of boxes of some kind of spelt flake. I was betting it tasted like crap. But forcing down a lousy breakfast that's good for your colon can't help but toughen you up a bit, I guess.

I actually found frozen pizza. It was an import, something from Germany called *Dr. Oetker's*. I grabbed a couple of spinach pizzas. Maybe Popeye was on to something.

Heading to the check-out area, I resolved to splurge and buy a few candy bars to compensate for the spelt flakes and spinach pizza. I was sorely disappointed. Unlike grocery stores in the rest of the country, this one didn't have any Snickers or Three Musketeers to tempt you while you waited to pay. What it had was endless varieties of gorp, otherwise known as trail mix. I grabbed a couple of bags with peanuts, almonds, cranberries, sunflower seeds, shredded coconut, and what appeared to be M&Ms. As they say, when in Rome, eat seeds and crunchy granola. Or something like that.

Driving back to Ogloskie in the rain, I started getting a sense of just how alien the environment was. Oregon had a rugged feel that I'm sure dated back to the days when Oquala Indians were masters of the forest, but it now was populated by pony-tailed dudes munching mixed nuts and berries with a ruggedness that seemed more mystical than manly. As I thought about it, I realized the only man I'd come across with close-cropped hair was Walker Treadman. No doubt we had a few other things in common.

Ruby was just getting ready to leave when I pulled up at the duplex. She was gussied up again. I figured she was heading off for another romantic interlude with her favorite outdoor sporting goods sales rep.

"Did some grocery shopping, I see." She stuck her head through the open window of the F-150 after I crunched to a stop on the gravel. "Beer, pizza, cereal and trail mix. Obviously, you know how to party."

"Just a few basics. Had to settle for this local beer, too. You wouldn't happen to know anyplace that sells Bud or Miller?"

"Miller around here? I think there' a law against selling anything but local beers."

"Well, at least if one of us gets tired of being a ranger, we can probably get a job with the local beer police." She kept leaning through the window, not in much of a rush to go. "Found a gym in Prestonville and worked out. You'll never guess who I ran into there."

"Don't tell me. You met the spirit of Vlad Ogloskie doing step aerobics."

"Not quite. Ran into John Alvarez doing bench presses."

"You don't say. I wondered how he stayed so strong. He's built like a wrestler. So are you two best friends now?"

"Well, he invited me over for dinner tomorrow night."

She stood there for a minute, not saying anything. "I'm still waiting for the punch line."

"No joke. Said he'd have his wife cook up something good to give me a break from Sven's swill."

"You're serious." She looked impressed. "That's a first. I don't think anybody else has seen the inside of their farmhouse."

"Well, you know what they say about guys bonding at the gym."

"No, I don't. What do they say about guys bonding at the gym?"

I could tell she was teasing me. I was beginning to get the impression that Ruby was wondering if she could do better than Walker. "They say guys bond when they work out together."

"Is that what they call it? Bonding?"

"Just what are you implying, Ruby?"

"Maybe I'm curious to find out whether you're gay."

"What if I am? You're not a homophobe, I hope. I think that's a bigger crime in Oregon than selling Miller."

"I wouldn't be upset or anything. Just disappointed." She winked.

"Don't worry. I'm straight. You should be careful."

"Really? Something going to happen if I keep provoking you? Sounds interesting."

"I mean the Department of Agriculture frowns upon supervisors soliciting sexual favors from their staff."

"Hah. That presumes you'd be the one doing me a favor." She gave me a look that said I should consider the possibility I was passing up something pretty special.

"Hmm. That's something to think about."

"You do that." She winked again. "Think about it all night while you drink this beer and eat these frozen pizzas. Me, I got a date. Don't wait up." Without another word she turned her back on me, hopped into the USDA vehicle she'd adopted as her personal property, and peeled off in the direction of Prestonville.

I did indeed spend the evening drinking Beavertail Pale Ale—it wasn't even all that bad—and eating frozen pizza, but I wasn't thinking about Ruby's sexual charms. Mostly I passed the time staring through the window at the dark edges of the Oquala, wondering how long I was going to be stuck in the middle of nowhere going stir-crazy. I needed to find my client.

Maybe I'd learn something at dinner with the Alvarezes.

Sunday morning I got up early again, although not because Ruby was pounding on my door. She'd apparently had such a great time with Walker, she didn't come home at all. A week of living next to a human alarm clock had conditioned me, though. I decided to go for a pre-breakfast run, see the town at first light, sweat out last night's pizza and beer. The cold, constant drizzle made working up a sweat a challenge.

Ogloskie was a quiet place early on a Sunday. I ran out to Wilson's motel and headed back through town without seeing a single sign of life. It wasn't much of a run, either; from the motel at one end of town to the ranger station at the other was a little less than a mile.

Still, it was better than nothing, and I could always head out to the service road that snaked several miles into the Oquala. I'd resolved to do that when I noticed someone sitting on the town's only public bench across the road from the Fey's store. As I got closer, I made out a disheveled, skinny guy with stringy hair matted and wet hanging from under a beat-up baseball cap down over the collar of his flannel shirt. Running in the rain is one thing; sitting staring into space while you get drenched demands an explanation, in my book.

"Everything okay?" I'd jogged right up to him; he never even glanced at me.

"Sure." He kept staring.

"Mind if I ask what you're doing, sitting here in the rain?"

That got him to look at me. He had big eyes somewhere between hollow and mournful. "Sitting in the rain."

My pulse picked up. I had a flash that maybe the tree-hugger killer I was hunting had suddenly had a pang of conscience, emerged from the woods and planted himself right in front of me while he wrestled with his guilt. Sure, it seemed far-fetched. Still, "You got any ID? You from around here somewhere? Prestonville?"

"You a cop?" He said 'cop' like it was an insult. Like I say the word, actually.

"Forest ranger."

"I ain't in the forest." He went back to staring straight ahead at nothing. "And I ain't breakin' no laws."

He was beginning to irritate me. I got in his face. "Look, buddy, I see a stranger show up acting odd, then giving me attitude, I start thinking about breaking something other than laws."

"Ain't no stranger, either." The hollow look shifted to a glare right back at me. "Sure, I recognize you now. You're that new Ranger working for Ruby."

"We've met?"

"I seen you at Sven's."

"I've never seen you."

"Guess you haven't made it back into the kitchen."

So this was Fred Walderman. I backed off, partly because I now had an explanation for his behavior, mostly because his alcohol breath almost knocked me over. "My mistake. It's Fred, right?"

"Yeah."

It occurred to me he really had wandered away from wherever he was living and gotten lost. Ruby had told me he drank around the clock and barely seemed to know what planet he was on. "Listen, you having trouble finding your way home? You sit here in this rain long enough, you'll catch a chill."

"I live right there." He nodded across the street toward the Fey's general store. "Upstairs."

I hadn't noticed the stairs around the side of the store. Apparently there was an apartment above it. "Well, sorry to have bothered you. Guess you can make it home on your own if you decide to."

"Yeah."

"Enjoy the rest of your morning."

"Yeah."

I resumed my run. From the look of it, Fred wasn't generally in any condition to be arranging skillful murders made to look accidental. But he had something serious on his mind, something he was anesthetizing with a bottle. Unanswered questions tend to nag at me. Guess I don't like loose ends.

Of course, the real mystery was how a guy who gets that far in the bag before seven in the morning can whip up such great pancakes. That was probably a mystery I'd never solve.

I got to the Alvarez farm at six that evening. After my encounter with Fred, it had proved to be an uneventful Sunday. At least I'd been spared having Ruby around making suggestive comments all day. It wasn't that I was offended. Mostly I was finding myself sorely tempted. Jumping in the sack with a woman in the middle of a job is an exercise in bad judgment—and I've got a long history of bad judgment where women are concerned. Walker keeping her occupied might just keep me from failing the common sense test again.

I didn't have anything to worry about that where Lucinda Alvarez was concerned. She was an impressive woman, too; two-hundred pounds and built like a linebacker—seeing her for the first time put into context Ruby's sarcastic comment about being the sexiest woman in Ogloskie. Maybe Ore-Fit had a special rate for families.

She met me at the door of their aging farmhouse—not a very impressive place, certainly not what you'd expect as the retirement castle of a formerly successful California attorney. It was wood-frame construction with blue-stained cedar-shake shingle siding and looked to be maybe twelve-hundred square-feet total. At least there were some appetizing smells emanating from the kitchen.

"Hi. Clayton Stillbridge." I introduced myself. "Something sure smells good."

She opened the door and admitted me without a word, then let the door close and walked back to the kitchen, still without so much as a hello. I got the impression she didn't like guests.

John Alvarez was waiting for me in a living room that looked like it had been furnished out of a consignment shop. I wondered if maybe he hadn't been such a successful lawyer after all.

"Welcome to my humble home, Stillbridge." He extended his hand for one of his vice-like handshakes. I braced myself and tried to match him. "Stillbridge. What kind of name is that, anyway? Your ancestors come over on the Mayflower?"

"I think one of my forebears translated it from some Polish name." Why Frank can't ever give me a phony identity like Smith or Jones is something I haven't figured out. Maybe stupid sounding names are considered more believable. "Alvarez. Italian?"

He arched an eyebrow, like he was trying to decide if I was joking. "Sure. My family came over from *Baja Italia*. Have a seat and I'll get us something to drink. You like beer?"

"Only when I can get it."

He walked back into the kitchen and emerged a few moments later carrying two bottles of something called *Web State Lager*. I took one from him and swigged some. It wasn't bad.

"This is about as close to Bud as it gets around here." He chugged some and made a face. "Oregonians won't drink beer if it isn't brewed locally by some vegan. I finally stopped buying Budweiser for fear a local lynch mob would come out here and string me up."

"Yeah, I went looking for Miller at the store yesterday. Couldn't find any."

"If you find it someplace around here and decide to buy it, pay cash. If you use a credit card, they'll probably enter your name in some database of enemies of the people."

He sat down in an ancient arm-chair and motioned for me to have a seat. I deposited myself on the beat-up sofa that might have been left over from pioneer days.

"Hope I'm not putting you guys out."

"I guess Lucinda wasn't very welcoming." He grinned. "Don't worry. She's not real social. She can cook, though."

"Yeah, something smells good."

"She's making an enchilada casserole. Hope you like spicy food."

"My momma always told me that's why there's beer."

"Smart woman." He sized me up for a minute. "So how you liking your new post? Must be a little different, being in such an isolated spot. You came from back East, right?"

"Georgia." Georgians don't think of themselves as easterners. "Being stationed in a national forest is pretty isolated whatever part of the country you're in."

"You like that, the isolation, being close to nature?"

"Sure. That's why I joined the forest service."

"Makes sense. Me, I'm more of a city boy." Funny. Walker had said the same thing.

"You picked an odd place to retire, then."

"Apparently, liking city life doesn't mean it's healthy. That's what my doctor said, anyway."

"So is it working?"

"What?" He gave me an odd look.

"Living here in the country. Is your blood pressure going down?"

"Well, yeah, actually. It's so low these days, I could hibernate in the winter."

"So I guess all these trees are therapeutic."

"It would seem so." He got a serious look. "Be a shame if somebody cut them all down."

I studied his eyes, trying to figure out if he was about to lecture me on environmentalism or whether he was probing me for a reaction. I couldn't tell. He wasn't someone I'd want to play poker with. "I don't know of anybody planning to cut down any of the Oquala."

"But you've heard the rumors."

"Me and everybody else within a thousand miles. But I don't pay attention to rumors. I even ignore the ones about Elvis."

"Elvis doesn't have several thousand employees hanging out in Prestonville . . ."

"You sure about that?"

". . . but Conifer Corporation does, and it's staging them there for a reason." He was probing, but not because he was concerned for the Oquala. I could tell he was more interested in what I was about to say, testing to see if I could sound believably like a forest ranger. I was getting the sneaking suspicion John Alvarez knew damned well I was a phony. Maybe ex-Army lawyers have a sixth sense for spooks operating in alias.

"Yeah, well the Air Force has a lot of planes in Alaska. Doesn't mean we're getting ready to bomb Canada."

He looked at me for the longest time with dead-serious eyes, a lawyer's eyes scrutinizing a witness, I guess. Then he broke into a big grin. "You sure we're not gonna attack Canada?"

"I'm sure I'd have been informed if we were. I'm a federal employee."

"Right." He stood up. "Dinner should be ready by now. Let's eat."

The dining room was on the other side of the kitchen and smaller than the living room. It had just enough space for a square table and four chairs, one of them with a little plastic booster seat so four-year-old Becky could reach the table. A large casserole dish sat square in the middle of the table with a bowl of salad next to it. I took the seat across from Becky, flanked by John and Lucinda.

"This looks really good." I meant it. The dish was bubbling with cheese and red salsa over blue corn tortillas rolled into enchiladas. It smelled great, too.

Lucinda scooped big portions with a metal spatula for me, John, and her, then plopped a smaller portion on Becky's plate. Becky was no more talkative than her mom, staring at her plate with big sad eyes.

"We haven't been introduced." Being friendly with other peoples' kids is supposed to make them warm up to you. I decided to give it a try. "I'm Clayton Stillbridge, the new forest ranger. You must be Becky."

The sad eyes went suspicious. She glanced over at her mom like a hostile witness looking for guidance from an attorney.

"Say hello to the ranger, dear." So at least Lucinda wasn't mute.

"Hullo." She went back to staring at her plate.

"Afraid my girls aren't very chatty." There was smug satisfaction in the lawyer's voice. "I'm a lucky man."

Lucinda didn't respond. She picked up a fork and started eating. As if on cue, Becky scooped a morsel of casserole into her mouth and started chewing silently.

I took a bite. The enchiladas were filled with chicken, cheese, and a hell of a lot of very hot peppers. I tried to maintain my best poker face while I chewed, but the tears welling up in my eyes gave me away for the *gringo* I am. I swallowed and took a big swig of beer in a vain effort to cool off my palate.

"Very tasty, Mrs. Alvarez." The words croaked out of my mouth, not sounding all that credible.

John Alvarez laughed. "Lucinda likes things on the spicy side. Here, this helps." He picked up the salad bowl and spooned a decent serving of lettuce and tomato onto my casserole, then did the same to his. I looked across the table at Becky and noted she was eating the untempered enchiladas with relish. It occurred to me that the Alvarez women didn't talk much because they'd scorched their vocal chords.

The lettuce and tomato did cut the heat some, but eating the casserole was still a challenge. Each mouthful had to be washed down with beer, and even that was like trying to put out a bonfire with a garden hose. I could only imagine what all those peppers were doing to my insides.

"This stuff will clean out your intestines, that's for sure." Maybe Alvarez had sensed my concern. More likely he'd just had plenty of experience with the aftermath of his wife's cooking. "Looks like you're getting low on suds, there, Clayton. Lucinda, honey, would you mind getting us a couple more beers from the kitchen?"

She looked up shooting daggers. This was no marriage made in heaven. Not many are, though. But she got up and fetched two beers, slamming one each heavily in front of me and her husband, who grinned broadly.

We finished eating in an uncomfortable silence. I couldn't help but wonder if Lucinda wasn't all that happy about moving to Ogloskie for her husband's health. I had to admit, there have to be other quiet places to live that aren't in the middle of nowhere. After dinner, she picked Becky up and disappeared somewhere in the tiny farmhouse. Her husband barely noticed.

"Now we can talk. I'll grab us a couple more beers and meet you on the front porch. It's real nice outside this time of year,"

I'd been finding the evenings a bit chilly, especially since it was always overcast and wet, but I figured I could take it if he could. It also occurred to me that a guy with high blood pressure isn't supposed to be pounding brews every evening. But, as I kept reminding myself, I'm no doctor. I made my way out to the porch and sat in one of the two ancient overstuffed chairs that afforded a view of the dark, drizzly, overcast night.

Alvarez came out shortly with the beers, handed me one and sat down with a satisfied sigh.

"It's so quiet out here in the evening. A man can really think."

"I guess so." Deep thoughts aren't my area of expertise.

"So how long you been working for the government, Clayton?"

I tried to remember what was in the Stillbridge file. It said I'd been in Georgia for three years. Before that,

I'd been someplace else. I hadn't gotten around to reading it that closely. "About ten years."

"Before that?"

"I was in the Army for awhile." I don't know if Stillbridge had served. But I had.

"Yeah, there's something about you that says ex-Army. How'd you like that?"

"Except for the officers, it was fine."

He laughed. "Yeah, officers suck."

"You in the Army too, John?"

He didn't say anything for a minute, like he was trying to remember. "Yup."

"Officer?"

"How'd you guess?"

"Just figured. I got a knack for sticking my foot in my mouth."

"Don't worry about it. I share your opinion of officers. Though I like to think I was different."

"You go to law school before or after the Army?"

"During, actually. Army put me through law school. Thought I'd make an ideal Judge Advocate."

"How'd that work out?"

"First day I'd completed my time of service required after graduation, I resigned my commission."

"Here's to you." I raised my beer bottle in salute. "Here's to life after the fucking Army."

He saluted back and took a long swig. The he lowered the bottle and stared at the mouth for a long time. "But you still work for the government, huh, Clayton?"

"Sure. Why not? I'm not a grunt anymore."

"Yeah." He sounded doubtful. "But you still follow orders."

"The forest service isn't like the Army."

"Forest service. Yeah." He looked up at me, a hard look. "You ever consider the private sector?"

"What, there are companies that hire forest rangers?"

He was staring at me, not blinking. "There are lots of opportunities for people with the right skill set."

"What skills are those?" I had a sneaking suspicion I knew what he was talking about. It couldn't just be coincidence that he was parroting my earlier conversation with Walker Treadman. Somebody was very interested in finding out if I could be lured away from government work.

"Keeping your head in tight situations, and knowing how to take care of problems."

"Too bad. I never was much of a Boy Scout."

"And yet that's exactly what you look like to me right now, running around in that ranger suit protecting trees and grizzlies."

"I'm not wearing the uniform right now."

"Yeah." He smiled. "I was speaking figuratively."

It wasn't adding up. I'd come to the Oquala to put a tree-hugger terrorist out of the EPA's misery, and I'd found Treadman and Alvarez. Both of them fit the goon profile, but I couldn't see either of them as an eco-loony. "I'm just saying I'm no Boy Scout."

"I can tell that, too." He nodded. "I'm just telling you, if you ever get tired of Uncle Sam holding your leash, there are people who would be glad to have someone with your abilities and who would pay you good money."

"I'll keep that in mind." I stared back at him, showing him I could restrain the impulse to blink, too. I'd suspected after my initial encounters with Walker that he was thugging for a rival government outfit.

Now it looked more likely that some corporate goon squad was in the mix. I wondered if Conifer's bosses had brought in a little private muscle to hedge their bets; hell, who could blame them if they lacked confidence in the government's ability to solve their problem. But I don't particularly like competition. Maybe Alvarez felt the same way, wanted to recruit me. Too bad. I'm not a team player. "Right now, I'm pretty content being a forest ranger."

"Sure." He looked away. The stare-down was over. So was the conversation. He'd invited me to dinner to deliver a message, and he'd delivered it.

"Guess I better be going. Ruby likes us to get an early start. Thank the missus for the great dinner."

"Enjoyed the company. Drive careful."

I finished the beer and headed back to my truck. So Alvarez and associates wanted to buy me off. I wasn't kidding myself that they were in the market for Clayton Stillbridge. That job offer had been for Richard Paladin. Before I finished this assignment and got the hell out of Ogloskie, I planned to figure out how my cover had been blown so fast.

Chapter V
Dead Ends

I WAS UP AND DRESSED BY SIX Monday morning. Actually I was up and in the bathroom at five. Lucinda Alvarez's enchilada casserole had me sitting on the toilet before sun-up wishing I had some sort of skin cream to soothe the fire that was consuming my asshole. Whoever was selling her chili peppers should have been working for the military developing chemical weapons.

I'd heard Ruby creep in about three in the morning. I wasn't complacent about her sleeping in anymore. Sure enough, she was banging on my door at six-thirty.

"You planning to sleep the day away, Clayton?"

"Just waiting for you to get up." I could read the surprise—and disappointment—in her face when I opened the door already fully uniformed. "Come on in. I made coffee."

"Don't mind if I do." She looked a little bleary-eyed. "Hope you made it strong."

"Just the way you like it. Looks like you had another late night."

She went to the kitchen and helped herself. "Walker wanted me to stay the night, but I prefer waking up in my own place. How about you? You and John Alvarez sit up swapping stories all night?"

"No. I was in bed before eleven."

"How was dinner? Lucinda know how to cook?"

"She knows how to make really hot Mexican food. If you're looking for a colon purge, try to wrangle an invitation sometime."

"Ooh. That doesn't sound good." She sipped some coffee and grimaced. I knew that meant she liked it. "So what are they like? Not many people around here have had a chance to meet the Alvarez's in their nest."

"I don't think I'd call it a nest. For a guy who's supposed to have been a successful attorney, he certainly didn't buy a mansion. It's a shack and it looks like he furnished it from garage sales."

"Well, I knew the place wasn't much to look at from the outside. One thing about money, you can never have too much of it. I know I'm not looking forward to living on a government pension." She looked pensive. I don't think she was contemplating the Alvarezes. "Think that's why they're so stand-offish, embarrassed that they're not living in luxury?"

"I think Lucinda is the one who's stand-offish because she doesn't like people very much. Including her husband, best I could tell. At least their kid seems well-behaved."

She made a face. "One nice thing about Ogloskie, there aren't a bunch of little brats running around."

"Ruby!" That made me laugh. "I thought forest rangers were supposed to be kid-friendly?"

"In my experience there are just two kinds; the ones who start fires and the ones who get lost in the woods. People should be required to pass a test to have kids, same as to get a driver's license."

"Becky doesn't seem the type to start any fires."

"Wait 'til she gets older."

"Anyway, I don't think you have to worry about them bothering you. Lucinda's the least social person I've met."

"Funny, though. When they first showed up a little over two years ago, John spent a lot of time in town. Seemed he wanted to get to know everybody. Then after a few months he got as reclusive as Lucinda."

"Maybe he found out everything he needed to know about Ogloskie."

"Still, it's curious." She was sitting on the sofa in the duplex I'd occupied. It looked maybe in slightly better shape than the one in the Alvarez's living room. I figured the duplex had been furnished out of some huge government warehouse.

"What's so curious?"

"First those guys from Conifer show up. Then the Alvarezes move here. Next thing there's a rash of accidents." She was staring into her coffee cup doing some serious thinking.

"Now who's acting like a cop?"

"You've got to admit, Clayton, it's an interesting sequence of events."

"You left one event out."

"Oh?" She looked up at me and smiled. "Don't tell me. The part where you show up and everything's okay?"

"No. In between Alvarez arriving and the accidents." I looked at her. She had a curious expression. I realized she didn't get what I was driving at. Love is a funny thing. Or sex, anyway. "Walker showed up. Right?"

It took a few seconds to sink in. Then her eyes went serious. She looked back into her coffee cup, like there were some answers in there. "Yeah, that's right.

Funny. I never really thought about him in relation to the other stuff."

"No reason you should. They were accidents and a suicide. That makes all this other stuff just coincidence."

"Coincidence. Sure." She put down her cup, then looked up at me with a curious expression. "What suicide?"

I'd forgotten that Roper hanging himself had happened in Portland. It might not even have made the news in Ogloskie. Even if it had, no one necessarily would have connected it to the other events. "Did I say suicide? I guess I meant Riefenthal getting himself lost."

"Is that what you meant?" She looked pretty skeptical. But her brain was grinding away at the new association I'd made for her. "You think there's a possibility Walker had something to do with those deaths?"

"No, I don't." My instincts are excellent where environmentalists are concerned, and they were telling me that neither Walker Treadman nor John Alvarez cared one wit about saving any trees. But until that moment I hadn't really pondered the fact that they'd both shown up before Conifer's managers started taking unplanned, early retirements, which seemed to eliminate either of them being part of a rival investigation. It was beginning to look like there was a lot to this job that my asshole boss hadn't filled me in on. Big surprise there. "Maybe Ogloskie's ghost doesn't like people who work for logging companies. Tell you what, if I run into him when I'm out there in the woods with Dewaldo, I'll ask him."

"You do that, Clayton." She grinned. But I could tell she was still pondering things. "Well, we're sitting here gossiping like old women. Waddya say we open the office and do what we're paid to do?"

"Sounds good to me." Except I was no closer to doing what I get paid for.

Ruby didn't stick around for long after we opened the office. She said she was headed to check the trail logs, but I figured she just needed time to think. I'd rattled her with my comment about Walker. She clearly had her suspicions about the deaths, and she'd admitted she wasn't all that sure about her boyfriend's bona fides. But sometimes it takes someone else to connect the dots for you no matter how long they're sitting in front of your face. And she was jumping the gun, actually. I still hadn't drawn any conclusions, and I wasn't going to draw any until after my expedition with Dewaldo to meet Blue Feather. I've learned over the years not to condemn the first suspect who acts suspicious; everybody acts suspicious and usually has something to hide. It's just human nature.

I logged on to the Internet as soon as she left and checked the Webmail address. There was no response to my queries. Washington bureaucrats don't work weekends, not even spooks. I typed in another entry.

One more local to check out: John Alvarez; says he practiced water rights law in California, retired for his health; wife Lucinda, four-year-old daughter Becky; earned law degree while in the Army; serious weight lifter.

Alvarez and Treadman look like the kind of people who work for you, Frank. Something you're note telling me?

I cleared the browser history and logged off quickly when I heard wheels spitting gravel outside. Figuring

Ruby had forgotten something, I got up and opened the door only to get a surprise. Walker Treadman was standing on the office porch.

"Walker. Didn't figure you'd be up and about this early. Not as late as Ruby got in last night."

"Thought I'd surprise her, take her out for coffee or something this morning."

"Sorry. She went off to check the trail logs." I stepped back so he could come into the office. I knew he was there to see me anyway. He knew damned well Ruby liked to check the logs first thing.

"My bad luck." He didn't seem disappointed. "Hey, she mentioned that you're planning to do some backpacking. You serious about heading up to Chalker Mountain?"

"Well, yes, I am." Alarms were going off in my head.

"Then why don't you give this baby a whirl." He pulled a black plastic box with a little display screen out of his coat pocket and laid it on the desk. I'd seen GPS devices before, and this was a nice one.

"You feeling civic minded, worried I might get lost?"

"Strictly commercial interest. I've been talking up forest service personnel all over my territory. Nice government contract would do wonders for my stock with Trailhead. Just try it out. The product sells itself."

"I'll be out almost a week. The battery in this thing will never last that long."

"Oh, you'd be surprised. These things don't use that much juice; runs on two double-As for a good fifteen hours. It's got a set of rechargeable Lithium-Ions in it fully charged right now." He reached in his other pocket and produced a little plastic pack with a strip of some kind of film attached. "Just keep a spare set in this little gizmo and stick it on your pack. Solar charger. You can stay out there for a month and never have any doubt just where you are."

"You know, Walker, there's more money in it if you'd try to market these things to the military."

"Aw, Garmin's already got that market locked. Tell you what, you don't like it, just tell me when you get back and no hard feelings. But I'm betting you'll find it's real useful. Then maybe you can write me a testimonial or something I can use in the contract proposal. I've already got a dozen other rangers who've done that."

"You don't say." He was almost pushy enough to be a real sales rep. "I don't know how to use one of these."

He produced an instruction booklet from the interior pocket of his jacket. He'd come prepared. "They're simple. Five-year-old could figure it out in no time."

"Maybe I'm not that advanced."

"Funny, Clayton. You got a sense of humor. I like that. Well, I'll leave it here. You don't want to take it, I can't make you."

I thought about it. "Ruby didn't seem too high on these."

"We don't need to tell her, do we?"

"I guess not. What the hell, it seems pretty light. I'll give it a shot."

"Hey, really appreciate it, Clayton. You'll be doing me a big favor."

"I have to pay for it if it gets broken?"

"What?" I guess he hadn't considered that. "They're pretty durable. But it's a demo. I can write it off if you break it or lose it."

"Good. I can't afford one of these on my salary."

"They're really not that expensive; only cost a couple hundred bucks. Trust me, once you use this thing, you'll never want to be without one."

"We'll see."

"Enjoy it. I'll talk to you when you get back." He headed back outside to his car and sped off while I sat examining the loaner GPS. He hadn't lied about it being durable. It had a plastic casing, but it was that heavy plastic that's designed to be lightweight and tough, and it was encased in a rubbery outer layer that provided extra shock-absorption. I picked up the operations booklet and checked out the features: it had about every bell and whistle you could think of; complete set of digital maps for North America; settings to store time and distance covered; a route planner that took terrain into account to map fastest, easiest, and most scenic; even doubled as an mp3 player in case I wanted to listen to Beethoven or Twisted Sister while I walked. About the only thing it wouldn't do was dig a hole to shit in. I wondered what else it could do that wasn't covered in the manual, like transmit it's location to someone who wanted to track my movements. I was sure of one thing; it cost a lot more than a couple-hundred bucks.

I stowed the GPS and accessories in the top desk drawer when I heard Ruby pull up. No need for her to know I had let her boyfriend loan it to me. She might think I was being corrupted.

"Things been quiet?"

"Quiet as a church on Saturday night. Walker stopped by."

"Yeah. He's picking me up this afternoon. We're driving over to Bend for some sorta folk concert. Might be late getting back. Don't wait up."

"Okay. I'll try not to worry."

"Sure." She sat across from me, pondering. "You know, you've only been here a week, and I'm gonna miss having you around."

"Sure. You'll have to go back to sitting here in the office most of the day."

"Right." She smiled. "You sure you're up for a week in the Oquala? Georgia's pretty tame compared to forests here in the West."

"I'll be okay. I'm pretty resourceful."

"You want to take my Smith & Wesson, you're welcome to it. There really are grizzlies out there, you know."

"If I can't stop a grizzly with my .44, I deserve to get mauled. Besides, I'll be with Dewaldo. He's managed to avoid getting eaten by bears. He must know a few tricks."

"Maybe it's the divinity degree. Maybe God protects him."

"Then I'll stick close to him so the protection rubs off." So she really didn't know about Dewaldo's Colt. I wondered what other secrets he'd been keeping. "Really, the only thing you need to be concerned about is how bad I'm gonna smell when I get back."

"I'll make sure to avoid you until you get a chance to shower." She sat back in the little chair and looked me over again. "So are you going to tell me why you're really so interested in meeting Blue Feather?"

"Like I told you, I'm interested in having a look around the Oquala. Paying a call on Blue Feather is just curiosity."

"Yeah, that's what you told me." She stood up. "Well, I'm gonna go have a nice long shower and a nap before my big night. You hold down the fort. See you tomorrow."

"Sure thing, Ruby." I couldn't begrudge her taking advantage of having a new assistant. It wasn't going to be permanent, after all.

It was getting dark early with winter approaching, which was good for what I had in mind that evening. I was pretty confident I had the appropriate suspects identified, but I've learned over the years that it's never a good idea to dismiss people if first appearances aren't damning. Fred the cook might very well be just a drunk who knew his way around a kitchen. I wanted to be sure, though, and the easiest way was to have a look around his place while he was at work burning bacon for Sven. That meant letting myself into his apartment, and that was best accomplished after dark. Ogloskie was just too small to count on bystanders not caring what goes on.

As far as I could tell, Fred's apartment above the Feys' store was one of only two apartments in the whole town. The other was above Ogloskie's and was occupied by Sven. The Feys lived in a log cabin just down the street from their store, Wilson resided at his motel, and Dewaldo occupied a two-room cabin on a hill behind the town's gas station that looked like it had been abandoned decades earlier. Townspeople needed gas, they drove to Prestonville.

I headed up the stairs after making sure the area was quiet; the Feys closed up at five in the off-season. The lock on Fred's door was a joke, of course. I often wonder why people bother to lock their doors when the hardware on almost every house in the USA can be defeated by a ten-year-old with a paper-clip, which is what I typically use. This time, though, I started working the lock and the door just opened. I froze at first, thinking maybe someone else had broken in before me and might be waiting inside. I stuck my head cautiously into the apartment and looked around, but it was empty. It seemed Fred not only didn't bother with the lock, he didn't even pull the door completely shut. Drunks can be like that.

I walked in expecting to be knocked over by the stench of a filthy sot's home. I got a surprise; Fred kept his place tidy. There wasn't a lot to it; a living area with a table, two chairs, a beat-up sofa, a kitchen that was clean and looked like it was never used, and a bedroom with a bed that had been made. I looked closer at the bed, wondering if Fred didn't even sleep there, but the sheets weren't clean and had obviously been slept on recently. He just made his bed after getting up in the morning. Lots of people do that, mostly people who have spent too much time in the military . . . or prison.

Wondering what kind of food a cook keeps on hand, I rummaged through the kitchen cabinets. I found a box of Cheerios and five bottles of Jim Beam Eight Star Whiskey. The trash can under the sink held two empty whiskey bottles. I guessed that Fred mostly ate in Sven's kitchen, and I was pretty sure he wasn't eating all that much. Fred was in the process of pickling his liver with rotgut, and guys who drink like that don't usually waste too much time eating.

There was nothing in the place to suggest that Fred was even aware the Oquala forest lay just beyond his door, much less that he was killing Conifer employees to protect it. Still, I was curious about anybody whose life seemed to be such a wreck and yet who was daily producing damned fine pancakes and other tasty items. I have a hard time accepting anybody at face value: maybe that's because almost everybody I work with or meet is living some form of elaborate lie. Contradictions are usually indications of a cover story. I went into his bedroom and rummaged around his closet, hoping to find a clue to what Fred was really up to.

I found answers. Fred had dumped his few personal possessions into a box in the bottom of his closet. Most of it was just crap, a high school yearbook, a bowling trophy, pathetic evidence of a not particularly noteworthy existence. I kept digging.

Near the bottom was a framed certificate of graduation from the California Culinary Institute. So he really was a cook. That didn't explain how he ended up as Ogloskie's Otis Campbell. I dug deeper. Then I hit paydirt.

Fred was the proud possessor of a Certificate of Discharge from the California Department of Corrections. I found this in a legal-size envelope containing a thick sheaf of papers related to his conviction on charges of reckless driving and manslaughter. So Fred had killed somebody. I could sympathize. But he hadn't meant to. From what I could make out from court papers and depositions, he'd fallen asleep at the wheel after working late—no doubt as a chef at some pricey eatery—and had plowed into a bus stop that unfortunately had been occupied by a single mother of three waiting for a bus to take her to her job as a maid on the other side of town. Fred got three years.

Also in the envelope was a newspaper clipping, a wedding announcement. Felicity Salinas married Roland Barnes just about a year before Fred got out of the slammer. The article mentioned that Barnes was a successful San Francisco realtor and Felicity was an up and coming chef who'd studied at the California Culinary Institute. Even I could do the math. Felicity had obviously dumped Fred when he got sent up the river. He had a lot of sorrows to drown.

All of which added up to Fred not having anything to hide except being a loser. I checked him off my list and let myself out, careful to leave his door slightly ajar, the way I'd found it.

Visiting Fred's apartment reminded me I wanted to stop in at the Feys' general store. Despite my earlier protestations to Walker Treadman that I could navigate the Oquala with a map and compass, I had omitted that I didn't have a compass with me. Back in Fairfax, Virginia I've got a standard issue US Army Lensatic Compass nestled in my sock drawer. I leave it there because it's got sentimental value—I lifted it out of the sock drawer of an officer back in my Army days after paying his wife a visit. He wasn't much of an officer; he could barely find his way from the latrine to the officers' mess, compass or not. I don't think he knew his way around the bedroom, either; at least, that's what his wife used to tell me. Anyway, his compass reminds me that if it weren't for officers and their wives, I might still be in the Army. Call it a good luck piece.

But I didn't want to wander off into dense forest without one, fancy GPS or no. I dropped by the store mid-morning the next day. Arthur was behind the counter looking bored. He glanced up when I came in.

"You're that new ranger." He sounded disappointed.

"Clayton Stillbridge. I've seen you and Myrna at Ogloskie's but never had the chance to introduce myself." I walked up to the counter and stuck out my hand.

"Nice to meet you." He looked at my hand with no indication he was interested in shaking it. I put it down. "What brings you in here?"

I looked around. His shelves were actually less than half full. Mostly it looked like he carried consumables; granola, power bars, freeze-dried entrees. There was a cooler with cold sodas and bottled water, two-thirds empty. I didn't notice a cooler for beer or much of anything in the way of real food. Apparently, he didn't sell groceries to the locals.

"I'm looking for a compass. You carry those?"

"Sure, I got a couple. You want a real compass or one of those cheap toys?"

"I'm planning to use it."

"Sure." He started rummaging through a drawer behind the counter, producing three different models. "This Suunto A-10 is twenty bucks and is reliable enough. If you want to spend close to a hundred, I can sell you this Brunton Eclipse. They claim you can practically survey with it, although I expect any serious surveyor would want something a little more sophisticated."

"The A-10 will be fine. I just want something to keep me from walking around in circles."

"Yeah. Only people who ever buy these Brunton's are tourists who probably never leave the highway." He rang up the sale. "That'll be $19.95. You need any maps?"

"No, we've got plenty of those at the Ranger station." I handed him a twenty. "Looks like your stocks are running low."

"Hiking season's over. I draw down inventory this time of year, then stock up again come March."

"Makes sense. Lucky for me you still had a few compasses."

"I've had these in this drawer for years. Mostly all I sell are these three dollar toys." He reached into the drawer and produced a little compass that looked like it had come out of a box of Cracker Jacks.

"I hope nobody ever buys one of those thinking it will work."

"About half the kids who come in here these days wouldn't know how to use a compass anyway. I had some smart-ass in here a couple months ago. His girlfriend asks him if they should buy a compass. He tells her not to worry, he's got a smart phone."

"Can you get cell service in the Oquala?"

"You can't get cell service here in Ogloskie. Closest cell tower is in Prestonville."

"I'm surprised more people don't wind up lost in the woods, then."

"The ones who strike out with no idea what they're doing get lost before they're half a mile in. Ruby checks the trail log. Anybody's still a no-show toward dusk, she usually finds 'em in tears a couple-hundred yards from the road."

"Well, there was that one incident recently."

"That guy was an experienced hiker. They found him several days march in."

"So he wasn't using one of these toy compasses?"

"No way. Not that guy." He arched his eyebrows, obviously wondering how I didn't know the complete

Garth Riefenthal story. "He came in here a couple of times. Forestry expert with Conifer."

"He was looking for hiking gear?"

"Nope. Usually he'd buy a soda or something. Just being friendly." One eyebrow stayed arched. "I think he was nosing around to see if people in town knew about Conifer's contract with the forest service."

"What contract would that be?"

"The one that's gonna let 'em turn the Oquala into wood siding and paper."

"Last time I checked, the forest service doesn't turn national forest over to private companies for clear-cutting." Ogloskie was lucky I'd been sent to take care of a killer and not plug the leak of a classified contract. I'd have been looking for a way to simulate a natural disaster wiping out the town.

"They train you rangers good. You said that with real conviction." He grinned. "But you should check again. Large parts of the Bitterspit Forest just over the border in Idaho are nothin' but stumps. I don't think it was a plague of beaver."

"Well, if you're so sure Conifer is planning to destroy the Oquala, maybe you should be organizing to get the state or Agriculture to step in." I was fishing. Could be he'd reveal himself to be a radical tree hugger.

"They can cut as much as they want. I do good business from hikers, but a bunch of logging crews working this area for six months? I'm betting I could bring in enough to retire." He stopped arching his eyebrows and got a distinctive twinkle. If there was any environmentalism in him, it was being drowned out by his capitalist persona, Mr. Greed.

"I'd be out of a job, though."

"Don't get too worried yet. Haven't seen any sign of Conifer since Riefenthal turned up dead. Maybe they're having trouble finding another forester willing to do their survey."

"Is that what he was doing? He told you that?"

"Said it was purely speculative." He laughed. "My ass. He was a talkative sort, though. Went on and on about how much he loved hiking virgin forest. Told me he'd hiked across Central Asia or someplace when he was younger. Real nature lover."

"Seems odd for a guy who makes his living cataloguing trees to be cut down."

"I don't know. Maybe he likes knowing he's the last guy who'll see someplace in its natural state. Anyway, I guess he died happy, out there doing what he liked best."

"How do you figure he got lost? I mean, he obviously knew how to use a compass and maps. Think he miscalculated the declination around here or something?"

"Declination?"

"Yeah, you know. The difference between polar north and magnetic north."

"Oh, I know what compass declination is."

"Miscalculating that can get you real lost real fast."

"You know what the compass declination is in this area?" Now he was smirking.

"I wouldn't be much of a forest ranger if I didn't. It's 17 degrees."

"And how'd you figure that out?"

"Hell, it's on just about every map in our office." I wondered if he was jerking my chain.

"And yet you figure Conifer's forestry expert, a guy who's hiked all over the planet, somehow would head out into the woods without making sure he knew a basic component of land navigation that, as you say, is on every halfway decent map."

"I'll admit, it's unlikely."

"Yeah."

"So how'd he wind up lost?"

"Dunno." He shrugged. "But the Oquala's haunted, you know."

"So everyone keeps telling me."

I spent the rest of the day in the office looking over maps. Not that I hadn't already memorized every detail of the Oquala. I was getting antsy, ready to get started looking over the terrain and Blue Feather and hopefully figuring out who exactly was my client. At least the sky had started to clear. Dewaldo turned out to be a good forecaster of the weather.

Ruby showed up around four, surprising me.

"What, no hot date tonight? Figured you were back at the duplex getting dolled up for Walker."

"He's off on a business trip early tomorrow and said he wanted to get a good night's sleep. So I'm free to harass you all evening."

"Sorry to disappoint, but Dewaldo's dropping off some gear later and I'll be getting kitted up. We're making an early start, too."

"Damn. What am I gonna do without a man to amuse me?"

"There's always Sven."

"Been there, done that." She grinned lasciviously. It was good I was striking out into the wilds. Being around a Walkerless Ruby and her healthy appetites for a few days would be a temptation I knew damned well I'd eventually give in to. "Besides, a few days on my own'll do me good. Maybe I'll catch up on some paperwork."

"Better you than me."

"I'll admit, Clayton, you don't seem too comfortable sitting at a desk." She eyed the maps spread out in front of me. "You look more like you're gonna pounce on those charts than study them. Anyway, I think I'll head over to Ogloskie's and have an early dinner. Then maybe I'll drive into Prestonville. Who knows? Maybe I'll find myself some young boy toy to occupy me while Walker's out of town."

"Check out that gym, *Ore-Fit*. The yoga instructor is quite the lady's man."

"From what I hear, he's into bored housewives. I'm probably more than he can handle." She turned to leave, stopped, and looked back at me. "If I don't see you before you head out tomorrow, just remember; I'll be real mad if you let yourself get eaten by a grizzly. I've been waiting for an assistant for a long time."

"No worries, Ruby. After a few hours hiking in the woods, I smell way too bad for anything to want to eat me."

Chapter VI
Backpackers

DEWALDO AND I had been hiking a good half hour when the sun came up, casting beams of light at low angles through the trees. Even I had to admit it was an inspiring sight: he stopped and just stood, drinking in the experience like some mystic in a trance. I stood quietly, letting him have his moment. It wasn't the first time I'd been in a forest at daybreak, but it was the first time I'd been with someone who just wanted to enjoy it. Previous experiences had usually involved humping too much equipment to a dawn attack in the Army.

I was humping a lot more weight than I'd planned, though. When Dewaldo had dropped off the gear he was loaning me along with a week's worth of freeze-dried entrees and granola bars, he'd included a case of Budweiser in cans.

"What the hell is this for, Dewaldo? I've never even seen you drink."

"Just pack as much of it as you can carry. It's for Blue Feather."

"This is what you meant when you said you were taking him some supplies?"

"Yeah. Usually I can only manage a few six packs. Figured you could carry some and maybe it'll be enough to hold him through the winter. If we get an early snow, it might be awhile before I can get back up there."

"Sure." I wasn't going to begrudge someone a Bud, although my image of a medicine man hadn't included a guy popping the top on a can of suds. "Where'd you find Budweiser around here, anyway? I thought the only beer for sale in Oregon was local craft brews."

"I drive over to Bend. There's one of those beverage outlet retailers there. Blue Feather prefers Bud. Like I said, just fit what you can carry. He'll be appreciative."

"Don't worry. I can lug the whole case. It'll be good exercise." I didn't point out that I'd enjoy having a few myself after hauling it all the way to Chalker. "Gee, Dewaldo, I didn't even know you had a car."

"Got a 1987 Buck Le Sabre, V-6, turbo-charged. Best car ever made."

"What's it get, three miles a gallon?"

"It's got a big gas tank." Dewaldo kept shattering my illusions that he was environmentally conscious. "Man, you pack that whole case, Blue Feather's gonna be happy."

"Me, too, once we get this stuff delivered and I don't have to haul a hundred pound pack anymore."

Dewaldo's pack looked pretty heavily weighed down with brewskies, too. I had to give him credit, he was wiry and didn't look all that impressive, but once we'd gotten kitted up and started out, I had to hustle to keep up with him. His earlier lecture about taking time to enjoy the hike didn't translate into slow walking.

He didn't walk fast because he was in a hurry, though. It was his natural pace, testament to the fact that he'd spent a lot of his life walking in the woods. He didn't talk, either, just walked determinedly in whatever direction his instinct and experience in the Oquala took him.

We'd been walking about three hours when I decided to test the GPS unit. I pulled it out of one of the cargo pockets of my fatigue pants—I'd decided not to wear the dork uniform for this excursion, although I had my ranger badge in my pack. It took a few seconds to make a connection with the satellite, then popped up our location on a detailed digital USGS map.

Dewaldo stopped and turned around. "GPS? I didn't figure you for a GPS type. Thought you'd be one of those old school guys who use a compass."

"I am. Walker Treadman loaned this to me, asked me to try it out."

He scowled, like he didn't approve. I couldn't tell whether it was the GPS or mention of Walker that got the reaction. "Where's it say we are?"

I held up the screen for him to look. "Says we're in the Oquala national forest."

"Hah. That's helpful." He looked curious. "Mind if I take a look?"

"No problem."

He hefted the device, then worked a few screen controls to zoom in on the map. He seemed familiar with it. "Not bad. It says we're about a hundred meters from Beaver Rock. Which is where we're headed, right over there." He nodded in the direction we'd been walking.

"Something special about Beaver Rock?"

"Nah. It's just a nice place to take a break. You'll see."

"Are there beaver there or something?" I didn't recall any streams or ponds marked on the map of this particular section of the forest.

"Nope. Somebody apparently thought the rock looks like a huge beaver or something. That's how it got its name."

"I guess you've been here enough, you don't need a GPS to find it. Or a compass, either." He hadn't been using one that I could tell.

"I've got a compass in my pack. Anybody can get lost out here. But I know the way to Beaver Rock."

"I'm betting you know the way to Chalker Mountain, too."

"I can get you there without a compass."

"Too bad that Riefenthal guy didn't hire you as a guide."

"Yeah. Too bad." He got quiet and started walking. I followed him the hundred meters to Beaver Rock.

It didn't look much like a beaver to me. More like a misshapen squirrel. I said as much.

"I think a lot of stuff got named by people who'd been wandering so long they were close to delusional." He dropped his pack and started climbing up the rock. It rose up about thirty feet and looked to be flat on top. I dropped my pack and scrambled up after him. By the time I got to the top, he was sprawled out on his back, head resting on his hands, eyes closed, basking in the sun. After days of rain, the sun felt pretty good. I sprawled out next to him. Maybe there is more to life than killing people.

"Ruby says you come from back East, Dewaldo. That right?"

"Yeah."

"How'd you wind up in Oregon?"

"How does anybody wind up where they are?"

"Most people wind up where they were born."

"Guess I'm not like most people." He didn't elucidate. I was finding out he was a pretty tough nut. "Guess you're not either. Where'd you come from again?"

"I was posted in Georgia before."

"Yeah." He was not a man of many words. "You're right about one thing. Ogloskie's a place where people wind up. They come here and then look up a few years later and realize they never left."

"You seem pretty happy here."

"Do I?"

"Sure. Seems to me you've become as much a part of the Oquala as Blue Feather."

"I've been thinking about moving on."

"Why? Seems like a nice enough place to me. Quiet, beautiful scenery." Lying there on the rock, it was pretty idyllic. A large hawk of some kind was circling overhead. I hadn't been so relaxed in years.

"Won't be like this forever. Conifer Corporation's got their eyes on all these trees. They're a big logging outfit."

That got my ears pricked up. The Conifer contract was turning out to be the worst-kept government secret since the Manhattan Project. "This is national forest. They can't just come in and cut it down."

"Yeah." He sounded far away. "My family runs a big mining conglomerate back East. Specialize in mountaintop coal mining. They're real tight with the Bureau of Land Management. Most of their concessions are on public lands."

"That why you came out to Oregon? Left home because you don't approve of the family business?"

"You think it would all just stop if my family got out of the strip-mining business? Shit, people are still gonna want to have lights and television. Yahoos in the Appalachians bitch about the mining companies all the time, then they run out and sign up for jobs at mines and power plants and come home and watch TV all night while they run their air conditioners. They don't want coal mining to stop. They just don't want the mines in their back yards." He sat up and looked over at me, then pointed out to the forest. "Same with all these trees. It's great while it lasts, but eventually these are all destined to be furniture, siding, resin, paper."

"You don't think people like us can stop it? Don't we have an obligation to try to preserve some of this for future generations?" It sounded stupid to me, but I was hoping I could convince Dewaldo I cared, get him to drop his guard and tell me what he really thought, how far he might be willing to go to save the Oquala wilderness.

"You sound like Blue Feather when he's had a few too many beers." He smiled, a tired smile. "Screw future generations. Let 'em plant their own trees."

"What would you do if they started logging all this, though? Where would you go?"

"Washington State is supposed to be nice. Lots of national forest up there. If they cut all that down, there's still lots of wild areas in Canada."

"Canada."

"Yeah. And there's always the Amazon Basin."

"That just sounds like running away from a problem to me."

"It is, Clayton. It is. You want to stand in front of a bulldozer to make yourself feel good, go right ahead." He grinned. "Time to get going. There's a nice campsite I know about twenty miles farther in. If we hump it, we can get there in time to set up camp before it starts getting dark."

"Sounds good." I was ready to start moving again. Relaxing is great for awhile, but I always start to get the feeling that someone is creeping up on me.

After two nights camping with Dewaldo, all I'd figured out was that he knew the Oquala like the back of his hand; and that he snored. It was an impressive, loud, stuttering snore that sounded like a chain saw in need of a tune-up. Dawn of the third day I finally said something.

"Jesus, Dewaldo. I don't think we need to worry about a grizzly attacking us in our sleep. The racket you make must have every animal within ten miles running for its life."

"Guess it's just as well I never got married." He was pouring boiling water into a little metal cup that he'd emptied a packet of instant oatmeal into. "Hope I'm not keeping you awake."

"I've slept better."

"Want some oatmeal?" He was sitting stark naked on a log. I'd quickly adjusted to the fact that he hung all his clothes on a tree before crawling buck naked into his sleeping bag. I understood that, of course. Clothes you sweat in all day can freeze you at night. But I like to put mine back on when I get up.

"No thanks. These granola bars you got are pretty filling. I'll take some of that hot water, though." He'd included instant coffee and instant cocoa in our kits. Mixed together, they made a great morning pick-me-up.

"We should make Blue Feather's cabin before sundown."

"Great. I'm looking forward to unloading all this beer."

"Yeah." He was scraping the bottom of his cup with his spoon. Dewaldo ate oatmeal the way a kid eats pudding, always looking disappointed when the last of it was gone. Yet he never seemed to enjoy it that much.

"Whatever they put in this stuff to make it taste like apple cinnamon, it just tastes like some kind of chemical."

"When was the last time you had a bowl of oatmeal you liked, Dewaldo?"

"I don't know." He got that pensive look again. "There was a place in Cambridge, they made really good oatmeal."

"Cambridge, Massachusetts?"

"Yeah."

"That's right. Ruby said you went to Harvard."

"She did?"

"So I guess you're really smart."

"Yeah."

I resisted the impulse to throw my hot coffee/cocoa on him. I wasn't sure it would have had much effect anyway. Instead I gulped the rest down and started collecting up my gear, packing up to get moving. Dewaldo stood up and grudgingly put on his clothes. I was betting he hiked naked when he was alone.

While he cinched up his pack, I policed our campsite, finding a scrap torn from one of the packages of last night's freeze-dried chicken cacciatore. Crumpling it up, I shoved it in one of the pouches of my backpack and took another look around to make sure I hadn't missed anything else.

"You take that 'pack it in pack it out' stuff seriously, Clayton. I'm impressed. Some of the people I bring out here would leave garbage scattered along the entire trail if I let them."

"Just figure we should leave the woods like we found 'em." If he thought I was some kind of tree hugger, all the better. I didn't point out that checking to make sure I wasn't leaving an obvious trail was because I cared about my own skin, not planet Earth's. "Looks clean to me. I'm ready to get moving whenever you are."

"Where's that GPS you're carrying say we are, by the way?"

"You afraid you're getting lost?"

"Nope. Just curious." He'd had me check it a couple of times every day. Maybe he was worried it was threatening his livelihood. I pulled it out of my pack and powered it up, handing it to him once it made contact with the satellite and displayed our position.

"Damn. These things really are accurate." He shook his head, handed it back to me. "You don't need me at all."

"Except it doesn't boil water or snore all night. I'd be pretty lonely by now with just this gizmo for a companion."

"Bet it doesn't know where Blue Feather's cabin is, either." He shouldered his pack, cinched it up, and started walking. I had to hustle to stay with him.

The sun was still shining strong, although it was pleasantly cool. We were climbing some now, right at the base of Chalker. It wasn't a huge mountain, certainly nothing by Rocky standards. The summit, I could see from a distance, was well under the tree line. It could have passed for mountains I'd grown up with in the Appalachians, except it was all evergreen.

A howl penetrated the air.

"That your ghost, Dewaldo?"

"Grizzly. Sounds like he's fifteen, twenty miles away."

"Sound really carries out here. What do you think, he's caught our scent and is complaining?"

"More likely he's caught the scent of a female in heat."

"How do you know it's a he?"

"Good point."

That was the conversation for the day. I was beginning to hope, whatever else I was going to find out about Blue Feather, that I'd discover he was a great conversationalist. Three days with Dewaldo and I was beginning to feel like a monk on a pilgrimage. I'm not usually much of a talker, but I'd always figured an expedition in the wilderness with someone meant you'd get to know them. With Dewaldo, I'd figured wrong.

The climb was finally starting to get a little steep, made harder by the fact that we weren't really following a trail. If there were well-worn paths anywhere in the Oquala, Dewaldo apparently liked to avoid them. Fortunately, evergreen forests don't tend to have a lot of underbrush, so at least we hadn't been bushwhacking cross-country; I'd done my share of hacking through kudzu in the southeast during my Army days. And not following set trails gave the added advantage of making it difficult for anyone to follow us.

Or so I thought. The trees thinned a bit as the terrain got steeper. We stopped to catch our breath on an outcrop of rock that afforded a decent view of the mile after mile of forest stretching out below us to the west.

"Think about it, Clayton. Forests like this dominated most of Oregon and Washington just a few hundred years ago. It must have really been something to see."

"I'm sure it was." I was more interested in what I'd just seen, a flash of sunlight reflected off what I suspected were a pair of binoculars about a mile away in

The Killer Trees

the direction we'd just come from. Dewaldo hadn't seemed to notice. He was a skilled hiker and naturalist, but he lacked my instinct for danger from the planet's deadliest predator, the human one.

Someone tailing us was actually good news, in my book. The only person with reason to follow us into the Oquala would have to be someone worried that I wasn't a simple forest ranger, someone suspicious that I was there looking into the deaths of Conifer's employees. Whoever was out there watching us relax on that outcrop of rock was likely my client—or a rival spook who'd decided the easiest way to find the client was to follow me to them. I still hadn't dismissed that possibility.

I had a pretty good idea who was out there. Walker Treadman hadn't planted that GPS on me because he wanted to make a sale. It was signaling our location to him. When it was switched on, that is. I realized I'd turned it off and put it in my pack after we'd checked it that morning. So Treadman wasn't without tracker skills himself.

"Hey, let's see what this little GPS says about where we are." I opened my pack, pulled it out, turned it on and held it out to Dewaldo.

"It's accurate again." He stared at it with disappointment. I don't think he enjoyed the competition. "I'm not sure where the adventure is if you've got one of these boxes to make sure you don't get lost. I wonder if they give these things to Boy Scouts now."

"I've gotta admit, they're easier to use than a compass."

"Yeah, just like calculators. Nobody knows how to add and subtract anymore. Pretty soon nobody'll be able to find their way home without one of these." He handed it back to me. I shoved it back in my pack, making sure I didn't switch it off.

I didn't want Treadman to lose us.

"How much farther to Blue Feather's cabin?"

"About another hour." He stood up and started cinching up his pack. "Cabin's a bit of a stretch. It's an old mining shack he's been fixing up."

"I didn't know there had been any mines up here."

"Not for about a hundred years. Like I said, it's an old mining shack."

"Well, let's go see it." I was ready to meet this self-declared Oquala medicine man. Walker trailing us or not, Blue Feather was still my prime suspect.

And I hadn't forgotten Dewaldo's assault and battery charge. Between the grizzlies, my divinity student ruffian companion, the con artist at the end of the trail, the mystery man with high tech surveillance gear behind me, and Ogloskie's ghost, the Oquala was sizing up to be a pretty dangerous place.

'Cabin' was indeed a generous description of the falling down shack that turned out to be Blue Feather's home. It was a one-room structure—'structure' being generous, too—that leaned precariously to one side. He'd obviously done some improvements on the roof; it looked like an odd patchwork of mud, twigs, and pine needles, although I noted a few pieces of sheet metal. Where he'd found sheet metal this far from anywhere was anybody's guess. An ancient tin pipe jutted out the top belching smoke. Apparently he was at home.

"Blue Feather! It's Dewaldo!" He called out from the edge of the clearing. I wondered if he was worried about getting shot if we appeared unannounced. I could understand his caution. Being mistaken for a 'revenooer' where I grew up could mean eating a load of buckshot. We stood waiting, watching the door. Nothing moved.

"Who's your friend?" The voice came from behind us. Blue Feather was light on his feet. Usually I notice someone approaching from my rear. Dewaldo turned around, a big grin on his face.

"New forest ranger assigned to work with Ruby. He wanted to meet you."

"Forest ranger?" He looked me over. I reciprocated. Delbert Blue Feather looked more redneck than redskin. Oh, his skin was red, but it's that red that palefaces like me get when they spend too much time unprotected in the sun. His arms and shoulders, visible jutting out from the sleeveless undershirt he was wearing tucked into a very old pair of jeans, looked like one huge freckle. I wondered if he'd ever heard of melanoma. Life in the mountains wasn't all that much of a hardship, either, if the spare tire hanging out of those jeans was any indication. Whatever he was finding to eat out here, he was eating too much of it. His hair, and he had a lot of it hanging down to his neck, was shocking white, again, a product of too much sun. If he'd had a full beard, he could have passed as a hillbilly Santa Claus. But he kept his face shaved—impressive for a mountain hermit. I almost laughed out loud at the sight of this fat gnome that Dewaldo worshiped. Then I looked at his eyes. They were steely blue, serious with a hard edge that told me I'd better not underestimate him.

"Clayton Stillbridge." I extended my hand. "It's a pleasure to meet you, Mr. Blue Feather. I've heard a lot about you."

"It's just 'Blue Feather.' 'Mr.' is what whites call each other, Ranger Stillbridge." He shook my hand. His grip was firm.

"Blue Feather it is, then. And call me Clayton."

"So, Clayton, you come all this way to tell me I'm trespassing on public land?" He was bracing for a confrontation. Some people respond that way to authority. Actually, it's how I respond to it.

"No, sir. As far as I'm concerned, you're the public and can stay out here as long as you want. I'm impressed that you can survive out here all alone. Most people would have died of starvation or frozen in the winter long ago."

"To an Indian, these woods are life itself. They provide all I need."

"I guess that's right. Indians have lived here a long time." I could have added that it didn't explain him. Ruby had been right. He looked to me like he had about as much Oquala Indian in him as Charlie McCarthy.

"So if you haven't come to try to evict me from my native lands, why did you want to see me?"

"Mostly I just wanted to get out and have a look at the Oquala, get to know the territory I'm responsible for. It just made sense, while I was out exploring, to have Dewaldo show me to your humble abode here so I could meet you."

He looked over at Dewaldo, not particularly pleased.

"We brought beer. Two cases. Clayton's got a case in his pack."

The edge went out of his eyes and he actually smiled. "Beer?"

"Budweiser." Dewaldo looked nervous.

"Well, let's not stand out here all day. Come on in. *Mi casa es su casa.*" I guess all legendary mountain creatures turn friendly if you know the password. Blue Feather's was 'beer.' Suddenly he was our best friend. Dewaldo was visibly relieved. I guess he hadn't entertained the possibility that Blue Feather might not appreciate his bringing me along.

The interior of the cabin was Spartan but cozy. The tin smokestack was connected to a pot-bellied stove that I figured was well over a hundred years old, but it had been cleaned and thoroughly polished. It would sell for a decent price at an antique store if Blue Feather ever decided to haul it out to civilization. Carrying it through the Oquala would be no mean feat, though.

I noted a few creature comforts. He had a radio, one of those crank jobs you see in hiking stores these days to be bought by tree-huggers who have decided batteries are evil. I picked it up and examined it; am, fm, and shortwave.

"You get any reception up here?"

"At night sometimes I get BBC. I don't use it much, though. One of Dewaldo's backpackers brought it last year and left it."

My eyes were adjusting to the dark cabin innards. I made out a variety of backpacking equipment—a camp stove, a couple of nice knives, a hand ax. Obviously I wasn't the first guest Dewaldo had brought bearing gifts. I was beginning to get an idea how the old redneck survived. With Dewaldo leading in pilgrims all summer to see the holy man in the mountain, Blue Feather had it made. He could just hand Dewaldo a shopping list and the next group of suckers would gladly acquire what he needed and pack it in.

He wasn't living totally off the charity of strangers, though. There were several deerskins hanging from the cabin walls, one that looked fairly new, all well-tanned. I rubbed my hand along one. It felt nice, and I was betting they helped keep out drafts in the winter.

"You tan these yourself, Blue Feather?"

"Yeah. There's an old mine shaft up the mountain a ways. I use it as a smoke house and tanning shop. Couple deer every year keeps me in meat, and the hides come in handy."

"What do you hunt with? You tell me you bring down a buck with a spear, I'm gonna be impressed."

Dewaldo had been unloading his pack, pulling out cans of beer. At my mention of hunting, he remembered something and started rummaging around in one of his pack's side pockets. "Almost forgot. Brought you a box of cartridges." He produced a carton of fifty .30-06 rounds.

"Appreciate it. I was getting low." Blue Feather took the carton and set it on a small shelf off in a corner. Leaning against the wall under the shelf was a rifle.

And then I was impressed. I hadn't noticed the rifle. It was an M1 Garand, the first semi-automatic rifle adopted by any military and the rifle that beat the Nazis and the Japs in World War II. It looked to be in vintage condition. A friend of mine who ran a gun shop outside of Kannapolis, North Carolina owned one. This was only the second I'd ever seen.

"Damn, Blue Feather. I know people who would pay you some serious money for that piece. Where the hell did you get it?"

"Won it in a poker game the same night I had my revelation."

"Revelation?"

"That's what I said." He didn't elucidate, just kept stowing away the cans of beer.

"The Great Spirit came to Blue Feather in a dream and told him to come here to Chalker Mountain." Dewaldo said this with the sincerity of a disciple. I suspected the Great Spirit who came to Blue Feather was named Jack Daniels. Then again, I had never been to divinity school. Maybe I'd have more faith if I had.

"Great Spirit deal you the hand that won that M1?"

"You play much poker, ranger?" If I'd hoped to get a rise out of the old medicine man, I'd failed. He grinned as he asked the question.

"A little. Not much."

"Take my word for it; players who rely on luck or the Great Spirit for winning hands never get them." There was a twinkle in his eye. I guess I could add card shark to con man on his rap sheet. "So you boys been eating that freeze-dried crap Dewaldo is so partial to?"

"It's health food, Blue Feather." Dewaldo looked offended.

"Well, since you fellas were so nice to bring beer, I've got a couple of venison steaks left from my last deer. How about I grill 'em up for us. Then tomorrow morning, Mr. Ranger, I'll show you where you can poach a decent-sized buck. Long as you promise not to arrest me for hunting without a license."

"Rest assured, Blue Feather. I'm not here to arrest you or even give you a citation."

"Guess I'll have to take your word for it. I'll go get those steaks." He stood up. "Want to come along, ranger? I got an ice house set up in the mine shaft, too. Nice and cool."

"Sure. Love to see it."

"You coming, Dewaldo?"

"No, thanks. Been walking enough today. I'll just hang out here."

I followed Blue Feather out and up a small trail that wound its way up the mountain, steeper than what we'd been hiking before. It afforded an even better view of the forest below than the clearing we'd stopped at earlier. I looked for more tell-tale flashes from binocular lenses, but the sun was getting low in the sky and I didn't notice anything. Still, I was pretty sure Walker was out there watching.

"You nervous about something?" Blue Feather had obviously noticed that I kept checking behind me.

"Just taking in all this great scenery." The grizzly had started howling again, somewhere in the distance. "Also hoping to catch a glimpse of this ghost that's supposed to be out here."

"Shit. Dewaldo been filling your ears with that crap about the ghost of Vladimir Ogloskie?"

"What, you don't believe in ghosts?"

"Don't figure it matters to them whether I believe in 'em or not."

"You're not worried Ogloskie's ghost is after you? He's supposed to be haunting these woods because of the Oquala Indians."

"Maybe I'm not an Oquala."

"Oh? I just assumed, with your revelation and taking the Indian name, moving out here in the Oquala . . ."

He stopped dead, turned around, and looked me in the eye. I had to admit, there was something about him, a presence, a sense that he knew things. "Any other assumptions you've made you want to share with me?"

"Yeah." I locked eyes with him. We played staredown for a minute, the grizzly howling in the background giving it a primeval atmosphere, like two cave-men getting ready to bash each other, winner taking the fresh meat and getting dibs on any woman who might be around. Which there weren't, of course. "I'm assuming as well that you've got some cold beer in this ice house you mentioned."

"Maybe I do."

"And I'm assuming you're gonna offer me one."

The twinkle came back in his eyes. Beer really was the way to his soul. "I was hoping you'd ask. A man gets tired of drinking alone." He turned around and resumed walking.

"So what did you do before you moved out here?" We'd broken the ice. I decided it was worth a try to get him talking about himself, see if I could get him to slip up about his past. He surprised me.

"I was a criminal."

"Huh?" Honesty is always unexpected. At least, in my line of work, I never expect it.

"Con man, card cheat, scheming to make a dollar any way I could." He said it matter-of-factly. "But you already knew that."

"What makes you say that?"

"Just a feeling I got when I first saw you. Like the feeling I got when Dewaldo introduced you, the feeling that said you're about as much a forest ranger as I'm an Oquala Indian."

"So you're not really Oquala?"

"So you're not really a ranger?"

"Of course I'm a forest ranger, Blue Feather. I've got a badge and ID to prove it."

"Then I must really be an Oquala Indian."

"If your funny feeling tells you I'm not a ranger, what does it tell you I am? Ruby's convinced I'm some kind of cop."

"You're no cop, I know that." He stopped again but didn't turn around. "I haven't figured out exactly what you are."

"Well, I'll tell you. I'm a government assassin sent here by the Department of Agriculture to kill you for poaching deer in a national forest."

He broke out into a big grin. "You've got quite a sense of humor, don't you, ranger."

"I try."

"But that's closer to the truth than you being a ranger, isn't it?"

"All this time living alone is making you paranoid, Blue Feather." It occurred to me I might have to kill him just to maintain my cover. "How much further to this mine shaft, anyway?"

"We're there." He walked off the trail and pushed his way through a big thicket. The entrance was well-hidden; I could have walked past it a dozen times without noticing. I had to feel my way in; the thicket blocked most of the light. Inside it was almost pitch black.

"Prepare to be impressed." Lights came on, not blinding lights but a whole series of low-voltage LEDs. After my eyes adjusted, I could see perfectly. The illumination stretched inward for about 100 yards.

"I'll admit it. I'm impressed. How the hell did you manage this?"

"I used to have to wander around in here with a storm lantern. I was always running low on kerosene, too. Then last year, Dewaldo talked a group of hikers into buying a couple of solar panels and some strings of these lights and hauling it in here. They don't take much juice. Fully charged, the batteries keep them glowing four, maybe five hours."

"I didn't notice the solar panels."

"They're just over the cave entrance, above the trees and that thicket. They're not big, like those you see put up by highway departments. Takes 'em the better part of a sunny day to fully charge the batteries."

"How about on the normal, cloud-covered Oregon day?"

"Takes a lot longer. But I don't spend that much time in here. Mostly I'm just in and out to get some meat from the smokehouse or ice house. Come on, I'll show you around."

It was damned impressive. Off to one side was a chamber with a vent shaft—courtesy of whatever mining company had been here a hundred years before. He'd build a fire-pit out of rocks and hammered a few hooks into the stone walls. A couple of venison roasts were hanging up, looking pretty well preserved. I wasn't sure I'd want to be in the place when he had a fire producing smoke, vent shaft or not. But it obviously worked.

"You can see my meat supply is getting a little low. A big buck should get me through the winter, though."

"You eat anything besides meat?"

"Forest is filled with berries, greens, herbs, even mushrooms, if you know where to look."

"Yeah, I know. A guy where I grew up used to brag about never having to buy fruits and vegetables, claimed he could live by foraging in the woods."

"It's not that difficult."

"He poisoned himself eating a toadstool."

"Don't worry, I'm not big on mushrooms myself. Except for the hallucinogenic ones."

He led me back into the main shaft, down another twenty feet and through a small entrance off to the left. I had to duck my head to get through. The cold was like an arctic blast.

"Ice house. I don't have a thermometer, but I'm betting it's damned near freezing in here even after the whole summer."

There were quite a few big blocks of ice. He'd packed the walls of the chamber with mud and pine needles. I also made out stacks and stacks of canned Budweiser. Dewaldo and company were quite the over-achievers. That explained why Blue Feather hadn't felt the need to lug his new supply up the mountain to chill it.

"So once you get a big freeze, you start packing this place with ice?"

"Yup. Winter, I make enough ice to keep this place cold all summer. Summer, I cut enough wood to keep from freezing in the winter. It keeps me busy."

"I'll bet." It sounded like a lot more work than I ever want to do.

"You sound skeptical, Mr. Ranger."

"Let's just say I'm not one of those romantics who believe the best life is working your ass off just to survive."

"Funny. Riefenthal said almost exactly the same thing."

That got my attention. "Riefenthal came up here?"

"Yeah. All on his own, too. Didn't get Dewaldo to show him the way, just hiked in on his lonesome."

"How'd he know where to find you?"

"I asked him that. Always figured I was off the radar up here except to a few folks like Dewaldo. Told me he'd been studying satellite imagery of the forest for weeks. Damn crazy world, if you ask me. Spaceships orbiting the planet so they can see my miserable little cabin from up there."

"What'd he want, anyway?"

He sat on a block of ice and thought. I guess he was considering how much he should tell me. I was shivering. It wasn't anticipation. The ice house was fucking cold. Maybe he wasn't Oquala, but watching him sitting on the ice, I wondered if he was part Eskimo. "You know Conifer's planning to clear cut most of the Oquala."

"Aw, that's just a crazy rumor." Actually, I was thinking that the only person for hundreds of miles who didn't know about Conifer's secret contract was Becky Alvarez. Then again, she'd probably heard about it, too.

"Not according to Riefenthal. He hiked all the way up here to tell me."

"Why would he do that?" I had a fleeting thought that maybe Riefenthal had a death wish. Maybe Conifer's employees were racked with guilt at all the nature they'd destroyed. That finance guy really could have hanged himself. Maybe Riefenthal confessed his sins to Blue Feather and then went off into the forest to die. Stranger things have happened.

"It wasn't out of the goodness of his heart, that's for sure." He laughed. "Conifer's worried that once they start operations, I'll find some environmentalist outfit with enough money to hire a lawyer and claim these are my ancestral lands."

"That's nuts. You said yourself you're not Oquala."

"Actually, I didn't say that. But whether I am or not, I probably could find some tree-hugger outfit willing to take 'em to court."

"Conifer's a subsidiary of Santomo Corporation. You wouldn't have a dog's chance in hell of winning a case like that against them."

"That's absolutely right. But Riefenthal said Conifer's worried they could get tied up in court and spend hundreds of thousands of dollars on legal fees."

"So he came here to tell you this and ask you nicely to leave?"

"No. He came here to tell me Conifer decided it would make more sense to buy me off for fifty-thousand dollars."

Up to that point, his story had sounded crazier and crazier. Then it made sense. Fifty-thousand was chump change to a company like Conifer. That was probably cheaper than paying someone to kill him.

"What'd you tell him?"

"You think I'd give up all this for money?" He sounded serious. It was too dark to see if that twinkle was in his eyes.

"I guess not."

"Then you're as crazy as those fucking tree huggers Dewaldo guides up here. Conifer wants to cut down all these trees, me and an army of tree huggers won't stop 'em."

"So you accepted the offer."

"Nope." He grinned. "I told him to make it seventy-five. And you know what? He agreed right off. I tell you, I've been away from the world too long. He was obviously prepared to go a lot higher."

He was appearing less and less like someone who would kill to protect his forest. Still, a con-man who feels he's been suckered can turn homicidal; or maybe he'd had a moment of remorse after accepting the offer. "Aren't you concerned that the Great Spirit will be upset with you, turning your back after being sent out here?"

"Don't joke about the Great Spirit, ranger man." He spit, I guess from some old superstition. "But the Great Spirit told me to come here and find myself. I did. So I figure the Great Spirit sent Riefenthal to buy me off. Maybe the Great Spirit finally got as bored with this Jeremiah Johnson crap as me."

He stood up and poked around under a pile of pine needles, producing three sizeable steaks wrapped in plastic. "These are just about thawed. You take these and I'll grab some beers. I keep some just outside the ice house in the runoff from the melt in here. Keeps 'em real cold." He handed me the steaks.

"You've got Saran wrap? Where the hell do you get that out here?"

"I am constantly amazed by what Dewaldo's people pack in."

We exited the ice house. I was looking forward to getting outside and warming back up. He disappeared around a corner for a minute and came out holding one of those reusable shopping bags you can buy at every grocery these days to make yourself feel better about slowing down the rate at which we turn planet Earth into an orbiting landfill. Dewaldo's hikers really had thought of everything.

"You feeling extra generous, Blue Feather? Two beers each?" Back outside I could see he'd pulled a sixpack from his stores.

"That's three apiece, ranger. Dewaldo don't drink."

"I wondered. I've only been around a couple of weeks, but I've noticed he hasn't had so much as a near beer. I guess it's all that religious training."

"From what he's told me, I think it has more to do with him getting belligerent when he has a few too many."

"Oh. I can understand that." Maybe that explained the assault charge from Cambridge. And I could indeed understand. I get the same way. But I've never thought of it as a problem.

On the way back down I noticed the boulder. It was big, sitting poised just above the trail. I looked down to see Blue Feather's cabin.

"You ever worry this rock is gonna get dislodged and destroy your hut?"

He didn't look up. I guess he'd seen the rock before. "That boulder's been there for a thousand years or more. It'd take a large earthquake or something similar to budge it."

"Yeah."

Blue Feather proved to be a damned fine cook. Hard to believe anyone could produce a gourmet meal using only a pot-bellied stove, but after he rubbed down the stakes with an herb mixture he created from stuff he foraged, the smell of them grilling in a cast-iron skillet was mouth-watering. He made some kind of mixed-wild-berry compote for a relish and sliced and grilled a wild root vegetable I'd never seen before as a side dish. Washed down with Budweiser, it was one of the best meals I've ever had. Of course, it helped that I'd been eating freeze-dried entrees that taste like cardboard for three days.

Even Dewaldo was impressed. "Tastes really good, Blue Feather." High praise from him, indeed.

"Sure you won't have a beer to wash that down?" Blue Feather liked needling Dewaldo. While he'd cooked, he'd provided a running commentary on the hiking guide's pricey Merrell boots and wick-dry socks, expensive Columbia hiking pants, state of the art pack. I had to admit, the "spare" pack Dewaldo had loaned me was a high-end internal-frame job that probably cost well over five-hundred bucks. "Getting back to nature cost's a pretty penny, eh, Dewaldo? I don't know how those Oquala natives were able to afford it."

"Guess we've learned a few things since then. I bet they'd have worn decent boots if they'd had them." He didn't seem peeved by the criticism, just responded in his matter-of-fact way. Maybe it was some kind of medicine man therapy Blue Feather was using, trying to get a rise out of Dewaldo, plumbing the depths of the internal anger he was allegedly battling. He wasn't the first to discover an inner grizzly looking for an excuse to go on a rampage. Whatever had released his, though, had obviously scared him into some serious life changes. I couldn't fault him for it, either. Grizzlies running amok usually wind up dead from somebody's high-powered bullet.

"Moccasins toughen up the feet so you don't need boots." Blue Feather, for what it was worth, was wearing steel-toed Dickies. I guess even medicine men have trouble practicing what they preach.

"They hunted with arrows and spears, too." I decided to try coming to Dewaldo's defense. "Or do you club deer to death with that M1?"

"Never said I was opposed to progress." He grinned and popped the top on a beer. "Even the white devils have made some useful innovations."

"I'll drink to that." I did.

"Alcohol's not exactly a modern invention, you know." Dewaldo could sound like a pinhead discussing sex, I figured. "The ancient Egyptians brewed beer."

"Beer? You sure about that?"

"Well, it was some kind of fermented malt beverage."

"All the more reason you should drink, Dewaldo. You're turning your back on thousands of years of human history." Blue Feather could be relentless.

"Maybe I've got an allergy." He got that withdrawn look again. He clearly didn't like to talk about drinking.

"I keep telling you, Dewaldo, your problem's not with alcohol." Blue Feather suddenly became serious. It was a remarkable transformation. He seemed to grow an inch or two and everything got quiet. Dewaldo sat up straight, his eyes locked on the old con man in rapt attention. "Alcohol, peyote, drugs dull the senses and blunt the rational tyrant disciplining the inner savage in us. You're containing the part of yourself you're afraid of, but it's still there. To master it, you have to confront it. When you do that, you'll be able to drink or not. But it'll be your choice from preference and not fear."

"I know. But how do I confront myself like that? You know I've tried. I've done yoga, meditation, studied Zen, spent hours out here alone in the Oquala."

"How many times I got to tell you, that stuff's all hogwash. Fucking Eastern mystics. Somebody tells 'em to look inside themselves, they sit around staring at their fucking navels."

"Then how do you look inside?" His voice sounded desperate.

"You gotta let go, Dewaldo, let yourself get angry again. Then maybe you'll figure out what you're so pissed off about."

"Yeah. I guess so." He looked doubtful.

"No, you don't. You're still a fucking pussy." Blue Feather shook his head in resignation. "If you weren't, you'd try to take my head off for talking to you like this. But you just sit there."

"Yeah. I guess so." He hung his head. Dewaldo was a complex guy, probably thinking about what he'd write about this in his notebook when he got the chance. I had to agree with our host. If he'd said that crap to me, called me a pussy, I'd have knocked his block off. Guess I'm in touch with my inner savage.

"This is some pretty heavy shit." I jumped in mostly because it was giving me a headache. Besides, I was worried that if Dewaldo got any more withdrawn, he might just disappear into that navel Blue Feather was trying to make him stop contemplating. "Mind tossing me another one of those beers so I can blunt my own rational tyrant and maybe get some sleep?"

"Sure thing, ranger." He grinned and threw me a can of Bud. "Sleep's a good idea. We're gonna need to get up early if we're gonna bag ourselves a buck."

"So you said."

It was, in fact, getting dark outside. We finished our beers and food, rinsed our dishes and hung them outside—Blue Feather didn't bother cleaning the skillet, just left it soaking up grease—and repaired to separate corners of the hut to crawl into sleeping bags. It had been a long day. I didn't figure I'd have much trouble sleeping.

I woke up in the middle of the night, sitting in the dark for the longest time trying to figure what had roused me. It was dead quiet. I listened for a sound, some disturbance. Then it hit me. Dewaldo wasn't snoring. I'd gotten so used to him sawing logs, the absence of it startled me awake. I looked over at his corner and made out a faint light coming from under his sleeping bag that he'd draped over himself. He was sitting up, scribbling in his notebook to the light of one of those mini mags sticking out of his mouth. Wilson had it right that night I checked into his motel; only lost souls come to Ogloskie. That had Dewaldo pegged to a tee.

Except for me, I thought. *I've know exactly where I am and what I'm doing here.* I curled back up in my bag and dropped off to sleep, wondering what the fuck anybody could think was important enough to sit up all night writing down.

Chapter VII
Hunters

EARLY MEANT PITCH BLACK. I heard Blue Feather rustling around the stove, adding wood to the embers barely glowing in its pot belly, blowing to get a real fire started. I didn't bother to check my watch. What difference did it make what time it was? We were heading out before dawn to bag ourselves a buck.

By the light from the fire in the potbelly stove I could make out Blue Feather boiling water in a big pot. I dug around in my pack for some of the freeze-dried coffee and instant cocoa. I needed caffeine. Across the room, Dewaldo was sitting with his notebook in his lap, the same position he'd been in when I drifted off to sleep. I wondered if he'd sat up all night.

"Glad to see you boys are awake." Blue Feather grabbed a tin from a cupboard behind the stove. "I'm making blackberry tea, if you're interested."

"Sounds great." Dewaldo actually sounded excited.

"If you don't mind, I'll just take some of that water in my canteen cup." I've never been partial to tea of any variety. "Instant coffee's not great, but it beats no coffee at all. I'm surprised Dewaldo's campers don't keep you stocked up on gourmet coffee beans, Blue Feather."

"Why drink that when you can get all the blackberries and blackberry leaves you need for free? Stuff grows wild not too far from here."

"I'll stick with a good-old-fashioned cup of American coffee."

"And yet, Mr. Ranger, coffee beans are one thing we don't grow in the USA." He was sounding smug. "While you're addicted to something we have to import from Africa or South America, I'm totally self-reliant."

"Last time I checked, we don't grow cans of Budweiser, either."

"At least it's made in the USA."

"So's this coffee I'm gonna drink. At least, as soon as I make it, it will be."

"Okay, I give up trying to improve your spirit today, Mr. Ranger. Pass me your cup."

I handed him the canteen cup I'd been using for days. It gave everything a metallic taste that mixed well with the buildup of dried coffee and cocoa sludge I'd been collecting. The taste took me back to my days in the Army, a bitter brew that made you tougher if you survived it. While I stirred my instant powdered product of the third world, he sprinkled a healthy portion of dried leaves and berries into the rest of the boiling water.

"Really, you should try the tea, Clayton." Always the disciple, Dewaldo hadn't given up on selling me the Blue Feather diet. "The dried blackberries give it a natural sweetness, and it's good for the stomach."

"Native Americans used it to cure everything from diarrhea to gout." I wondered how Blue Feather had gotten so knowledgeable about Indians. More likely, he had a con-man's instinct for bullshit.

"Tell you what, I get the runs or turn up lame, I'll look you up." I swigged my concoction. He poured his brew into two big ceramic mugs, both with Starbucks logos. Somebody had hauled those a long way. I hadn't seen a Starbucks since the Portland airport. "So how far you think we have to go to find this buck of yours?"

"About an hour north of here there's a big pine with antler markings all over it. Doe tend to gravitate there when they're in heat, so there's usually a good chance a buck'll wander by at some point. Lotta estrus scent. I stake the place out at dawn every day when I need meat. Longest I've had to wait is four days."

"Let's hope we get lucky today. I'm not sure I want to hang out here for almost a week."

"Afraid your instant coffee supply will run out?"

"You should be more worried that I'll deplete your stock of beer."

I didn't see much reason to haul my pack with all its contents. Instead I rummaged around and pulled out the Sam Brown with the .44, clipping a canteen to the belt and shoving a couple of power bars in the cargo pocket of my pants.

"You expecting trouble, ranger?" Blue Feather had a smirk. I guess he wasn't worried I was planning to shoot him.

"I don't like leaving a loaded weapon lying around. Besides, the grizzly out there howling might catch our scent and decide he doesn't like humans poaching on his hunting ground."

"Don't worry. I'm a pretty good shot with that M1."

"I don't doubt it." I was betting he'd had lots of practice. The deerskins hanging all around us testified to that fact. "And a thirty caliber round is just great for bringing down a buck or a Nazi. But do me a favor; if a grizzly comes at us, leave him to me. Forty-four magnum's got a little more stopping power."

"Guess you never figured to be surrounded by armed men, eh, Dewaldo." Blue Feather winked at his disciple.

"Just try not to shoot me." Dewaldo shouldered his pack. Maybe he felt more comfortable with all his supplies on him. More likely he hadn't shared with Blue Feather that he was packing, either, and decided to haul everything with him rather than pull out his Colt Peacemaker.

Blue Feather grabbed the Garand, a box of cartridges, and a clip, feeding bullets expertly into it. I expected him to shove the clip into the magazine—you load an M1 by inserting the clip through the open breech—but he surprised me, tossing me the rifle and clip. I've got good reflexes; that's the only reason I caught the rifle rather than letting it hit me in the face.

"Ever loaded one of these before, Mr. Ranger?" I could see the glint in his eye.

"I'm sure I can figure it out." So he was testing me first thing.

"Go ahead."

I laid the rifle in my lap, pulled back the bolt until it locked, placed my right thumb over the bolt to hold it in place, then slid the clip into the breech and shoved it down with my left thumb until it snapped into place. The M1 has one design flaw. Once the clip is fully inserted, the bolt releases. Unrestrained, it'll fly forward and snap the top cartridge into the chamber, taking your left thumb with it if you're not careful. That's why you hold the bolt with your right and then let it charge the first round after you've gotten your left out of the way. Few people know about this the first time they load one; they get a bruised or broken thumb for their efforts. This was a common enough occurrence during

WWII that GIs coined the term "Garand thumb" to describe it. I'd watched my North Carolina gun dealer buddy who owned the only other M1 I've seen let unsuspecting newbies learn this the hard way numerous times. I guess it's not a surprise that people who like to play with guns generally have a mean streak.

"I'm impressed." Obviously Blue Feather knew about Garand thumb, too.

"Huh?" Dewaldo didn't. "What's the big deal? Loading a rifle's not exactly rocket science."

"Not as long as you've got a medicine man around who knows how to set a broken thumb. Right Blue Feather?" I gave the old con-artist a wink and handed him back the loaded weapon.

"Aw, it don't break your thumb, Mr. Ranger." The twinkle in his eye was still there. "First time I loaded it, I just got a big bruise."

"You and a few thousand GIs."

"Okay, so you two have your little inside joke." Dewaldo was clearly irritated, the way a disciple gets when they think their master has a new favorite. "If you're through, though, maybe we should get going. The sun'll be up in about an hour."

"Yeah, best get going." Blue Feather got up and headed outside. We followed him into the pitch black. Once outside, we stood for a few minutes, accustoming our eyes to the lack of light. There wasn't much of a moon, but with no cities for miles, the stars punctuated the night and almost provided enough illumination to see.

"I know the way, so just follow me." Blue Feather was whispering. "Try not to make too much noise."

"Right." Dewaldo's whisper still had a tinge of irritation, but I could hear eagerness, too. I suspected this was the first time Blue Feather had taken him along hunting.

"Just inside the forest line, we'll stop to piss. Once we get close to that big pine, we don't want to do anything that'll give off a strong human scent."

"Sure, Blue Feather." I'd had my share of deer-hunting expeditions as a kid, including hearing this little gem of wisdom. I doubt if a buck can tell the difference between human piss and the animal kind. But I like to humor people. Still, "I hate to tell you two, though, but you're both giving off enough human scent to knock over a buffalo."

"That's where this stuff comes in." He held up plastic bottle filled with something. "Deer urine. After we piss, I'll shake some of this over us."

"Great. Something to look forward to." This was probably some native American lore. Every hunter I've ever known has some ridiculous secret to bagging their prey that is really little more than superstitious nonsense. Personally, I figure the best technique is to practice until you're a good enough shot you can hit something before it gets close enough to smell you. "By the way, Blue Feather, how do you get a deer to piss into that bottle?"

"Funny, ranger. I collect it from the bladder when I butcher 'em."

"Right. I knew that."

Dewaldo had gone quiet, obviously drinking in Blue Feather's store of cunning. The old con-man headed into the woods, Dewaldo trailing, me bringing up the rear. We stopped inside the tree-line as he'd promised, emptied our bladders of human piss and then let him shower us with deer urine. I'm sure I'd felt stupider in my life, but I couldn't remember when.

The Killer Trees

But Blue Feather knew the way in the dark and was damned quiet. I'm pretty good at sneaking up on things, too, but he and Dewaldo were stealthy enough to make me self-conscious every time I blindly brushed against a pine-needled branch. Living in the city leaves you sounding pretty ham-handed when skulking around a forest with practiced woodsmen, no matter how stealthy a life you lead. Finally the first dim rays of morning crept around us after what seemed an eternity.

"This is the place." Blue Feather pointed. Through the trees I could just make out the big pine. "Find a place to settle in. We might have a long wait."

Dewaldo undid his pack and sat on a boulder, pulling out the big notebook. I wondered how he had enough light to write. I sidled up next to a tree, figuring it would break up my profile. Standing, I knew, would also give me a better view. Blue Feather watched me for a minute, then came up close.

"Tell you what, Mr. Ranger. Since you loaded the rifle, I'll let you have the honor." He held the M1 out to me.

I thought about it for a moment. He probably wanted to see if I could shoot the piece as well as load it. Maybe he was also thinking that if I really was a ranger, I was just waiting to bust him for hunting without a license. Could be he'd decided I'd have no grounds for a complaint if I did the shooting myself. Or maybe he wanted to see how I handled killing something.

"Thanks." I took the rifle from him. "So where do you prefer I shoot it?"

"Wherever it is that you get a good shot." He looked puzzled.

"I mean, do you want the head for mounting, or do you prefer a quick kill to keep the meat tender? Wounded animals pump out a lot of adrenalin."

"It won't get close enough for you put the muzzle between its eyes. Just shoot at whatever part you get a clean shot at."

"Okay. I'll see what I can do."

We waited, and waited. Hunting requires patience. I've got it. Blue Feather, too. We both stood perfectly still, scanning the woods out by the big pine, looking for movement. Dewaldo scribbled. He wasn't making a lot of noise, but once when he turned a page, Blue Feather glared at him. I understood. This was serious business, meat to get him through the winter.

It was maybe an hour before I spotted movement, not in front of us near the deer-mating tree, but off to our left, maybe two-hundred yards away. Blue Feather didn't seem to notice; Dewaldo had his head in his notebook. I didn't turn to look, just shifted my eyes. Whatever it was had stopped dead.

"There." Blue Feather pointed straight ahead. I'd picked that movement up, too. We froze. Dewaldo stopped writing, slowly raised his head. Blue Feather hissed, "Dewaldo, don't move."

Straight ahead through the pine needles and thin underbrush I could make out the tip of an impressive set of antlers about fifty yards beyond the big pine, maybe a-hundred-fifty yards from our position. It was standing there, considering. I doubted Blue Feather's deer piss had managed to completely mask the scent of human. It was probably picking up a trace, getting suspicious. Any movement or sound and it would bolt.

Off to the left I caught another movement, something looking to get a better position. It was possible, of course, that a rival hunter also knew about Blue Feather's secret buck-on-the-prowl site. Possible, sure, but I had a better idea about who was out there. And whoever it was, he was about to spook our prey.

Blue Feather decided to risk another whisper, thinking I needed guidance, I guess. "Give it a chance to clear those bushes . . . "

The report of the M1 cut him off like a teacher's ruler on the back of a smart-mouthed brat's hand. He stood there, mouth hanging open, watching the antler tip jerk back. It was a big buck. The sound of it hitting the ground was almost as loud as the rifle shot.

"You got it!" Dewaldo' shout was triumphal. For someone who wasn't into hunting, he got pretty excited about it.

"Damn, you sure did, Mr. Ranger." Blue Feather shook his head. "I never saw anything except an antler and rustling pine needles."

"Lucky shot. I was afraid it would get spooked." I didn't mention the source of my concern.

"Let's go see how big it is." Dewaldo ran toward the downed buck like a kid.

"Careful." Blue Feather turned paternal, worried about his charge. "If it's wounded, it can be dangerous. The hooves are sharp."

"It's dead." I don't know why I said it. I knew I'd killed it, but there was no reason to act cocky.

Blue Feather shot me a respectful glance. "We'll see."

Dewaldo reached the deer first, undeterred by Blue Feather's warning. When he got there he let out a whoop like, well, an Indian.

"It's dead, alright. Damn, Blue Feather. He shot it right between the eyes. Unbelievable."

"Lucky shot?" There was fresh appraisal in the con-man's voice.

"Guess I've got natural skill with a gun."

"White men always do."

We stood around the buck admiring for quite some time. It had a six-point rack and looked to weigh well over two-hundred pounds. Blue Feather wouldn't be wanting for meat. We were also procrastinating, putting off the hard part of a deer hunt. We'd have to drag the thing back to Blue Feather's butcher shop in the cave and get to work skinning and gutting it. All told, those are demanding, messy jobs.

I thought about calling out for Walker to give us a hand. But I figured he'd already satisfied his curiosity about what we were up to and cleared out.

Later that afternoon we dropped exhausted to the floor of Blue Feather's hut. Dragging the carcass through the woods had been a hell of a job, even after our expedition leader had produced a rope, tied it to the back legs, and attached it to a yoke he fashioned out of a felled pine branch. That allowed the three of us to pull it as a team, still no mean feat. And we'd dragged it all the way up to the entrance to the cave where we hung it upside down from a tree and then watched Blue Feather gut it. He did indeed carefully remove the bladder and empty its contents into his plastic bottle. One thing was certain; between our sweat, dirt, and deer piss, we all stank to high heaven. Blue Feather sported an impressive sheen of the buck's blood to round out the effect.

Dewaldo dozed off as soon as we hit the floor of the hut. Maybe he could hike all day and sit up all night writing, but hauling deer carcasses apparently pushed him to the limit. I had to admit, I was tired, too. But I haven't dropped off to sleep from exhaustion in a long time. Something always keeps me awake. I think it's some inner sense warning me that things like to creep up on those who are too tired to care.

Blue Feather tossed me one of the cold beers he'd retrieved from his freezer-cave. He didn't seem particularly spent. Living like Grizzly Adams had obviously toughened him up quite a bit. I made a note to add the occasional backpacking expedition to my gym-oriented fitness regimen. Watching Blue Feather casually sipping his Budweiser reminded me that people in my line of work can wind up dead if they run into someone just a little tougher than they are.

"You're an interesting fella, Mr. Ranger." Blue Feather wanted to talk.

"Not me. I'm just your average government worker."

"Sure, who shoots like Davy Crockett." He stared, waiting for me to say something. I didn't. Finally he got impatient. "So you gonna tell me who that was bird-dogging us today?"

"I don't know what you mean." So he had noticed. He had a damned good poker face.

"Come on, you saw that guy plain as day. Or does your X-ray vision only work when you're lining up a buck hiding behind a bush?"

"Didn't think you'd seen him, Blue Feather."

"You don't give me much credit. Or maybe you think I survive out here because the Great Spirit protects me."

"Well, Dewaldo didn't notice him."

"Dewaldo's too busy trying to capture the great outdoors in verse."

"Okay. So maybe it was another hunter. I'm sure you're not the only person who's noticed all the antler markings on that tree."

"This deep in the Oquala this late in the season? Not likely. Whoever that was, they followed you two up here. And don't try to tell me they did it without you noticing. I watched you today. You're one of those people who can sense someone tracking you."

"Don't give me too much credit." I didn't tell him I still had the remnant of a nasty bruise on the back of my skull from not sensing someone behind me a little over a month before. "But you're right. We were followed all the way from Ogloskie."

"Who is it?"

"I don't really know for sure." I grabbed my pack, dug out the GPS unit and tossed it to him. "But that little gizmo tells me it's a wholesale sporting goods rep named Walker Treadman."

He looked over the device. "I don't follow."

"Well, he does, courtesy of that thing. He loaned it to me, said he wanted me to give it a trial. He's been following us like a bad cold the whole way, but he hasn't been staying close enough to be tracking us the old-fashioned way. That fancy GPS is signaling our position to him."

"Why didn't you throw it into the woods somewhere?"

"Anybody that interested in knowing where I'm going, I get curious to know why."

He turned the GPS on and stared at it for awhile. "I'm still amazed how accurate these things are."

"Hard to get lost with one, I'll admit."

"So how did Riefenthal get lost, then?"

A cold sensation formed in my gut. "He had one of those?"

"Looked exactly like this one."

"You're sure?"

"He showed it to me. Said he'd never used one before. Told me it would be the death of real excursion backpacking, but that since he'd started using it, he couldn't stop himself from checking it all the time."

I kicked Dewaldo's foot to wake him up.

"Hey, what'd you do that for?"

"You found Riefenthal, didn't you, Dewaldo?"

"Sure." He rubbed his eyes. It was taking him a moment to wake up completely. "About fifty yards from Stickler's Creek, just where it turns west."

"How'd you know where to look?"

"I didn't. I guessed he might head for water if he was in trouble. An experienced hiker who's gotten lost usually looks for someplace where they can get oriented. Find a creek, you can follow it downstream and maybe it'll lead you someplace."

"That's what he'd done?"

"I doubt it. I think I just got lucky that he wandered close to the creek before he died. He obviously wasn't thinking straight at the end."

"You found his gear, too. Right?"

"Yeah. Again, I got lucky. Ruby'd issued me a radio, but it was useless where I found him. The creek runs through a hollow there. So I climbed up out of the hollow, figuring maybe I'd climb a tree and see if I could raise her. I walked right into his campsite."

"You go through his stuff?"

"Why would I do that?" He glared at me. "What the hell are you driving at, Clayton? You think I stole money or something out of his pack?"

"I'm just wondering why the GPS he had with him didn't show up with his effects." I'd gone over the itemized inventory in the police report Frank had provided, curious what an experienced hiker who gets lost leaves behind when he decides to abandon everything and head off naked into the woods. I'd have remembered a GPS on the list.

"What makes you think he had a GPS with him?"

"He showed it to Blue Feather."

"Well, if it wasn't in his stuff, then one of the state troopers must have lifted it. I don't need one and I sure as shit wouldn't steal one off a dead guy." He sounded pretty indignant. I doubted he was lying. Of course, really good liars always sound sincere.

"You know, Mr. Ranger," Blue Feather interrupted my interrogation, "this GPS you've got looks exactly like the one Riefenthal was carrying."

"Maybe it's the same one." In fact, I was pretty sure it was.

"How's that possible?" Dewaldo's voice was pure puzzlement. Blue Feather had been right; his head was so deep into his book of poems, he was oblivious.

"That's what I plan to ask Walker." I'd had the sales rep on my list of suspects, but honestly, I'd marked him as more likely a rival spook or maybe even a freelance investigator. He just hadn't struck me as some sort of eco-loony willing to kill to protect his precious trees. It still didn't make any sense. But he'd obviously arranged Riefenthal's death, then retrieved the tell-tale GPS-beacon.

"Well, you'll have to wait awhile to do that. It'll take us three or four days to get back to Ogloskie." He wasn't glaring any more, but he kept looking at me. "So I guess Ruby was right."

"About what?" I had an idea.

"That you're some kind of cop."

"Of course I am, Dewaldo. I'm a forest ranger. We have law enforcement authority."

"You don't sound like a ranger when you're asking questions. You sound like a cop." Dewaldo laid back and closed his eyes, dropping back into dreamland. I realized he was about the most Zen person I'd ever known, making the assault and battery conviction an even bigger puzzle. But that could wait. I had a client at last. Now it was just a matter of getting the drop on him.

Of course, I wasn't happy to find out I sound like a cop. I don't like to think I come across as a nitwit.

"Dewaldo is such an innocent." Blue Feather was watching his sleeping acolyte, smiling. "Men like you and me have to look out for ourselves, Mr. Ranger, because the Great Spirit is too busy protecting innocents like Dewaldo."

"Right." I remembered the Colt in Dewaldo's pack. I'd eliminated him as my client. But, in my experience, no one's innocent.

"But you're no cop."

"You already came to that conclusion, Blue Feather. Remember? You decided yet what you think I am?"

"Somebody I wouldn't want to piss off."

"Then I suggest you toss me another can of beer." I was losing patience with the guess-what-Clayton-Stillbridge-really-is game. It was time to finish the job and disappear leaving everyone to play whatever-happened-to-Ranger-Clayton.

Blue Feather handed back the GPS along with the beer. "You hold onto this. I feel better knowing your friend Walker is tracking you, not me."

I stowed the GPS and then downed the beer. Might as well let the old con-man think I'd drunk myself into a stupor. I shed my boots and lay back on my sleeping bag, feigning sleep.

After a couple of hours it was quiet except for Dewaldo sawing logs. I decided to take a chance that Blue Feather was asleep, too. I reached quietly into my pack and located the GPS. Then, quiet as I could manage, I crept over to where Dewaldo was snoring and tucked it into one of the pockets of his backpack.

Walker turning out to be a killer meant I'd rather have him drawing a bead on someone else. And, with any luck, I could surprise him before he actually killed Dewaldo.

Chapter VIII
Killers

WE SAID OUR FAREWELLS early the morning after the hunt. I made it to be Monday, not that it mattered much. I don't punch a clock, and, besides, I figure I'm always on the clock, anyway.

Blue Feather wasn't too broken up about us leaving. He made some more blackberry tea after giving me some water for a real morning beverage. Dewaldo had a hang-dog look while he drank his.

"If the weather holds for a few more weeks, I'll try to make it up one more time, maybe pack in some more beer."

"Always appreciated." Blue Feather didn't sound all that grateful. "Don't try to brave a blizzard, though. I get desperate this winter, I can always ferment some blackberries."

"Or maybe give up booze altogether like you, Dewaldo." He shot me a glare, not appreciating my effort at humor.

"We'd better get going. I know you're impatient to ask Walker about Riefenthal." He slung his pack over his shoulder and stalked outside. I figured he was in a hurry to get me back to Ogloskie so he could go back to being Blue Feather's number one pupil. There was little point in telling him we'd be meeting Ruby's boyfriend a lot sooner than expected. If Walker was up to what I thought, he'd be trying to make sure we didn't make it back to Ogloskie at all.

Outside the grizzly had resumed wailing somewhere in the distance. It was getting downright spooky. "Is there a record for how many consecutive days a bear can go on like that, Dewaldo? If that's some kind of mating cry, then that must be one desperately horny grizzly."

"Maybe it's hurt or something." He didn't seem concerned.

"Well, I hope we don't run into it if it is. Even this .44 I'm lugging is a popgun to a wounded grizzly on a rampage."

"Just shoot it between the eyes. You can do that." Dewaldo grinned. I had to give him credit; moody poet and all, he didn't rattle easy.

"That's not a cry of pain." Blue Feather had followed us out. I think he wanted to watch us go, make sure we left. I guess people who seek solitude in the wilderness can only stand company for so long. "Sounds more like a warning of some kind."

"You speak bear now, too?" I'd had enough conman wisdom for one expedition. "If so, tell me how to say 'shut the fuck up' in grizzly lingo."

"Dewaldo already told you that. It's a bullet between the eyes." He stood in front of his hut, arms crossed, glint in his eye, like some redneck caricature of a medicine man. I almost laughed. "You boys hike safe."

"Enjoy the venison." We set off. I didn't look back. Dewaldo did, several times. I wondered how he'd managed before finding his own personal Jesus. Of course, there had been that assault and battery charge.

Following Dewaldo the way we'd come, I ran over the trail in my mind, considering ambush points. As thick as the Oquala is, Walker could be laying for us anywhere, pick us off with a high-powered rifle if he had one. If that's how he played it, he'd shoot me first, then finish off Dewaldo. That's how I'd have approached the problem, anyway. Always take out the bigger threat with the first shot.

But I wasn't expecting him to turn sniper on me. Walker had shown a preference for subtler handiwork, not all that different from the way I approach jobs. He'd be reluctant to leave two bullet-ridden corpses with no easy explanation for cops to latch onto. Considering his problem from a professional perspective, I mulled over how I'd do the job. First step would be to put us both out of commission, maybe use a taser or something like that tranquilizer gun Ruby had back in the station. Then drop Dewaldo off a cliff somewhere and dump me naked in the middle of the forest like he'd apparently done Riefenthal. Easy explanation for the cops; guide suffers unfortunate accident, rube newby ranger gets lost in the woods, goes whacko and expires. Neat. And Conifer would still get the point once their CEO learned the bad news that the spook sent by his puppet president to clean up the mess had become one of the statistics.

I didn't plan on letting any of that happen. With Dewaldo packing the GPS, all I had to do was put some distance between me and him and then wait for Walker to make an appearance. I had a few ideas how to make that happen. So, of course, events took an unexpected turn.

Thwump!

I stopped. Years of instinct and training kick in pretty fast when you hear something familiar.

"What the hell was that?" Dewaldo spun around. The noise had come from behind us.

"Don't know," I lied. An explosive makes a pretty distinctive noise. This one had been farther away from me but bigger than the blast that blew out the windows in Rudy Larson's garage apartment a few weeks earlier.

A large crashing sound followed the explosion by a few seconds, like a very heavy object falling on something fairly fragile. Blue Feather's comment about the boulder popped into my head; *an earthquake or something similar.*

"Something similar. Yeah."

"What?" Dewaldo looked confused.

"Nothing." I was sizing up the situation fast, but not really coming up with a plan of action.

"Maybe we'd better go back and check on Blue Feather. That noise came from the direction of his cabin."

"Sounded to me like it was more to the north." I'd come up with something. "Listen, I think I'm getting a cramp in my calf. Why don't you run back and make sure Blue Feather's okay. I'm gonna sit down and try to work the cramp out. Once you've satisfied yourself your guru is still alive and well, I'll meet you at that overlook we stopped at on the way up. Okay?"

"I guess so." He was antsy to race off and make sure his friend didn't need rescuing, but years of being a guide and having far-and-away too much conscience for his own good ... "You sure you're gonna be okay? I hate to just leave you here."

"I'll be fine." I'd be safer, too. People who go racing toward the sounds of explosions and crashes are well-intentioned but not destined to live long. He turned and started running back toward Blue Feather's cabin.

I counted out a minute and then took off after him at a leisurely—and quieter—pace. It was time to bird-dog Dewaldo so I could catch Walker bird-dogging me.

There was no need to keep Dewaldo in sight; I knew where he was going. I paid more attention to the surrounding woods, paralleling his track and watching for any appearance by Walker. Not that I expected to see him. He hadn't been tailing us that morning; obviously he'd had other business.

"Noooo!" Dewaldo's wail told me he'd made it back. I had a good idea what he'd found. Still, I made my way through the trees to the edge of the clearing, staying out of sight as best I could.

The boulder Blue Feather and I had discussed was sitting in the middle of the mess that had been the old con-man's home. Half the cabin was completely caved in—although the pot-bellied stove with its smokestack seemed undamaged. Disasters are like that; nature seems to have as much sense of irony as the God of the *Bible* my mom tried to beat me into fearing, without much success.

There was actually enough of the hut left that an industrious individual like Blue Feather could probably have rigged some temporary cover from the deer skins, boards and roofing remnants that lay scattered from the force of the impact, maybe even ridden out the winter. And, of course, the redneck medicine-man's complex of mine-shaft larder, ice-box, and tanning shack was probably still intact. But he wouldn't be needing them.

"Blue Feather!" Dewaldo stood in front of the mess calling his mentor's name for what seemed an eternity. It wasn't that unreasonable to hope he'd been outside somewhere when the boulder struck. Not unreasonable if you assumed it was an accident. Which

I knew it wasn't. I could have saved Dewaldo a lot of breath. Blue Feather was lying dead inside that cabin. He'd been there in that state when the boulder came crashing down. That's how killers who arrange accidents to cover their handiwork operate. Dislodging the boulder with an explosive placed to send it tumbling directly onto the cabin was an expert piece of work done just for show. Walker had undoubtedly snapped Blue Feather's neck as soon as we'd vacated the premises. That's how I'd have done it.

"Blue Feather." The last was more a sob than a shout. I understood. Dewaldo had suffered a hell of a loss. He'd been trekking the Oquala to learn from the wise man at the foot of the mountain for a couple of years. I guess that's a tough break to handle. Not that I'd know. I make it a point never to develop a close relationship with anybody. Too many people I meet in life don't have long to live.

He went into what was left of the hut, disappearing from my view around the back of the boulder. Then he let out another long wail. He'd obviously found the body.

He stayed in there for awhile not making a sound. Maybe he was trying to render first aid. Hell, maybe he was praying—there was that alleged divinity degree. I waited, still looking for any sign of Walker. He was likely somewhere watching. Dewaldo racing back after the explosion was pretty predictable. Maybe he figured I'd come bounding out of the woods, too. He was going be disappointed. For the time being, we could both watch to see what Dewaldo would do. Personally, I was betting he'd go into shock, sit there next to Blue Feather for a long, long time.

I'm a pretty good judge of human behavior. And yet people still surprise me every now and then.

Dewaldo came out from behind the boulder with the Garand—amazingly intact—in one hand and a clip in the other. While I watched, he pulled back the bolt and shoved the clip into the breech. I almost called out a warning, but thought better of it. The bolt slammed into his thumb. It's really a serious design flaw. In fact, after the war, somebody in Congress introduced a bill to reward John Garand, father of the M1, $100,000 to compensate him for not getting any royalties from the design he'd developed as an employee of the government-owned Springfield Armory. The bill failed. I'm betting there were a few ex-GI Congressmen still smarting from their first experience with his handiwork who got a particular pleasure killing that measure.

Dewaldo gingerly slid back the bolt with his other hand and freed his thumb. I was impressed. He didn't cry out in pain, just released the bolt to chamber a round, wiped some blood off his damaged digit, and headed up the mountain behind the hut with blood in his eye.

So the naive hiking guide wasn't quite as innocent as he appeared; he knew Blue Feather's death was no accident. That raised the question of just how much else he knew. I stayed hidden and watched him disappear up the trail. Then I waited some more. All things come to those who wait, they say.

After fifteen minutes, my patience was rewarded. Walker exited the woods from the other side of the hut looking like something out of a hiker's catalog, rip-stop fabric cargo pants, sun-resistant shirt and hat, a bush jacket that probably cost over five-hundred bucks, and a state-of-the-art internal frame pack. Maybe phony sales reps get merchandise wholesale, too. He scanned the area, a puzzled look on his face, checked an electronic gizmo in his hand that looked like my loaner GPS on steroids, obviously the tracker. Staring at the screen, he shook his head, looked up toward the mountain, then took off up the trail after Dewaldo. I guess he'd figured out that I wasn't carrying the beacon anymore. Following Dewaldo at this point was a mistake, though; he should have stayed focused on me. But I'm betting he wanted to make sure he retrieved the beacon like he'd done with Riefenthal.

I gave him ten minutes to get out of sight before I sprinted out of the woods to the hut. Call it professional curiosity; I wanted to see how well he'd arranged things to look accidental. It was pretty convincing. He'd left Blue Feather's body in the middle of the cabin, and the boulder had landed on the lower part of the torso, crushing everything from the waist down. A sharp investigator, or one of those brilliant coroners you see on TV, might notice that the neck that was snapped clean was the only damaged portion of the upper part of the body and gotten suspicious. Fortunately for guys in my line of work—and Walker's, too, it seemed—those brilliant forensic specialists only exist in screenplays. Whatever local or federal police force got stuck with jurisdiction for Blue Feather's demise would be more than happy to write off this particular event as an unfortunate act of nature that had rid the world of one more miscreant. When somebody finally made it to this remote part of the Oquala to find the body, that is. There was a good chance the death wouldn't be reported for months. I wasn't going to be filing any police reports, and I didn't expect Walker would, either. Of course, there was always Dewaldo.

I left Blue Feather in peace and started quietly up the trail. Dewaldo was up there looking to kill the murderer of his medicine man. Whether he knew that was Walker was still up in the air. Walker, of course, was headed up there to kill Dewaldo. There wasn't much doubt who'd win that contest. If I got there fast enough, though, I might be able to take care of Walker before he took care of Dewaldo. Then I'd have to decide what to do with my pony-tailed guide.

"Walker! God-damn-it, Walker, I know you're up here!" Dewaldo's voice echoed down the trail. That answered that. He knew about Walker. He'd been a convincing liar. I mentally tipped my hat to him. Everybody's a liar, in my experience, but lying well is a skill most people lack.

"Walker!" He wasn't being particularly smart, though. Yelling for a professional killer to show himself is kinda stupid. It just tells him where you are and that you're planning to do him harm. A professional killer's response to that will be to . . . well . . . kill you.

I skirted along the edge of the trail as fast as I could while staying in the cover of the trees that lined the path. They were still fairly thick at the base of the mountain. Up where the boulder was—had been—was more exposed. I'd have to move slower approaching that spot, which from the sound of Dewaldo's voice is where I figured he'd gone. Maybe he thought Walker had just stayed there after blowing the boulder. Divinity school is obviously not good preparation for predicting the actions of murderers in the woods.

"Dewaldo." Walker had reached him. The phony sales rep's voice was calm, almost playful. I'm betting he enjoyed his work. "Where's your hiking buddy?"

"You killed Blue Feather!"

I was getting close. Dewaldo wasn't yelling anymore, but I could make out every word. The woods were eerily quiet. For the first time I noticed that the grizzly had stopped howling. Thinking back, I realized the howling had stopped when I'd heard the explosion. Maybe the loud blast had scared it off.

"Now that's a bit of an assumption on your part, Dewaldo, if you don't mind my saying so." Walker was playing it cool, making conversation, trying to get the kid to drop his guard. I wasn't close enough to see, yet, but I assumed Dewaldo was pointing the M1 at Walker's gut.

"Alvarez said nobody was gonna get hurt."

Now things were starting to take shape. Alvarez. He was obviously in charge. Dewaldo was his eyes and ears in town and in the forest. Walker, of course, was the muscle. The only real question was what group of eco-loonies could afford such expensive talent and had the know-how to find it. The answers now lay just around the next bend. I dropped to my belly and crawled the last few meters to a small rock by the trail that would give me cover to see what the two of them were doing.

"Accidents happen, kid. Forests are dangerous places."

I could see them both. Every time Walker spoke, he took a step closer to Dewaldo, who was indeed standing right where the boulder had been, aiming the rifle at the hit-man's stomach. Most people get weak at the knees when a gun is pointed at their gut. It didn't seem to bother Walker at all. I noticed as well that he'd dropped his pack, freeing himself of the weight, readying himself for action.

"You didn't have to kill Blue Feather. He was gonna let Conifer buy him off. We could have bought him off, too."

I'd been thinking I'd just about figured things out. But this didn't fit with tree-huggers turned violent. Eco-terrorists wouldn't need to buy off some redneck squatter to save the Oquala from a lumberjack-wielding corporation. Blue Feather had only been a threat to forces that wanted to cut the forest down.

"You gotta learn to see the big picture, Dewaldo. Riefenthal died before he could tell anyone the old Indian had agreed to a settlement. A lot of people are gonna assume Conifer blamed Blue Feather for what happened to Riefenthal and sent somebody up here to kill the old fraud in revenge. Conifer's going to be tied up in investigations for years."

"Yeah, well they'll also be looking for who was sent up here to kill Blue Feather. And they're going to come up with your name." Dewaldo was sounding less and less sure of himself. Walker's plan was working. He was filling the guide with doubt while he got close enough to make a grab for the rifle. He was a real pro.

"Nah, kid. They'll pin that one on your hiking buddy, the government spy."

I felt my face flush. Damn, I hate it when people think I'm a spy. I unholstered the .44.

"Not when I tell them he was with me. Not when I tell them I know damned well it was you."

"Yeah, kid, you'd be the one person who could screw all this up." Walker's back was to me, but I could tell from his voice he was smiling, almost laughing. He was less than two feet from the muzzle of the Garand. Dewaldo had missed his chance.

I had the .44 pointed right at the small of Walker's back. I could have shot him and saved Dewaldo right then and there. But I was curious to see how skilled Walker was. And, to be honest, since Dewaldo had revealed himself to be part of whatever the hell was going on, I suspected the safest course of action was to let events play out so that I'd only have one client to deal with.

Walker grabbed the rifle by the muzzle and spun all in one quick motion, jerking the M1 out of Dewaldo's hands, whirling full circle until the rifle butt cracked Dewaldo on the side of the head. I remembered Ruby's comment; Walker was indeed very light on his feet. Dewaldo staggered back and stumbled over the same outcrop that the boulder had gone over just an hour or so earlier. His body impacted somewhere below with a sickening thud.

"Fucking amateurs." Walker's voice dripped with disgust. He walked to the edge and looked down, still gripping the M1 like a club.

I stood up and pulled the hammer back on the .44. This is really unnecessary. It's a double-action revolver; simply squeezing the trigger cocks the hammer and releases it to fire the round. But cocking the gun manually makes a distinctive sound that anyone with firearms experience recognizes instantly. Walker froze.

"That you, Ranger Spook?" I didn't answer. Let him wonder. He stood there perfectly still for almost a minute before saying something else. "You mind if I turn around so we can talk face to face?"

"First put the rifle down."

"Sure." He placed the rifle on the ground right at his feet.

"Now kick it over the side where you sent Dewaldo."

"Right." He complied. It clattered down the slope. "Now can I turn around?"

"Not until you toss the other piece you're carrying."

"Don't you think, if I had a gun, I'd have used it rather than let Dewaldo almost shoot me?" It was a nice try. Some people might have bought his logic.

"Just get rid of your gun, Walker. I don't play games."

He shrugged and started to reach inside his jacket.

"I want to see just two fingers on the butt. Otherwise you're gonna have a big hole between your shoulder blades."

His hand came out slowly, a sleek black little automatic dangling from his thumb and forefinger. It looked to me like a .38. Something else we had in common, not feeling the need to carry a large caliber gat to prove our manhood. Although I had to admit, training the magnum cannon I'd been issued at Walker felt pretty reassuring.

"Toss it over the edge like I said."

"Give me a break, ranger. This is a Beretta Cheetah. Untraceable, too. These things ain't cheap."

"Put it on your expense report. Or if you prefer, I can shoot you."

"You're gonna do that anyway." It was a probe. He was wondering why I hadn't shot him already, going over in his mind whether I was after something else or maybe just not capable of shooting a man in the back. He was right about one thing, I wanted to talk, fill in some missing pieces, buy a little time to figure out some way to make his death look like something other than murder.

"Maybe not, Walker. Could be we're in the same line of work. Toss the piece and we can talk shop."

He flipped the pistol over the edge. It didn't make as much noise going down as had the rifle, or Dewaldo.

"Now can I turn around?"

"Slowly. I got a good look at your dazzling footwork already. And keep your hands where I can see 'em."

He turned to face me very slowly, a big grin on his face. "Nice work planting the GPS on Dewaldo. Guess you figured out it does more than help you navigate."

"I'm the suspicious type."

"So why don't you do me a favor and ease the hammer down on that cannon you're pointing at me. Cocking a .44 like that gives it a hair trigger."

"I haven't shot anyone accidentally yet."

"Well, you know what they say about there's always a first time."

He was good. He'd taken two small steps toward me while making conversation, the same trick he'd used on Dewaldo. I lowered my aim and fired a round into the dirt six inches in front of his left foot, then pointed the gun back at his chest.

"How's that? Feel more relaxed? Take one more step and I'll demonstrate how light the action is on this piece even with the hammer down. But you'll be too busy dying to notice."

"Okay. Then let's talk shop."

"Sit down first, legs crossed in front of you."

"Damn, you don't give a guy much of a chance, Clayton." He was still grinning. "Or should I say Dick?"

He'd meant that to rattle me, get me to flinch so he could make a move. I pulled the hammer back again instead. "Sit."

"Sure thing." He sat down, extended his front legs, crossed them and put his hands on the ground behind him to keep from falling backwards. Making someone sit on the ground and cross their legs throws them off balance, forcing them to keep all four limbs occupied. It's not as good as hog-tying a client, but it's the next best thing. "So what do you want to talk about, Dick?"

"Maybe first you can tell me why you keep calling me Dick. That your idea of an insult?"

"It's your name, ain't it? Dick Paladin." His expression was pretty smug. I didn't blame him. His boss obviously kept him better informed than mine kept me.

"It's Richard."

"Oh. Sorry. Your file didn't say you were touchy about it."

"I'm real sensitive. Hurts my feelings to know somebody's leaking classified information about me. Makes me want to shoot somebody. Tell you what; you tell me who leaked my ID to you, I'll go shoot them instead of you."

"Geeze, you think they share information about sources with me? I'm the operations guy, not management."

"Then at least tell me when you got my file."

"The day after you arrived." He feigned a look of real concern. "It's a waste, a talented guy like you working for the government. They can't even protect your cover. They sent you out here compromised, gave you no chance at all."

"Yet it seems I'm pointing the gun at you."

"Like I said, wasted talent." Worry crept into his smile. Guys like Walker go through life convinced they can handle any situation that gets thrown their way. The realization that this time might be different was dawning slowly on him. "Believe me, I know. I used to work for the government."

"That doesn't surprise me."

"Lousy assignments, stupid bosses, crappy pay. Sound familiar?"

"Must have been awhile back you quit, Walker. All that's changed. Civil service reform, you know. We're even getting pay for performance." They'd been feeding us this bullshit in Washington my entire career. Maybe it would convince Walker I was really a contented employee more than happy to kill him in the line of duty. That part was true, anyway—not the contented part, but more than ready to blow his ass to Hell.

"Private sector's a lot more lucrative, Richard." He wasn't taunting me with the name anymore; it was a psychological ploy—*Richard, pal, fellow axe-man, colleague*—to make me think he was really offering me a deal, sincerely holding out a better way of life if I'd just listen. "Be your own boss. Take contracts you like, pass on ones you don't. Did I mention it's a lot more lucrative?"

Maybe his appeal would have been more effective . . . if my name was really Richard. "I'm not interested in working as a mercenary for tree-huggers."

"What?" He looked shocked. "Is that what you think, I'm working for some environmentalist group?"

"Who else would want to stop Conifer from cutting down the Oquala?"

"You're kidding, right?" It took him a minute. Then he laughed. It's funny when somebody acts stupid, even when they're pointing a gun at you. "I'll tell you who else would like to stop Conifer. Just about any of a half-dozen other big corporations that do commercial logging."

I'm really not a moron, but like everybody, sometimes it takes me awhile to see the forest for ... well, I finally got it. I wasn't protecting Conifer's contract from environmental terrorists, I was stopping a rival company from muscling in. And that they'd made their play by hiring some ex-spooks and assassins; well, why should corporations act any different than the government? Not that any of this made any real difference to me. Conifer's contract was with the government. I work for the government. I was in the Oquala to deal with clients who were interfering with a government contract. To be honest, I kinda like doing what I do for the government.

Something must have conveyed to Walker that I wasn't going to be bought off; worry spread back across his face. And I'd decided to forego my usual methods; let Frank and company sort things out if I didn't make it look like an accident. It's the least they could do for letting my file leak to a bunch of for-hire goons. I aimed square in the middle of Walker's chest and started to squeeze the trigger.

Except the big grin came back, the worry in his face disappeared. That caught me unawares. I released the pressure on the trigger for just an instant. It was an instant too long.

Something bashed into the back of my head, right about the same place where I was still sporting a bruise from a couple of months before. Before the lights went out in my skull, I had the fleeting realization that I'd been cold-cocked by a woman . . . again.

Every superman has his own personal kryptonite, I guess.

I came around surprised that I was still among the living, but the throbbing in my head assured me I was indeed alive if not well. I restrained the impulse to groan and stayed perfectly still; no reason to attract the attention of the professional killer I'd been about to dispatch or the very stealthy person who'd tried to bash my brains in.

" . . . leave the gun on the ground, Walker. I'm serious." It was Ruby's voice. Someday I'll figure out why I never hear a woman sneaking up behind me. Of course, women have always been trouble for me— behind me, in front of me, underneath or on top of me. If I didn't develop a better warning sense for the one's with blunt objects, though, I was gonna be in serious need of a head transplant one of these days.

Not that I had much expectation to live long enough to get beaned by a third broad down the road. Ruby's comment told me Walker was reaching for the .44 I'd dropped at lights out. I had a pretty good idea what he planned to do with it when he got it.

"Come on, Ruby. You didn't save me from that government goon so you could shoot me."

"Don't be so sure, Walker. I saw you take care of Dewaldo."

"Then you saw that he was threatening to kill me. Self-defense. Somethin' must have addled the poor kid's brain."

"He was pissed because you killed his pet Indian."

"Aw, are you gonna start with that too, hon'? A rock fell on the guy's cabin. It was an accident."

"I've been following you for five days, Walker. You may be good at tracking someone who's carrying a homing device, but, honestly, you're lousy at spotting someone following you. I watched you set that charge."

So Walker wasn't perfect. Confidence is a great thing for a hit-man, but too much of it can be a flaw, leave you thinking no one can get the drop on you. But I have to say, I found myself wondering why Ruby had just watched while he did away with Blue Feather. Some people would expect an armed forest ranger to intervene when they see a homicide in process. Ogloskie was turning out to have one interesting cast of characters. I decided to risk opening my eyes a tad to assess the situation. If Ruby and Walker were going to rumble, I might get a chance to wriggle out of my predicament.

Ruby had the balanced posture of an experienced handgun artist, the Smith and Wesson 500 sitting lightly in her right hand supported by her left and pointed directly at Walker. Her eyes darted quickly between Walker, me, and the .44 lying about a foot away from where I'd sprawled. Walker was crouched over, frozen, fingers inches from my piece, watching Ruby intently.

"Ruby, baby. It's me, Walker. Your bay-at-the-moon beau. You and me, we're like ginger and molasses, a sweet pair." I had more trouble stifling a groan at that line than from the pain in my head. "Now I'm gonna pick up this gun in case Spooky here comes out of it. I'm telling you, he's the dangerous one. You don't need to worry 'bout me. I'm your sugar."

It worked. He slid his fingers around my pistol and slowly picked it up. Ruby kept the Smith & Wesson trained on him, but she didn't shoot. Still, Walker was smart enough to keep the .44's muzzle pointed to the ground. Ruby was pretty edgy.

"I won't let you shoot him, Walker." She sounded serious, but I could detect a hint of doubt. She hadn't made up her mind whose side she wanted to be on.

"Aw, why not, darlin'? Heck, you probably killed him anyway when you hit him with that cannon." He glanced over at me. I guess he noticed my eyes slit-open. "Or not. Looks like Ranger Hatchet-man has a pretty thick skull."

Government goon. Spooky. Hatchet-man. He was giving me lots of reasons to kill him. All I needed was an opportunity—just a miracle, nothing much. I sat up, slowly.

He leveled the .44 at me. Ruby cocked her piece. "I mean it, Walker."

He didn't say anything for a long while. Then he lowered the muzzle again. "You're right, sugar. Better if you do it."

"Are you crazy?" Ruby was getting pretty confused.

"Like a fox." He had that grin back. "You shoot our phony ranger, and believe me, once he's a corpse, people will find out real fast that he's no ranger. He's just a bureaucrat sent here to remove a few impediments blocking Conifer Corporation from clear-cutting these woods. You'll be a local hero. Ranger Ruby who killed the spy who worked for the evil government that wanted to destroy the Oquala."

"I'll be in jail, Walker. He's carrying a federal badge, in case you forgot." She didn't sound really convinced it was such a bad idea. I was getting the impression that

Ruby had followed Walker not so much because she was concerned about what he was up to but more out of curiosity whether she could play it to her advantage. She'd said it herself; government pensions aren't much these days. It's not a surprise when career civil servants start thinking about feathering their nest a little. I've got that freezer full of cash, after all.

"Just for a time, honey. And I'll be there waiting when you get out. Partners. We're the perfect pair." He winked at her. "Plus, the people I work for, they'll make it worth your while."

She thought about it.

"Just how much might that be?" She was sounding alarmingly mercenary.

"Name your price, sugar."

Things weren't looking good. Ruby was considering his offer. I decided to get into the bidding.

"Ruby, he didn't have to kill Blue Feather. Riefenthal negotiated to pay him seventy-five grand to get out of the Oquala and not make waves. Walker knew that. He killed Riefenthal and Blue Feather. Why would he kill them both if his leash-holders are willing to shell out big bucks in bribes?"

She hesitated. "That's a good question. Walker?"

"Damn, Ranger Dick." The grin gave way to a sickly smile. I could read deadly seriousness in his eyes. "You're just determined to ruin my day, aren't you?"

He moved quicker than I'd seen with Dewaldo before, spinning, dropping to the ground, raising the .44 all in one motion and blowing a big hole in Ruby's chest just below and between her lovely breasts. To her credit, she fired reflexively when he moved, but her .50 cal round passed harmlessly through the air where Walker had been and into the forest beyond.

Ruby stood for the longest time, disbelief in her eyes. I've never been shot, but I've seen it happen enough that I know it takes a moment for the victim to realize what's happened. If it's a well-placed shot, they never do. She fell over backward like a tree finally succumbing to a logger's axe, sprawling, the Smith & Wesson still clasped in her right hand. I eyed it, sizing up the distance, getting ready to spring for it.

"Yeah, go for it, Ranger Dick. You might even get a finger on it before I blow your fucking head off." Walker was back on his feet, laughing. He was one cold-blooded son-of-a-bitch. I've never killed anyone I had sex with. I don't think even I could laugh about it.

"So it's back to 'Dick,' I see. I guess we're not best buddies anymore."

"Don't worry. You're gonna have an eternity to sulk about it."

He was in a damned fine position to make good on that promise. All I could do was stall for time.

"Since I'll have so much time for reflection, you mind satisfying my professional curiosity so I don't spend the hereafter wandering the Oquala as a ghost looking for answers?"

"It won't work, Dick. Making conversation won't get me to drop my guard long enough for you to get Ruby's gun." He was smug about it. That was good.

"Then it won't hurt if you fill me in on how you pulled off all those jobs; Langford, Riefenthal, Roper. I'm pretty good at arranging accidents, but those were works of art." A little ego-stroking couldn't hurt; even highly-trained assassins get distracted when they're given a chance to brag about how good they are. He took the bait.

"Langford was easy. Drove like a bat out of Hell. Running a bad driver off the road into a tree is child's play. And his buddy was asking for it. Drove out to the tree to lay a fucking wreath, for Christ's sake."

"I'm assuming you used the same trick as Blue Feather, broke his neck and then dropped a heavy object on him."

"That's right out of the manual."

I'd never seen the manual he meant. Maybe the USG really has a *Manual for Staging Accidental Deaths*. It's got publications for everything else. "You got creative with Reifenthal, though."

"Yeah." His chest swelled. He was proud of that one. "That guy was a regular Daniel Boone. Looked more at home out here in this damned forest than most people are in their own houses. I'm betting you could have dropped that guy in the middle of Siberia with nothing but a Swiss Army knife and he'd have shown up in Moscow a week later looking like he'd just gotten back from vacation."

"So how'd you get him disoriented?"

"Nothing to it. Waited for him to go to sleep one night. He slept pretty sound. Snuck up on him, used a taser, then gave him a big shot of Thorazine. Stripped off his clothes, dragged him a mile through the woods to that creek, and dumped him in. I'm guessing he woke up about two a.m. freezing his ass off with no idea what continent he was on."

"So you took the GPS out of his pack . . . "

"I'm not gonna leave a thing like that lying around."

" . . . and told Dewaldo where to look."

"You must not give me as much credit as you say. Dewaldo was just a spotter collecting information on the Conifer folks in the area to help us decide who and how. He wasn't briefed on the entire scope of the project. I sure as shit wouldn't tell him something that would get him thinking I'd been out here stalking Riefenthal. He just got lucky and stumbled on the guy's body."

"So he was reporting to Alvarez? Still, he seems to have known about you."

"You ask a lot of questions for someone's who's not gonna live long." I'd touched a nerve. Pissing him off so he'd shoot me immediately wouldn't be smart.

"What about Roper? Getting him out of his house in his pajamas in the middle of the night without his wife noticing? That's got me stumped."

"Bob Roper. He was one strange dude."

"How'd you pick him? He worked in the corporate office."

"Yeah, well, we were beginning to worry Conifer wasn't taking it seriously with just field people winding up dead. Decided to hit a little closer to home."

"You picked Roper because he was in finance? Some kind of message?"

"Nah. We just stuck video surveillance on the homes of all the top Conifer brass looking for an easy set-up." He had a big smile, remembering something special. "I'm scanning through the video files, and one night this guy Roper comes out in his PJs with a stool and a noose. Ties it to a tree and does that weird auto-suffocation thing until he gets aroused enough to jerk off."

"Oh." That made a lot of sense. I've watched plenty of clients, spotted them doing something particularly stupid and found a way to make their stupidity lethal. That's probably in that manual Walker mentioned, too.

"Just penned that clever little suicide note about his guilt at being such a tree-killer and waited around a few nights until he got amorous again."

"Still, his wife must have known what he was doing out there in his back yard at night. If she'd told the cops, they might not have bought the suicide, started looking for who planted the note."

"Yeah, just blurt out *My husband wasn't suicidal, he was a pervert.*" He mimicked a woman's voice, enjoying his moment of theater. "The guy was loaded. She's doing fine. Probably happy to be rid of the sick bastard. Who knows? After I finish up here, maybe I'll pay her a call, see if she likes to go dancing."

"You know, sounds like I could learn a few tricks from you, Walker." He could certainly teach me a thing or too about being a remorseless killer. That crack about cutting a rug with Roper's widow while Ruby lay sprawled a few feet away gave whole new meaning to the term sociopath.

"Yup, I sure could teach you a lot. Too bad."

"I guess it's too late to say I accept your offer of employment?"

"Hey, you're quite a character, Paladin. Cracking jokes in the face of death and everything. Yeah, too bad. Too bad we never got a chance to get to know each other."

"Still not too late."

"Oh, yes it is." He aimed the .44 at my chest. I had a pretty good idea how big a hole it was going to make, having just seen the result on Ruby.

"Just one more question, if you don't mind."

"Make it quick."

"Blue Feather and Dewaldo will go down as accidents. But how do you get the cops to believe Ruby and me are anything but homicide victims?"

"Ranger and phony ranger kill each other. You were up here with Dewaldo. Police'll probably figure Ruby saw you throw him off that cliff, shot you but not before you shot her."

"How's she supposed to have shot me with the same gun I used to shoot her?"

His jaw sagged. Then the grin came back. "Damn, Ranger Dick, I must be tired or something. I almost made a fucking amateur mistake. Thanks." He glanced toward Ruby, toward the Smith & Wesson. Still leveling the .44 at me, he started toward her. This was the only chance I was going to get. I lunged toward Ruby and rolled when I hit the ground, hoping I'd get real lucky and maybe Walker would hesitate to shoot me with the .44. It was a pretty empty hope.

And then things just got weird. For the record, I'd realized I needed a miracle to escape winding up very dead. But I didn't pray for one. Prayer's for grandmothers and losers who can't accept the fact that they're ... well ... losers. I'd put myself in this predicament. I'd accept the consequences all on my own. But...

The bear started howling again. It sounded like it was right on top of us. It wasn't really a howl, either; more a throaty, angry scream.

Walker looked away for just an instant. I kept rolling toward Ruby. It was a desperate move. I had almost no chance of getting to her gun, grabbing it, spinning, and firing with any accuracy before Walker regained his composure and killed me with the .44, consequences be damned. But it beat sitting waiting for a bullet. Three rolls and I was at Ruby's corpse. I grabbed the gun, spun back toward Walker, took aim . . . and realized why I wasn't dead.

The bear had burst out of the woods no more than ten feet behind Walker. Instead of shooting me, the killer-for-hire had turned to face the attacker. And there they stood, bear mysteriously stopped in its tracks, screaming and waving its paws, Walker aiming the .44 at the bear's chest. Why he didn't shoot, I'll never know. Maybe he was stunned by the size of the thing, or taken aback that it didn't charge. Now that I got a good look at a grizzly in full rage, I began to doubt my earlier confidence that a .44 slug would stop it. Even Ruby's howitzer felt like a toy before it.

But I wasn't worried about the bear.

"Walker!" I could barely hear my own shout over the noise the grizzly was making. But Walker heard me. It brought him to his senses, too. He spun around as quick as before, realizing too late that he'd forgotten the deadliest predator in his vicinity. And if I'd been Dewaldo or Ruby, he'd still be around somewhere plying his trade as corporate mercenary, or maybe making Roper's widow bay at the moon. But I'm no hiking guide or forest ranger. I'd seen him make that clockwise spin twice. This time he spun his chest right into the path of the .50 caliber slug that belched from Ruby's revolver. He looked pretty surprised just before he collapsed in a heap.

He was dead when he hit the ground. I'd punched a hole right through his heart. Like I told Blue Feather, I've got natural skill with firearms.

I turned my attention to the grizzly. Nothing would be worse than finishing an assignment with an Annie Oakley shot only to be mauled to death by a bear. The

Smith & Wesson had three rounds left. I had no idea if it would be enough.

The bear stopped screaming. No shit, it was standing over Walker, calmly looking him over. It kicked him, I guess to make sure he was dead. I'd never seen anything like it.

Then the bear looked at me and my little .50 cal pointed at him, glared, daring me to shoot. This was the first grizzly I'd ever seen. I don't know, maybe they all have hard eyes looking like there's some intelligence behind them. Or maybe that's just Oquala grizzlies who appear out of nowhere and save your ass. Somehow shooting it didn't feel like a smart play. I lowered the weapon.

The eyes softened. It snorted, turned around and walked into the woods. As big as it was, it didn't make much noise striding away from me. Maybe I'd expected the ground to shake when it took a step. To be honest, I was still a little amazed how things had turned out.

"Clayton." Ruby's voice was barely a whisper. I turned back to her. Somehow she was still alive. But not for long. I could almost see the ground through the hole in her chest.

"Ruby." I knelt down over her. "Don't try to talk."

"Why . . . not? Not . . . got . . . anything . . . to save . . . my breath . . . for."

"I'll get you back to Ogloskie. You're gonna be fine."

"You're . . . a . . . lousy . . . liar." She had me on that one. I'd been doing a lousy job of lying the entire assignment. I hadn't fooled anyone in Ogloskie about being a ranger, hadn't fooled Walker, probably hadn't even fooled the damned grizzly. "You . . . really . . . a . . . government . . . killer?"

There was no reason to lie to her anymore. After all, if you can't be honest with the dying, who can you be honest with? It's a rhetorical question, of course. Who's to say the truth is of use to anyone at anytime? I lied. "No, Ruby. I'm just a federal cop. You had me pegged all along."

"Great." She tried to grin. It came out as a grimace.

"What were you doing following Walker anyway, Ruby?"

"Got thinking . . . what . . . you said." She was having trouble breathing. "Business trip . . . my ass . . . followed him from . . . Prestonville . . . tracking you."

Walker was lousy at spotting a tail. Or maybe he'd been stalking people so long, he gotten blind to the possibility of being stalked himself. "You just watched him kill Blue Feather."

"Curious . . . what he . . . up to."

"Yeah." Greed's a powerful temptation, even to a real forest ranger. "You were thinking maybe there could be something in all this for you."

"Can't . . . blame a girl . . . for trying. Didn't think . . . Walker would . . . shoot me . . . though."

I looked over at him splayed out on the ground like a rag doll. "That's what he did for a living, Ruby. Kill people. He was a pro."

"Yeah . . . well at . . . least he was . . . pretty good . . . in the sack." She coughed up blood. Her eyes were losing focus. "Bet . . . you'd have . . . been some fun . . . too . . . Clayton."

"Sorry I didn't get the chance, Ruby. Guess I'll always wonder what I missed."

"You sure . . . will . . . I'm a . . . hell of a . . . good lay." Her last breath wheezed out. She was gone, her eyes open, vacant. I thought about closing them, reconsidered. No reason to get sentimental. I put the Smith & Wesson back in her right hand instead, tucking her forefinger into the trigger guard. It would look just like Walker's shoot-out scenario, except with him the other victim, not me. Lucky, too, that Ruby had gotten off a shot before she fell. Cops probably wouldn't run any fancy forensics, but if they did, a paraffin test would confirm she'd fired the gun. Everything nice and neatly laid out, a lover's quarrel ending badly. Of course, there'd be the question of whatever happened to Ranger Clayton Stillbridge. But he'd have vanished from the face of the earth.

Maybe the locals would start another legend, say he'd been spirited away by the ghost of the Oquala. That was fine by me. The sooner I could dump the ranger persona and get back to Washington, the better.

I just had a couple of loose ends to tie up.

Except the Oquala had other ideas.

Chapter IX
The Haunted Wood

THE SHOOT-OUT SCENE looked believable enough, but there were a few artifacts I couldn't afford to leave lying around. Foremost was the tracking device Walker had been using. He'd dropped it when he grabbed the Garand from Dewaldo. I picked it up and shoved it in my pack. While I was at it, I went through Walker's pack. He'd told me what I was looking for. As I expected, I found a taser, very nice model, state of the art. It had a display telling how much battery power was left that showed just over three-quarter charge. So he'd used it on Blue Feather. Digging deeper, I found a box marked first aid. Inside was a syringe and two ampoules, one marked Thorazine, the other Haloperidol. I'm betting he'd planned something like Riefenthal's fate for Dewaldo and me.

There was a spare magazine for the Beretta Cheetah and a box of .38 cartridges. I shoved those in my pack along with the taser, drugs and syringe. No reason to get someone asking why a guy who'd shot his girlfriend with a .44 was carrying .38s. The taser and the drugs would raise even more questions. I made a note to look for the Cheetah back down the hill. I'd pack that out, too. Hell, it might come in useful down the road. Maybe it was really untraceable; certainly it couldn't ever be traced back to me.

After planting my spare .44 rounds in Walker's pack, I turned to the business of going through his pockets to make sure he wasn't carrying more .38 ammo or something else that would look out of place, like an ID with something other than his Walker Treadman identity. Actually, I was hoping I'd find some other identification on him. I always carry spare IDs and credit cards. Never know when I might need to change on the fly.

His wallet was clean, though. Drivers license, credit cards, even a social security card, all emblazoned with "Walker Treadman." Whoever he was working for, he had access to high-quality forgeries. He also had about fifteen-hundred bucks cash. I left it alone and shoved the wallet back in his pants pocket, then patted down the body. Sure enough he had one of those security pouches people wear under their clothes to hide extra cash and credit cards when traveling. I unbuttoned his shirt, reached inside, carefully undid the belt and removed it, then rebuttoned the shirt and tried to make him look as unmolested as possible. I dropped the pouch in my pack. Plenty of time to examine the contents later.

The beacon GPS was down with Dewaldo where he'd landed near Blue Feather's cabin. I needed to retrieve that in addition to the Beretta. Then there'd be nothing to distract the local authorities from concocting an explanation for the four bodies. It'd be interesting, I was sure. Cops can come up with very amusing theories when they're trying to wrap everything up nice and neat. I'd have to find an anonymous Internet connection sometime to look at a few newspapers and see how creative Oregon cops could be.

Before heading down, I stopped for one last look at Ruby. It was too bad the way things had worked out. The forest service would have to find themselves another ranger. I doubted her replacement would fit in as well as she had with Ogloskie's characters. But I reminded myself that it wouldn't be for long. Conifer would probably get to work pretty quickly, now that I had solved their problem. Ogloskie wouldn't last much longer than the Oquala.

Making my way back down the trail, I was feeling pretty good. Really, the job was done. I just needed to collect the Beretta and the GPS, make my way back through the Oquala to my truck, shed Clayton Stillbridge and resume my Richard Paladin life. The hardest part of that was getting out of the Oquala, and that was just a walk in the woods. Underscoring how easy things were looking, I spied the Beretta as soon as I rounded the last switchback toward the cabin. It was maybe fifteen feet from Dewaldo. I picked it up and tucked it into the waistband of my trousers, then made my way to the hiking guide's body and removed the GPS from the pocket in his pack. It was indeed pretty rugged; it came right on when I thumbed the switch, displaying my position almost immediately. At least I'd have no trouble navigating.

I stood up and noticed the Garand lying off to one side, still intact. I'd forgotten that detail. Leaving it lying there might raise questions about just what had transpired. I thought about taking it with me; really, they're fairly valuable. But getting it back to Washington unnoticed wouldn't be easy. I decided the best choice was to put it back in the remnants of Blue Feather's cabin; walked over and started to pick it up.

"Unhhh."

At first I thought the rifle had groaned. Then I realized it was Dewaldo.

"Clay . . . ton?" Amazing. He was still alive. Ogloskians are tough. I went back and kneeled over him.

"Dewaldo. Thought you were dead."

"Yeah." He groaned again. "Maybe I am."

"Apparently not."

"Think . . . I'm pretty busted . . . up." I looked him over. It was an understatement. But he wasn't coughing up blood. That was a good sign. Or a bad one, depending on your perspective. A dead or dying Dewaldo would just be another corpse for the authorities to explain; alive, he might offer up a few facts that could complicate things.

"Where's the pain?" Best to figure out right away how serious the situation was.

"All over." He tried to grin, failed. "Think I . . . busted a rib. And . . . pretty sure . . . my leg's broke."

I ran my hand down his left thigh, squeezing gently.

"Yaaiiooeee!" Sweat popped out all over his face.

"Busted femur. Feels like it broke clean." He was breathing heavily, a reflex against the pain. "You got a serious bruise on the side of your head, too. Probably got a concussion."

"No . . . shit." He closed his eyes, opened them again. "Walker . . . walloped me . . . good."

"I'll go get help." I didn't mean it, but no reason to tell him I was going to leave him to die.

"Sure." He sighed. "It's . . . three days back. Another . . . day to get . . . word to . . . hospital . . . closest helicopter . . . Roseburg."

"Yeah."

"I'm . . . not gonna . . . last . . . that long."

"Best I can do for you, kid." It occurred to me I could put him out of his misery.

"That's . . . the breaks." He finally managed a grin. "Do . . . me a . . . favor . . . put me next . . . to Blue Feather . . . get notebook . . . outta my pack."

"Moving you is going to hurt like a son of a bitch, Dewaldo." Not to mention possibly causing someone to wonder who had placed him in such a position.

"Please."

I considered it. Hell, no set-up is ever perfect, anyway. And if he wanted to spend his last hours seated next to the moldering body of his spiritual mentor writing a few final lines of verse, maybe I owed him that much. He'd led me out here, after all, and unwittingly played clay pigeon so I could get Walker in my sights, although that hadn't gone exactly to plan. I stood up, grabbed the straps of his pack, and dragged him as fast as I could to the cabin. Best to get the painful part over and done with before he had a chance to reconsider.

"ShitshitSHIT!" He screamed a lot more before he passed out. I leaned him against the boulder, Blue Feather's vacant eyes staring up next to him. It was even possible, I realized, that whoever found them would assume Dewaldo also had been injured when the boulder hit the cabin.

One last act of kindness before abandoning him; I gingerly removed his backpack and set it down beside him. At least he'd have easy access to water and a few power bars while he lingered. There was even the Colt if the pain got so bad he decided to kill himself. Feeling just a bit smug that I was being so uncharacteristically nice, I pulled the notebook out of the pack to place it in his lap for when he came around. But even I have a streak of curiosity. From what Ruby had said, no one but Dewaldo had ever seen a word of what he'd been scribbling for years. It was thick, too, a big sheaf of loose-leaf lined paper neatly bound in one of those three-ring binders enclosed in a zipper cover to protect the contents from the elements. I unzipped it and started flipping through the pages, all three or four-hundred of them covered in ball-point scrawl. I thumbed to the last page with an entry. Maybe he'd written something about me.

... trees witnesses so much death and now comes death himself robed as justice but death in his eyes in his steely cold eyes;

yet the trees the killer trees have swallowed so much that was before history before the time-marking men entering in their ledgers,

and death's bolt cut down the majestic stag Olympus-like, tolling death

for the trees that swallowed and will themselves be swallowed by the ledgers ...

I'm no literary critic. Maybe it was great poetry. Mostly it looked to me like the ravings of somebody who had spent too much time hiking the Oquala. But I kinda liked that *death robed as justice* line, not to mention the *death* in my *steely cold eyes*. So he had some skill for judging people. I zipped the notebook shut and placed it on his lap.

"It was nice knowing you, Dewaldo."

I shouldered my pack and headed across the clearing toward the tree-line and the path back to Ogloskie, feeling more than a little smug, in fact. This assignment had turned out to be a lot more complicated than Frank had figured. I can't say I was happy that I was walking away from so many bodies, but I'd gone up against a real pro and come out on top. Thinking about how I'd break all that to Frank had me smiling.

I stopped in my tracks when I heard what I now recognized as the distinctive howl of a grizzly. A sinking feeling in the pit of my stomach told me I'd gotten ahead of myself and started celebrating prematurely. The big beast emerged from the woods directly ahead of me, blocking my way.

"Fuck, not you again." I slid my hand slowly to the holster on my Sam Brown, reaching for the .44. And, of course, I realized almost immediately that it was up the hill in Walker Treadman's dead hand. What I was carrying now was a .38 Beretta.

The bear snorted, like it was reading my mind, following my thought that I'd have about as much chance stopping it with a BB gun. I'm not dismissive of lesser calibers. I've got a nice .22 Bersa Thunder back in Fairfax that I still believe I could have used to kill that grizzly. But I load it with hollow-points. The teflon-coated armor-piercing .38s Walker preferred—I'd checked his extra ammo and the rounds in the magazine when I'd retrieved the handgun—would be great for bringing down a cop wearing a bullet-proof vest, but they'd probably pass through my hairy nemesis without doing much immediate damage.

Besides, the bear wasn't charging me, just standing in my way. I tried circling around it, but it mirrored my move and growled.

"Okay, you must want something. How about we talk?"

That elicited another growl. Conversation probably wasn't going to be very informative.

"Afraid I don't speak grizzly like Blue Feather."

It waved it's snout around. I got the impression it was trying to point to the wreck of the cabin.

"Blue Feather's dead. There's really nothing I can do about that." I retreated slowly back toward the boulder, remembering the Colt .45 in Dewaldo's pack. A piece with that kind of stopping power might do the trick. I'd never actually seen it, but Dewaldo said he always packed it . . . "Dewaldo."

The bear grunted.

"Dewaldo's still alive. Yeah, I get it." Maybe, rather than concluding the bear wanted me to save Dewaldo, I should have started questioning my sanity. I was standing in the middle of nowhere talking to a seven foot grizzly, after all. Dewaldo's earlier comment about most explorers getting delusional crossed my mind. But hallucination or not, the bear looked real enough to me at that moment; I wasn't going to ignore it. "You know, I can try to drag him back to Ogloskie, but he'll never survive the trip."

The bear's expression turned distinctively homicidal.

"But what the hell. At least I can try, right?"

I walked back to Dewaldo to assess the situation. The bear remained where it was, watching. It wasn't going to give me any choice. Looking over the banged-up guide, it was obvious hauling him back to civilization was going to be a hell of a job. And his leg would have to be set first or else the misaligned bone would keep destroying tissue and blood vessels and causing mind-numbing pain, any of which might kill him.

He was still passed out. If he came out of it while I was setting the bone, he'd experience real agony. I dropped my pack and dug inside for Walker's sedative kit. Thorazine and Haloperidol are more than simple sedatives; both have psychoactive effects as well. I didn't really know which one was better for what I needed, knocking Dewaldo out cold. I'm no doctor.

"Eeny meeny miny moe . . . "

I gave him half a hypodermic of Haloperidol, injecting it into his arm. That'd keep him unconscious for awhile, assuming it didn't kill him. If it did, I guess I'd be digging for the Colt.

But after fifteen minutes he was still breathing and sleeping soundly. I looked over my shoulder. The bear was staring intently.

I'd need a splint. Nothing much seemed at hand; the cabin's wood framework was in splinters and there didn't seem to be any decent branches lying around. Heading into the woods to cut a branch or strong sapling was a non-starter: the bear wasn't going to let me go wandering off. Then I saw the M1. That'd do nicely. I got up and walked over to it, leaning down to pick it up. The bear started growling again.

"Easy, boy." I looked up at it, trying to appear as sincere as possible. "Just need something strong and straight." I grabbed it and raised it slowly, pulled back the bolt and slowly eased out the clip, shoving it in my pocket. "See? Completely harmless."

It grumbled but stayed put. I walked slowly back to Dewaldo, laying the rifle parallel to his broken leg. I'd need something to strap it to the limb. Digging through his pack produced quite a few handy items including parachute cord. Cinching that tight around the splint would eventually cut right through his skin. I dug deeper and came up with a spare cotton t-shirt, then looked in the pack for something to cut the shirt into strips, found nothing, rifled through his pockets. Sure enough, he was carrying one of those Swiss Army knives in a pouch on his trousers. I'd have been disappointed not to find one; Dewaldo was the "always prepared" type. Me, I've never carried a camping knife, not even the one issued to me in the Army. Guess I wouldn't have made a very good Boy Scout.

This was just the set-up for the tough part. Rifle by the leg, strips of cotton t-shirt slipped under the rifle and limb at key points, I could splint it quickly as soon as I set the bone. I crossed my fingers hoping the Haloperidol had really knocked him out, got a good grip on the ankle with both hands, and yanked as hard as I could. No drug masks real pain completely. He woke up briefly and let out a scream that trailed off into a sob, then mercifully passed out again.

"Sorry, kid." I surprised myself. Apologies are wasted on the unconscious and meaningless with everyone else. This was no time to go soft. I tied the strips securely, hoping I wasn't cutting off too much circulation.

Some kind of make-shift stretcher was needed. I sure as shit couldn't throw him over my shoulder and haul him through the woods for days. Of course, most stretchers are designed with two bearers in mind. I looked back at the grizzly, still watching me.

"Any ideas, Booboo?"

It snorted.

"Don't suppose you could help me carry him?"

It turned and moseyed back into the woods.

"Thanks. Big help you are." But maybe it was satisfied that I'd rendered some first aid. I thought about grabbing my pack and making a dash for it, catch it unawares and make a clean escape.

A very intimidating-sounding snarl echoed out of the woods. Who knew bears could read minds? I went back to looking over the remnants of the cabin for something I could use. There was one sheet of tin from the roof that hadn't been too badly mangled. In fact, it was just about Dewaldo-sized. All I needed was to fashion some kind of harness and I could drag it along like a sled. The parachute cord would work for that.

All the metal sheet lacked, in fact, was a couple of holes at one end to run the cord through. I pulled out Walker's Beretta and fired two rounds, one apiece into two corners, making nice neat holes like they'd been bored with a metal drill. It's the reason I don't carry a camping knife or other exotic tools. Most of life's problems, I've found, are like the clients I deal with: a little ingenuity and muscle power resolve about ninety percent; for the rest, there's always a ballistic solution.

Getting the sled/stretcher rigged up took awhile. There was a nip in the air, which told me it was going to start getting cold at night. Placing Dewaldo directly on the metal bed for several days with night temperatures dropping would probably cause him to die of hypothermia if he didn't succumb to his injuries. I dug some of the cured deerskins out of the cabin wreckage, lashing a couple to the stretcher to provide some insulation. Then I removed Dewaldo's sleeping bag from the stuff sack he hung it in from his pack and spread it out. It was a mummy bag. Inserting him into that would be impossible with the splint on his leg. I ripped it open at the bottom seam so I could spread it out and laid it over the deerskin-covered piece of metal.

He was still knocked out from the drugs. Pushing the make-shift stretcher next to him, I rolled him onto one side, slid the stretcher close, and rolled him onto it. He groaned some, but that was all. Wrapping him up in the sleeping bag as best I could, I lashed him to the contraption so he wouldn't fall off once I started dragging him. At least he'd be warm and securely in place. That was about the best I could do.

The sun was starting to get low in the sky. Amazing how long it can take to win a shoot-out with a client, face down a grizzly, and render first-aid to a busted-up hiking guide. I decided it would be best to build a fire, eat some of the freeze-dried crap we still had on us—maybe even see if I could get some into Dewaldo—and set out early the next morning. We'd both be more comfortable passing the night sheltered somewhat by the destroyed hut and the big boulder that was now its centerpiece. I collected wood and kindling—the boulder had done a nice job reducing Blue Feather's home to just that—and got a decent fire going near enough to the boulder that it would reflect some heat but not so close to torch the rest of the edifice. I dragged Dewaldo in between the fire and boulder where he'd stay warm. Now I just had to pass the night.

I got an idea.

"Be right back, Dewaldo." So now I was talking to the unconscious in addition to grizzlies. I wondered if Riefenthal had spent his last hours talking to the trees.

I headed back up the trail behind the cabin, back up the mountain. The bear didn't protest. I guess it knew I wasn't trying to escape, there being no way off the mountain except back by Blue Feather's resting place. I came quickly to the clearing where Ruby and Walker were still staring peacefully at the dimming sky. Soon they'd be staring vacantly at stars. It was going to be a clear night. I expected there'd be an impressive display.

Some people might have paused, thought about the twists of fate that leave two people shot stone dead on a mountain with winter approaching. I kept going, up the trail to the old mine shaft. There was still a lot of cold beer in there. A few of those might even make freeze-dried turkey cacciatore edible.

Dewaldo's moaning woke me up shortly before dawn. The shot must have worn off sometime in the night. Honestly, I'd kinda been hoping I'd wake up and find him dead. That would have simplified things greatly, although I'd have had to explain to the bear that it wasn't my fault. And the grizzly didn't come across as the understanding type. Actually, before dropping off the night before, I'd dug through Dewaldo's pack for the Colt he'd claimed to be carrying, figuring it might make a good equalizer if the grizzly confronted me again. One look at it had dashed that hope. The piece looked a hundred years old and probably hadn't been cleaned and oiled since the Spanish-American War. Dewaldo was lucky he'd never had to use it; if the firing pin wasn't rusted through, it probably would have blown up in his hand.

"Try to hang in there, kid. Soon as it's light enough for me to see what I'm doing, I'll give you another shot."

"Clayton?" He groaned again. "You . . . tied me to . . . this?"

"So you don't fall off when I'm dragging you through the woods."

"Thought . . . you were gonna . . . leave me . . . get help."

"It'd take too long to get someone back up here. Figured this is your best chance. I couldn't very well just leave you to die, buddy." I heard a snort off in the distance. The bear thought that comment was pretty funny.

"You'll . . . die trying . . . air smells . . . like winter."

"Don't sell me short." I had a feeling he knew what he was talking about, though. There'd been a definite wind shift from west to north. If a decent snow hit before we made Ogloskie, we might both wind up ice statues in the middle of nowhere. "But you're right about one thing. I'm gonna have to make good time. Afraid that means I'm gonna bounce you around some. That'll cause some pain."

"Okay." He got quiet. You don't argue with someone who's trying to save your life, even if you think they're being stupid.

The sun's rays crept slowly over Chalker, giving me enough light to give him another shot. Looking at the vials, I figured I had two, maybe three more doses of the Haloperidol. That had worked pretty good; I'd save that for if he really started feeling it again. The Thorazine bottle was full. Might as well see if that would work, too. Using both drugs, I might be able to keep him doped up almost all the way back.

"What . . . hell's that?" He was eying the syringe.

"Morphine." No reason to tell him I was shooting him up with sedatives developed for schizophrenics and depressives.

"Where'd . . . you get . . . morphine?"

"Oh, I always carry it. Don't you?"

"Right." I stuck him with the syringe before he could ask any more questions.

The fire was almost out. I threw dirt on it to smother the last of the smoldering embers. It's not that I cared if I started a fire that burned down the entire forest; tough luck for Conifer and their bottom line. But I didn't want to get caught in a blaze whipped up by the wind out of the north if it picked up any. I'd already made enough mistakes on this assignment.

I tied the make-shift parachute-cord harness to the straps on my pack; hopefully that way the load wouldn't dig into my shoulders so bad. Shouldering the pack, I started what was promising to be a long trek. It wasn't going to be fast going; I'd just have to plod steadily as long as I could, take breaks when exhaustion crept up, then get going as soon as I'd grabbed a breather. It'd be mindless, brutish work, the kind oxen and other draft animals do all the time. What the hell, as the saying goes, what doesn't kill you . . .

It was time to see what the fancy GPS could do besides pinpoint my location for professional killers. I'd marked the location where I'd parked my truck on the service road before we'd left almost a week ago. Thumbing threw a few menus, I managed to mark that as our destination, then had it plot the quickest route. The on-screen map showed a few zigs and zags for the first fifth of the journey, obviously routing us around some of the more difficult parts of the Chalker foothills. After that it marked a straight line. In the lower left corner of the screen was a little text box telling me that if I averaged three-and-a-half miles an hour for ten hours a day, I could be back to the F-150 by the end of day three.

Pulling Dewaldo, I'd be lucky to manage two miles an hour. I pressed the compass button; a digital compass-face appeared on the screen with a bold red arrow pointing the direction of the route I'd programmed. Fortunately, I'd remembered to hang the solar charger and spare batteries off my pack the way Walker had suggested. I'd need the gizmo to keep working until we reached the straight-line part of the way back. Then I could just remember the compass bearing and use the Suunto. If I got that far. And, hell, at least it would be downhill.

"Hang on back there." Dewaldo was snoring. That was good. I started pulling. It really wasn't so bad, just taking it one step at a time. The sled/stretcher actually slid along the forest floor fairly easily.

Three hours later, drenched in sweat, I had a better appreciation for what I'd gotten myself into. Dropping the pack, I collapsed against a tree, panting. At least I'd had the presence of mind before striking out to fill every water bottle and canteen we'd brought, along with a couple of bottles I'd found strewed around the wrecked cabin, with water from the rain barrel Blue Feather had fortunately kept several feet away from his home. I'd shoved those into Dewaldo's pack and lashed it to the stretcher. I'd shoved two of the six-packs of Bud in there, too. I grabbed one of those and sucked it down. Hydration's important. Numbing the common-sense part of my brain that was screaming at me to abandon the dead weight and make a run for it seemed like a better idea.

Sitting there, I started wondering why the bear would care so much about Dewaldo. Obviously, it wasn't your ordinary grizzly. It apparently had something against Walker, for example. And that had been no delusion; Walker hadn't been distracted by a figment of my imagination. Of course, maybe it was all part and parcel of the same thing: the bear had appeared after Walker sent Dewaldo flying down that slope, after all. I concluded that this grizzly was partial to poets. Exhaustion and beer lead the mind to bizarre conclusions.

The Killer Trees

Resting too long was a recipe for failure. I pulled on my pack and started up again, plodding determinedly with the sled in tow. The Thorazine was doing the trick, anyway. Dewaldo was still snoring. Occasionally he'd break into incoherent rambling. I caught something about Blue Feather, then some bizarre utterings in what sounded like Russian that terminated with "Vladimir!" If that was the Thorazine, Walker had probably been right about Riefenthal not knowing what planet he was on when he came around.

I towed Dewaldo well past sunset, following the arrow on the GPS, pausing every three hours to rest, making it past the point where the route stopped zig-zagging. Finally, with it pitch black and my legs trembling, I just dropped the pack and collapsed against a tree.

When I woke up, it was still pitch black and I was shivering. I'd been stupid, of course. No matter the circumstances, falling asleep at night in the woods without taking measures to stay warm is a great way to freeze to death. Fortunately, I had the presence of mind to fumble around in the dark for my pack, find my sleeping bag, strip off my clothes and climb in for whatever was left of the night. I didn't get back to sleep, but after awhile at least I warmed up.

At first light Dewaldo started groaning again.

"How you feeling, kid?" I was just making conversation. Obviously he was in a lot of pain.

"Hurt . . . all over. Leg's . . . killing me."

"Yeah." He was right about that. Hopefully a doctor could repair it some if I got him to a hospital in time. But I doubted he'd ever be the hiker he was. "I'll give you another shot in a minute. I need to get you to eat something first, though. And drink some water.

I've got a packet of dried chicken-flavored noodles in my pack. I'll heat some water and you can drink the broth."

"Oatmeal." At first I thought he'd started talking nonsense again. "It's time . . . for breakfast."

"Okay, Dewaldo." I had to stifle a laugh. Maybe he was feeling better, getting back to his old self. More likely he was making a final request for his favorite meal. "I'll make you some oatmeal, see if you can swallow it."

"Thanks." He said that with a lot of effort. I dug his camp stove out of his pack and got it working. He needed to eat something fast so I could knock him out again, before the pain sent him into shock.

"Clayton." Urgency had crept into his voice.

"What is it?"

"Walker." He was struggling to talk. Obviously he had something important he wanted to say. "Where's Walker?"

This was probably his first really lucid moment since getting knocked off the side of the mountain.

"He's dead, kid. Back up on Chalker."

"Oh." I guess he'd been worried Walker was still out there, was trying to warn me. "He . . . killed Blue Feather."

"I figured that one out already, Dewaldo."

"He . . . worried . . . you . . . cop."

"Right." I was stirring one of the oatmeal packets into a cup with boiling water. It was almost done. "Actually, he knew I was no cop. He knew exactly who I work for."

"Who's . . . that?"

"Government, kid. It's just I'm no cop." It was getting light enough to see. I looked over at him. He was watching me. There was something in his eyes; fear, remorse, regret, all of the above? "And you were working for Alvarez, who was holding Walker's leash."

He didn't say anything.

"Collecting information on Conifer employees who showed up in Ogloskie, keeping him informed about what they were doing, where they went. Right?"

"Yeah." He looked away from me. "It seemed . . . harmless."

"Sure. Just a little harmless targeting." Pros love to enlist civilians to do the menial work. I've been known to do it myself. "When did you figure out Walker was murdering the people you told Alvarez about?"

Another pause. "Riefenthal . . . I guess . . . no . . . way . . . he . . . gets . . . lost."

"Why'd you help them in the first place?" I'd have believed it of just about anybody in Ogloskie before Dewaldo. "Money?"

This time he went silent for a considerable length of time. I figured he'd passed out from the pain again. I kept stirring the oatmeal. Maybe I'd try it.

"Family." I'd given up on an answer. It caught me off guard. "Davis . . . Industries."

A little light went on inside my head. "Davis has a logging subsidiary, too."

"Yeah."

"So Alvarez is working for Davis Industries. Lucky for him, finding you out here when he showed up, knowing you'd cooperate because it's the family business."

"Family . . . sent me . . . look over . . . Oquala . . . bid."

So Dewaldo had been a spy from the beginning, pretending to be a free-spirit hiker getting back to nature, in reality making an estimate of the Oquala's worth so his family could figure out how much to bid for the right to cut it down. And when Conifer got the bid instead, they did what entrepreneurial families in America have always done when they lose out on something; they decided to change the rules of the game, bring in some muscle. Corporations never have any trouble finding goons, either. Most of them have decades of experience battling unions. Of course, the really big corporations don't bother with mercenaries; they just get the government to send in the National Guard. Or, in the case of Santomo/Conifer, me.

"So let me see if I've got this right. You knew Walker was knocking people off. And you knew he was worried about me. Gee, Dewaldo, I thought we'd gotten to be friendly. Yet I don't remember you warning me there was a professional killer gunning for me."

"Came . . . along . . . protect you."

I couldn't help myself. I laughed out loud. "Do me a favor, kid. You survive this, stick to writing poems."

"You're . . . not . . . mad?"

"I'm not the type to hold a grudge." That's not true, by the way. I'm a firm believer in payback. But I couldn't work up any anger at Dewaldo. He was just a lost kid. I shifted closer to him on the stretcher, propped his head up, and spooned up some of the oatmeal. "Now eat some of this. And I don't want to hear you complain about how it tastes."

Two days of plodding like a plough horse got us all the way to Beaver Rock, and damned if under a full moon after exhausting, back-breaking labor it didn't start looking a little like a beaver. I was beginning to believe Dewaldo's theory about the American west having been conquered and named by explorers in serious states of delirium.

At least it had been an uneventful day. No one had tried to kill us. The grizzly hadn't even put in an appearance. Maybe it had decided after watching me drag the sled like some kind of obsessed mule that I'd be too stubborn to abandon the effort less than a day from my truck. It was right, in fact. I was invested in getting the kid to a hospital. Besides, abandoning him this close to Ogloskie would make it likely he'd eventually be found and raise all sorts of questions about how he'd wound up there too busted up to move.

If he survived, of course, there was the uncomfortable possibility that he'd tell the local authorities things that might get them curious about recent events, too. That wasn't looking likely, though. He seemed to be deteriorating. The drugs had been wearing off the last hour before I made camp, and he was raving pretty good while I made a fire. I'd held out hope of getting some more food down him before I doped him up again, but that was appearing unlikely, too.

"*Old brass . . . Las Americas . . . wind coming off the marsh land . . . death-chill from the mountains!*" Whatever he was trying to say, he sounded pretty desperate about it.

I got the fire going and gave him an extra-large dose of the Haloperidol. I needed some sleep. His rantings weren't very soothing. The drugs kicked in and he went silent again. I dug around in my pack and found a couple of power bars, retrieved the last few cans of beer from his pack attached to the sled, stripped off my sweat-drenched clothes and settled in leaning up against the rock with my sleeping bag over me. A high-protein, high alcohol dinner and some sleep might actually get me ready for the final part of the trek.

Nursing the last beer, enjoying the heat of the fire, I finally started to relax. That's always a mistake.

"Hello there." The voice came out of nowhere. "Nice fire you got. Mind if I join you?"

My hand went reflexively to the Beretta next to me under the sleeping bag.

"Sure, buddy. Come on over by the fire." I tried to sound as friendly as possible. What I was thinking was: *Come on out of the shadows where I can see you and decide whether or not to shoot your ass.*

A man stepped out from the trees. He was smallish, no more than five-foot-six, wearing a thick, wool coat. Long, stringy hair draped out from a fur hat. The light from the fire as he got close revealed gray hair, gray skin. He seemed old, although he moved easily, almost gliding. I sure hadn't heard him approaching through the woods.

He wasn't carrying a gun that I could see. But he could have been hiding a piece of field artillery under that coat. I thumbed the safety off the Beretta. There was already a round in the chamber. I've never understood people who leave the chamber empty: anyone who's afraid of shooting themselves with their own gun shouldn't carry one. I kept the Beretta out of sight under my sleeping bag, pointed right at his gut.

"It sure seem winter coming. You are enjoying a last camping trip before the snow?" He had a pretty thick accent. I couldn't place it, though. Honestly, I was close to complete exhaustion. My mind wasn't functioning too clearly.

"Yeah. We've been out on a nature hike." Maybe he really hadn't noticed that Dewaldo was strapped to a makeshift gurney. "How about you? You set out on a day hike and get lost?" I'd noticed that he didn't have a pack.

"Lost? No, not lost." He grinned. It was a hollow grin. "Know these woods good, Kyle."

The hair on my neck stood on end. Walker had seen my file, knew all about Richard Paladin. There nothing in that dossier about Kyle. As far as I was aware, only one person at the EPA knew my real name, and he'd been packed off to a sanatorium for running an unauthorized lethal program. And this guy sure wasn't somebody I knew from the earlier part of my life. "Sorry. You must have me confused with someone else."

"Yes. Confused." He was still grinning. "You have not much time. Poor Dewaldo is bad hurt."

"You know Dewaldo?" My finger was squeezing the trigger ever so slightly. Whoever this guy was, he had to be some kind of spook, someone who'd been stalking us all along, maybe stalking me for even longer. He had some guts, though, walking in on us so brazenly. If he knew so much he even had my real name, surely he was aware I'd kill him without blinking.

"Oquala my home. Know all those who enter these woods."

"Too bad for you. You know too much." I pulled the trigger. Or I should say I tried to pull the trigger. Something stopped me.

He squatted next to the fire. "You think you going to kill me, Kyle?" He laughed.

"Any reason I shouldn't?"

"Sure you bet. I friendly. Come tell you better get going."

"I plan to, as soon as the sun comes up."

"Too late." He shook his head slowly, like a patient parent talking to a slow-witted kid. "Morning too late."

"If you're so worried, maybe you should get going yourself." I was still trying to figure out why I couldn't pull the trigger. The gun wasn't jammed, and underneath the sleeping bag, it wasn't cold enough to have frozen up. It actually felt like I just couldn't move my finger.

"Be going soon. Finished here."

"Finished with what?"

He smiled. There was a light in his eyes. "You know, Kyle."

"Why do you keep calling me that?"

"Being friendly. Friends use first names."

"Sure. And what's yours, Mr. Friendly?"

"You not know?" He shook his head slowly again, this time as if with great sadness. "Vladimir."

"Vladimir Ogloskie."

"Yes!' He smiled broadly.

"The ghost of the Oquala."

He didn't answer, just sat there beaming.

"So I really am hallucinating. Christ, I knew I'd gotten dehydrated. Now I'm seeing fucking ghosts." And talking to them, too. "Tell me, did I hallucinate the bear as well?"

No response. He seemed content to stare in silence. Maybe ghosts learn that in Haunting 101.

"So Blue Feather, the last of the Oquala tribe, is dead, and you don't have to wander the Oquala anymore. I get it." The silent treatment was starting to annoy me. "Except he wasn't an Oquala Indian."

He laughed. It echoed all around me. I was getting mad.

"He was a con man, you idiot! Don't you get it? Are ghosts as stupid as Dewaldo there, sucked in by professional bullshit? WHAT'S SO GODDAMN FUNNY?"

I was yelling at nothing, at no one. There was nobody in the clearing except Dewaldo and me. The Beretta was in my hand, pointing into emptiness. I checked the safety; it was off. I'd actually thumbed it off safe during the dream or hallucination or whatever the fuck I'd just had. Lucky for me I hadn't blown my foot off.

And then I noticed the snow, small flakes falling lightly all around, melting on contact with my skin. It wasn't even sticking to the ground yet. But something in the air—the smell, the eerie quiet—was telling me this was the beginning of a significant storm. By morning we'd probably be under a foot or more of snow and ice. I might be able to wade through it back to my truck, but I'd never make it with Dewaldo in tow.

"Time to move, kid." I pulled on my clothes, shoved the Beretta—safety back on—into a pocket, switched on the GPS to get our direction, and pulled on the pack/harness. The fire was still burning, but the snow would take care of that. The muscles in my legs were twitching from exhaustion; our only chance was that I could make the last leg on adrenalin alone.

Plodding along in the dark, stumbling into trees, bouncing Dewaldo horribly and listening to him groan constantly, all I could think was what a good, long sleep I was gonna have when I got back to that crappily-furnished duplex.

"Or when I'm dead." That seemed more likely.

There's a basic combination of things that kills you when you're caught out in a blizzard: the only way to stay warm is to keep moving, keep burning energy; exertion and the wind start dehydrating you, making your brain play tricks on you; exhaustion begins nagging at you, telling you to rest; your brain-fried-by-dehydration starts thinking your exhausted muscles pleading for a break are making sense; once you stop moving, hypothermia sets in and your mind just goes off on holiday; finally you freeze to death with a great big smile on your face. The remedy for this is . . . don't get caught out in a blizzard.

I had one thing going for me. I'm a stubborn son-of-a-bitch. I despise losers and quitters. I'm not sure why. Maybe it's being the product of a broken home. My old man disappeared on a drinking binge when I was ten. He was a loser, that's for sure. Could be that had a lasting impact on me.

You'll never amount to anything, Kyle. You're a loser just like your father.

"FUCK YOU!"

It was still dark and cold with snow blowing in my face. Some corner of my brain was rational enough to recognize that yelling at my mom for something she'd said years ago was a sign that the first stage, dehydration, was kicking in big time. Next would come the voice trying to kill me.

Take a break, Kyle. Just ten minutes. Give your muscles a chance to recover. Then you can start walking again.

"SHUT THE FUCK UP! AND STOP CALLING ME KYLE! THE NAME'S CLAYTON! OR, DEXTER! OR, RICHARD! FUUUUCK YOOOUUUU!"

The wind grabbed my words and whipped them away to nothingness before even I could hear them. But it worked. Despising every thought that even hinted at weakness, shouting down every internal whisper about stopping, I kept pushing, dragging the sled, following the arrow on that fucking GPS Walker had given me so he could track me and kill me.

At some point—I have no idea how long I'd been walking—I noticed the batteries in the GPS had given out. Still raging, I smashed it against a tree, threw it to the ground.

Better pick that up.

Who'd said that? I looked back at Dewaldo. He looked frozen, dead. There was no sign of the bear, of Ogloskie's ghost.

"I've lost it. I'm talking to myself."

I picked up the dented gizmo and shoved it in my pocket next to the Beretta. I still had the Suunto, buttoned in my shirt pocket. Did I remember the right heading? Yeah, sure.

Compasses don't work out here.

"That's near Chalker. We're far enough away it won't throw the compass off."

So what? It's pitch black. You can't see it.

"It's got a luminescent dial."

You sure about that? It's a cheapy. Maybe you're just imagining you can see it. Sit down for a minute. Think things through. Don't just keep walking blindly in the snow.

"SHUT UP!" I'd almost let the weakling that hides in all of us trick me.

The numbing cold wind would have cut right through the only outerwear I'd packed for this expedition, a rain slicker Dewaldo had included in the gear he'd loaned me. Instead, I'd cut a hole in the bottom of my sleeping bag and draped that over me like a cape. It had kept me from freezing to death, but just barely. My face had finally stopped burning from the snow blowing into it, a sure sign that frostbite was setting in. Dewaldo was much better insulated than me with the deerskins and his sleeping bag wrapped around him, but I'd stopped looking back to check on him. His moaning had ceased. I kept getting the bad feeling I was killing myself dragging a corpse.

I'd long passed the point where the people you see on TV who have survived near-death experiences talk about having realized that they were religious after all, describing prayers and mystical experiences with angels and visions of Jesus H. Christ. I didn't drop to my knees and start praying for salvation. I'd already had a grizzly threaten me if I didn't embark on this fool's errand, then had a ghost appear and laugh at me. I wasn't feeling like the supernatural was my friend. Like I said, I'm stubborn. I'd make it out on my own or die trying.

Which is the point I thought I'd reached when I finally stopped and sat down. And I wasn't kidding myself that I'd just rest for a moment and start back. I was spent.

"Sorry, kid. Looks like Mother Nature's gonna win this round. Fucking bitch that she is." I doubt if Dewaldo heard me.

And then the wind let up for just a brief moment, stopped whipping snow around so I could see more than a few inches in front of me. A tiny ray of pre-dawn light crept through the clouds somehow. Ahead of me through the trees I saw something that looked familiar. I squinted to focus as best I could. And there it was, a Ford F-150 pick-up. My F-150 that I'd parked at the end of the service road a week ago.

"Son of a bitch." I was thinking how stupid I would have looked if I'd been found frozen stiff just fifty yards from my truck. I'm not afraid of dying, but looking stupid in death would have pissed me off for eternity. "Scratch the defeatist speech, kid. We made it."

Well, I'd made it, anyway. I wasn't holding out much hope for Dewaldo. But I got back on my feet and dragged him the last few paces to the truck, then somehow found the strength to haul him up into the bed. Driving with him in the exposed back wasn't going to do him much good—assuming he was still alive—but unstrapping him from the gurney and sliding him into the cab didn't seem like such a good idea either.

Of course, remembering where I'd put the keys turned out to be pretty damned difficult, too, given that my brain was functioning at minimal levels. I'd placed them in a small zippered pouch on my pack before we'd set out. So, needless to say, I tore through every nook and cranny of the pack before finally finding them. At least I had the presence of mind at that point to collect the contents that I'd strewn all over the truck bed and shove them back into the now mangled pack. Hauling evidence of spooks and killers away from the crime scene wouldn't have made much difference if I'd scattered it all along the road on the drive back.

I hadn't made any deals with gods or demons to get us out of the Oquala, so I sure wasn't saying prayerful thank-yous to any deities. But I made a vow to write a testimonial someday to the Delco Corporation when I turned the key and the engine sputtered to life. It had occurred to me when I inserted the key in the slot that the ultimate joke on us would be to freeze to death in the truck because the battery was dead. I guess I'm not destined for an idiot's demise.

There was a good foot of snow on the road. I got the truck turned around and drove slowly back toward town. A pick-up isn't exactly the best thing for driving in a blizzard. But it was only about five miles to Ogloskie; if Dewaldo wasn't already dead, another twenty minutes in the bed of the truck wouldn't kill him. Reflexively I looked in the rear view mirror to make sure he was still in the back. Behind us I spotted the grizzly standing in the middle of the road, waving good-bye.

I wasn't going to miss the Oquala forest one damned bit.

Chapter X
The Lives I Save

OF THE MULTIPLE-THOUSAND CATEGORIES of public servant in the USA, I know of two who really excel at their work. The first is me. And I could collect a thick file of testimonials to attest to that, except all my clients are dead. Because I excel at my work.

The second are EMTs, Emergency Medical Technicians. Wherever you may happen to be in this country, if you're sick or injured and a couple of EMTs get to you before you're dead, there's a good chance you won't be. It's actually a nuisance for people in my line of work. If I don't make absolutely sure of a client, some EMT team will show up and undo all my efforts. I generally consider them adversaries.

So I watched with mixed feelings as the two who'd driven through a blizzard from Prestonville worked on Dewaldo. They knew what they were doing. After twenty minutes of poking him, prodding him, listening to heartbeat and pulse, giving him injections, stabilizing his leg with an inflatable splint, wrapping him in a shimmery space blanket, one of them pronounced to me that he had a pretty good chance of pulling through. That's where the mixed emotions came in. I still couldn't help thinking that a dead Dewaldo would be less of a complicating factor. But I'd made my bed, as they say.

It's not like I'd raced him to the nearest emergency room, either. Once I got back to Ogloskie, I headed for the ranger station. The grizzly's jurisdiction ended outside the Oquala, I figured, so I wasn't going to risk my neck further by slip-sliding the F-150 another forty miles to Prestonville. There was a phone at the station. If the lines were up and someone was willing to brave the storm, I'd give Dewaldo that much of a chance. I even dragged him out of the truck bed into the station where there was some heat. Having finally warmed up in the cab on the drive back, I guess I was feeling generous.

It surprised me when I picked up the phone and got a dial tone. I punched in 911.

"Roseburg Public Safety Response." It was a woman's voice. She sounded tired. "What's the nature of your emergency?"

"I need an ambulance for a seriously injured hiker."

"What's your location?"

"Ogloskie." That question struck me as strange. "I thought that information popped up automatically based on the phone I'm calling from."

"I've got an address that just says 5 Ogloskie. Is that a street?"

"It's a town." So even Oregonians only a hundred miles away had never heard of the place. "It's forty miles north of Prestonville."

"Oh." From the sound of it, she was having a bad day. "Yeah, I see it. Why didn't you call Prestonville?"

"I dialed 911. It connected me to you."

"Try to remain calm." I almost laughed. She was running on fumes, giving canned responses. "Pull the vehicles off the road. We'll get to you as soon as we can."

I was guessing the storm had hit the entire region. Obviously Oregon drivers are no better in bad weather than anybody else in the country.

"Like I said, I've got a seriously injured hiker. There were no vehicles involved."

"Uh huh." She considered that for a moment. "What are the nature of the injuries? Can you possibly render first aid?"

"Let's see. Broken leg, busted ribs, probable concussion, frostbite, hypothermia."

"That sounds pretty serious." I could hear the sound of keys clicking on a computer. When she spoke again, there was panic in her voice. "I'm having a little difficulty finding an emergency contact in Ogloskie."

I took a deep breath and reminded myself that, in any emergency, most people are useless. When it's a 911 operator who goes foggy, the tendency is to get pissed. But she was clearly overwhelmed. I'd have to walk her through it. "Ma'am, this is Ranger Clayton Stillbridge of the US Forest Service. I'd be that emergency contact in Ogloskie. And I'm calling you."

"Oh. You're a forest ranger?" That calmed her a bit. Some titles automatically impress people. I wondered if I should have told her I was an astronaut, since I was lying anyway.

"Yes. And what I need you to do is try to raise someone at the nearest medical facility and see if they can send an ambulance to the Ogloskie ranger station."

"That'd probably be the Settler's Creek Medical Center. It's in Prestonville."

"Great. Think you could contact them?"

"Although the fire department there has an emergency response medical service, according to the medical services directory on my computer."

"Fabulous. Maybe you could call them?"

"Sure. I'll see if they can get to you."

"Thanks."

"Try to remain calm, sir."

I could have mentioned to her not to worry since at the time I was seated at poor Ruby's desk with my feet up enjoying a cup of bitter coffee that I'd brewed before calling. I didn't. Might as well let her think she was doing a swell job, talking me through the crisis. Like I said, I was feeling generous.

It took the EMTs exactly one hour to arrive, which told me they jumped in their ambulance and headed right for us as soon as they got the call. Prestonville must be the only city in America where people are smart enough to stay off the roads in a blizzard, leaving their emergency response personnel available to handle actual emergencies rather than running from fender-bender to fender-bender to sew up cut lips.

Even more annoying than EMTs gung-ho save-everybody-they-can attitudes is their tendency to act a little too much like cops. These guys were no exception.

"What happened?" The taller, more chiseled looking of the two techs asked me this while his partner, a shorter, serious-looking Asian guy examined Dewaldo.

"He fell off a cliff."

"Where?"

"In the Oquala forest."

"I didn't know there were any cliffs around here."

"There aren't." I guess he was suspicious that I'd beaten Dewaldo within an inch of his life before calling for help. "It was up by Chalker Mountain."

"How'd he get here?"

"I dragged him here after the accident."

"How'd you find him out there?"

"I didn't find him." I could feel myself getting pissed. I don't respond well to authority. "We were hiking together. He slipped and fell."

"You set the bone and splinted it?" This from the other tech.

"It didn't set itself."

"Never saw a rifle used as a splint before."

"Seemed like a good idea at the time."

"He's lucky you were with him. Guess they give you rangers emergency medical training."

"Yup." I assumed this to be the case. What I'd learned, I learned in the Army. That and watching old movies on TV as a kid.

"You give him something for the pain?" The first tech again. They were switching back and forth like a trained interrogation team.

"Shoved some aspirin down his throat when I could. Mostly he'd wake up and pass out again almost immediately." I couldn't very well tell them I'd been shooting him up with a professional killer's knock-out kit. Hopefully all the Thorazine and Haloperidol would be out of his system before anyone got a chance to run a tox-screen. If not, I wasn't planning on being around long enough to get sucked into an investigation.

"How are you feeling?" Tech two again. He glanced up at me. "Actually, you don't look so good."

"I'll be okay. Just a little tired from the hike."

"Get some fluid in you. You're probably dehydrated."

"Thanks. I will." I was thinking *no shit*. I was also remembering that I still had about half a case of Beavertail Pale Ale back at the duplex. "Soon as you guys get on the road with him, I plan to head home and get some sleep. I'll be sure to drink a lot of fluid before I sack out."

"Good idea."

"Any idea how long this storm is supposed to last?" I was counting on not having to worry about any cops or killers coming after me until the heavy snow stopped.

"Weather report says it should blow through by this evening."

"Good luck driving back."

"No problem." Tech one again. He sounded dismissive of snow-clogged roads. "We got snow chains."

"You taking him to Settler's Creek Medical Center?"

"Yeah, that's the closest." The Asian guy was obviously the most medically proficient of the two. "We've got him stabilized. They've got a decent surgeon, probably will want to open up the leg and make sure the bone's set right. But it feels like you did a pretty good job. He'll be okay. It'll be awhile before he's out hiking again, though."

They loaded Dewaldo into the ambulance. Tech one got behind the wheel, fired up the siren, and spit a lot of snow and gravel hauling ass out of the parking area. Dewaldo was in for a thrilling ride.

Before getting some sleep I decided to check in with Frank's encrypted e-mail site. The phone lines were up, so the DSL connection would be working. Since I'd been out of touch for a week, I figured there'd be news. I wasn't disappointed.

Having a good time? You've been there screwing off for more than a week. Stop playing house with the ranger chick and get to work.

Have identified your client. Walker Treadman an alias. Only backstopped to 1998. Ran photo from Florida driver's license against Federal and state databases, correlates to Harold Demarco; graduated West Point 1977, ten years special forces, black ops; retired 1989; staff employee FEMA 1990-2001, file restricted; employed by Darkmatter Corporation 2001-2003; currently freelance contractor. Looks like environmentalists are finally getting smart enough to employ real talent.

Now that we've done the hard part of your assignment, how about you finish the job and get back here. Work's piling up.

Treadman turned out to have quite a pedigree. Interesting to note as well that FEMA was also playing murder incorporated. But I shouldn't have been surprised. Just about any aspect of public service brings you in contact with people who serve no real purpose except being flies in the ointment. Every organization has to have a department to take out the trash. And there was obviously a thriving market for experts in my field out in the private sector. Treadman—Demarco—had told me as much. So had Alvarez.

"Yeah, Alvarez." He was still a loose end, even if Frank hadn't turned up anything. I'd have to get some sleep before dealing with him, though. Mention of Treadman working for Darkmatter had given me pause, too. I'd run into goons from that company before. They're somewhere between spook outfit and organized crime. If Treadman had worked for them once, no doubt they were still in the mix.

First, I figured I might as well take a minute to let my boss know how useless he was—and that I was still alive.

Appreciate the timely info on Treadman. You can add to his file that he retired again three days ago, this time permanently.

FYI, Treadman was working for Davis Industries, not tree-hugger terrorists. DI was miffed Conifer got the Oquala contract instead of them. I'll put the details in my report when I get back. Or you could wait for your research department to figure all this out sometime before the next millennium.

Picked up a couple of souvenirs I don't want to carry through airport security. Will figure out ground transportation back. Might take a week or more to cross the continent. Any chance you'll have been fired by then?

It wasn't just the Beretta I wanted to bring back. I had Walker's extra papers. Frank's researchers might find those useful, figure out who was turning out high-quality forgeries and maybe give them a government job. There was also the Garand. The medics had left it after replacing Dewaldo's splint. I hadn't decided whether to keep it or not. I couldn't think of any time I'd ever use it; taking an M1 rifle on a job isn't exactly subtle. Selling it could bring in a couple thousand bucks, but it's not like I needed the money.

Something else to sleep on. I headed to the duplex to unwind with a few beers and cut a few Zs. At least I wouldn't have to worry about Ruby and Walker waking me up.

The snow had stopped by early evening when I woke. I was starving but otherwise felt pretty good. There was still a frozen pizza in my freezer. I stuck it in the oven and took a shower. It felt good to be clean again.

I wasn't in a rush. Outside it looked like a little more than a foot of snow had dropped. The sky had cleared, too, a half-moon reflecting off the fresh, white powder. I washed down the pizza with a couple more Beavertails. Then I made another pot of coffee and sat drinking it until just after midnight. I wanted to be alert.

A pick-up's not the best vehicle for driving in snow, but if you know what you're doing and take it slow, it'll suffice. Pulling away from the duplex, I was grateful for once that Ogloskie was so isolated. I wouldn't run into any other traffic. I kept the lights off, too. The moonlight reflecting off the white snow was providing enough illumination to see where I was going, and I knew the way, anyway. About a mile from Alvarez's house, I pulled over to go the rest of the way on foot. Sneaking up on a pro isn't easy, but with any luck he'd be unsuspecting. I figured he'd be confident that Walker had taken care of me.

The farmhouse was dark. I stayed in the trees and worked my way around to the back, then crossed the snow-covered clearing as quickly and quietly as possible to the back door. Fortunately, Alvarez hadn't upgraded the lock. Overconfidence is a killer. Making a mental note never to get complacent, I let myself in.

Standing just inside the door while my eyes readjusted, I heard the sound of soft footsteps upstairs. I'd made almost no noise opening the door, but obviously Alavarez was a light sleeper. Heavy sleepers don't live long in our profession.

I could just make out his steps coming down the stairs. For a muscle-man, he was light on his feet. I moved into a dark corner of the living room and waited for him to come to me, Walker's Beretta in my hand, safety off, round in the chamber. He took his time, stopped at the foot of the stairs. I'd positioned myself to be behind him when he entered the living room, just off the door. Before I saw him, I saw the muzzle of a pump-action twelve gauge. Alvarez followed it in, sweeping it across the room like a SWAT-cop. Even so, I could have killed him before he saw me. That would have been the safest course.

"Freeze." I was taking a real chance. Pointing a gun at a trained killer and not shooting immediately is usually a recipe for suicide. I'd made that mistake with Walker and almost paid for it. He'd gotten cocky and done the same with me, and he'd never make that error again. But I was counting on the fact that Alvarez had probably been in management for awhile. Maybe his field reflexes were a tad rusty.

He stood motionless, no doubt trying to decide if he wanted to risk spinning and firing. In the dark, unsure of exactly where I was, it'd be a risk. But I've been in that situation: anything beats dying helpless.

"You'd be dead already if I wanted to kill you." I was primed to empty the Beretta into him if he so much as flinched. But I was hoping it wouldn't come to that.

"That you, Mr. Forest Ranger?" He sounded surprised. "I'm impressed."

"Take your right hand off that shotgun or you'll be dead." He complied, holding his hand up over his head where I could see it. "Now set it down gently on the floor with your left and back away from it." He did as instructed. "Okay. Go sit in your armchair. I get edgy with you standing, and this Cheetah has a hair-trigger I'm not used to."

"Mind if I turn on some lights?" It was a nice try. He gets to stay on his feet just a bit longer and maybe gains an advantage when the lights temporarily blind me.

"I can see fine. Sit down"

He sighed, moved slowly to the arm chair, and lowered himself into it. I walked to the shotgun and slid it behind me with my foot. Bending over to pick it up would have been just the stupid move he was hoping for, giving him a chance to spring out of the chair and snap my neck with those powerful arms. Even in the dark I could read his disappointment that I'd stayed balanced with the Beretta aimed dead at him.

"Beretta Cheetah. I know someone else who carries one of those."

"Knew. This is his gun."

He let out a long, slow whistle. "Walker was a pro. Now I'm really impressed."

"Don't know who you mean. I took this off a guy named Harold Demarco."

"Harold Demarco. Yeah, I've heard of him. Real American hero, you know. West Pointer, served his country for more than twenty years."

"Too bad. Arlington cemetery's getting pretty full. But maybe your Darkmatter colleagues can arrange something, since you've been holding his leash these last few years."

"You're very well informed. I had no idea the Forest Service had an intelligence department."

"You can drop the act, Alvarez. Treadman—Demarco—filled me in about how quick you guys blew my cover."

"Hey, don't blame me if your EPA buddies can't keep a secret." He smiled. "Loyalty's a wonderful thing. Too bad it always loses out to money."

"That's what I wanted to talk to you about."

"Money?"

"Loyalty. As in, who sold me out?" Not many people had access to my file. Finding out who had leaked it was important to me. I planned to make sure they didn't do that again.

"Now, why would I tell you, even if I knew? A well-placed mole is somebody you protect."

"Somebody you'd be willing to die for?"

He thought about that. "No, not really."

"Then give me a name."

"I don't know it."

"That's really too bad." I let him consider things. "I'd hoped to get outta here without waking up your kid. But Walker didn't seem to have a silencer on him."

"How about we make a deal?" He was sounding nervous. I have that effect on people.

"Sorry. I happen to be quite satisfied with what I make from the government." It was true. I've become an expert at padding expense reports over the years. My freezer in Fairfax was stuffed with cash—and a couple of frozen pizzas.

"Maybe I can offer you something else you could use?"

"Like what? You don't know the name of the traitor in my office. That's all I'm interested in right now."

"I can tell you the name of the person at Darkmatter who knows."

"Interesting." Maybe he was stalling, waiting for his wife to get curious, come down the stairs and whack me over the head. But I wasn't making that mistake again. I had my back to the wall. "Why should I trust you to tell me the truth?"

"How about I tell you something else to build trust?"

"I'm listening."

"Lucinda and Becky aren't here. I sent them away yesterday." It didn't strike me immediately why that should make me believe him. "I'm really not stalling while one of them calls the cops or anything. You can shoot me with that popgun and you and I are the only ones who will hear."

"Why send them packing?" I didn't care if he had a lousy marriage. Mostly I was just curious what he was trying to tell me.

"Because their job here was done."

"Job?" Things were getting clearer. "Just out of curiosity, where do you go to rent a wife and kid for a few years?"

"Hey, that's the free market. Where there's demand, somebody's going to go into business on the supply side."

"So you're just hanging around for . . . what?"

"I was waiting for Walker—Harold—to get me word that he'd taken care of you. Then we were going to pack it in and vamoose. Mission accomplished."

"Sure." I noticed he'd cut off the long ponytail, cropped his hair nice and short, the way Walker kept his, and me. So he was through trying to look Oregonian. "Dead fed guarantees enough red tape for Conifer to call it a day. Then your Davis Industries pals re-bid the contract and somebody else gets to turn the Oquala into pulp. I get it."

"I wondered if you'd put all the pieces together. Nice work." He nodded his head slowly, like he was finally deciding I'm not a complete rube. "The way I see it, you've got enough information to backtrack to Davis and figure out who they worked with at Darkmatter on this contract. So eventually you'll find my boss there, the one who put this operation together."

"And the one who knows the name I want."

"Exactly."

"Which makes you telling me valuable exactly how?"

"I save you a lot of trouble. I also save you having to inform anybody in your department about the existence of a traitor in your ranks. Because you probably don't want to risk having your mole figure out you're aware of him."

"Whoever it is will know that as soon as his Darkmatter handler tells him, which he's gonna do as soon as you run back and reveal you blew the handler to me. Sounds like I should just shoot you and go threaten a few people at Davis Industries to find out who your boss is."

"I'm not going to tell my boss about this conversation, whether you shoot me or not."

"Oh, don't tell me. You're gonna give me your word." We both laughed. Maybe there's honor among thieves, but there sure isn't any between killers.

"No." In the dark I could see a big, malicious smile on his face. "I'm not going to tell him because he's a sniveling ex-CIA bureaucrat who spent his entire career on the European cocktail circuit and now thinks he's got the chops to give orders to people like me. After you take care of him—assuming I can convince you not to kill me—I've got an excellent shot to get his job, which pays seriously more money and doesn't involve spending two years in places like fucking Ogloskie."

That I could believe. Field guys always despise their bosses. When the boss is a know-it-all who's never flown anything but a desk, it usually develops to outright hatred.

"So give me the name." He didn't answer immediately. Once he told me, of course, I might just kill him anyway. He was considering that. "By the way, since I'm not really sure I can trust you, I won't kill you after you tell me. If you're dead, I won't be able to take pleasure hunting you down and killing you real slow if I find out you lied."

"That's a fair point, Paladin." We'd finally dropped all pretext. "The name is Karsten Felix Caruthers. Actually, he makes a point of telling people it's Karsten Felix Caruthers 'the third.' He works out of the Darkmatter office in Raleigh."

"Thanks." Just the name made me want to find the guy and kill him. I hate people who want you to know they come from families that think so much of themselves they pass names from generation to generation. "I'll have to pay him a call."

"So are we done here?"

"Not quite."

That made him nervous again. "What else you got in mind?"

I let him sweat for a minute. I don't know, maybe I enjoy scaring goons and spooks. It's probably a character flaw. But I didn't wait long enough for him to get desperate, start getting ideas.

"You're gonna deliver a message for me."

"Okay. I'm listening. Who to?"

"Davis Industries. Let them know my assignment here was to clear obstacles to Conifer executing its contract. I've succeeded. They're gonna stop being an obstacle."

"You want me to tell them that?"

"I want you to tell them if I find out I haven't completed this assignment, my next move will be to attack the problem at its source." It was a bluff, of course. I doubted Frank would authorize hits on a corporation's execs, even if they were at odds with one of the President's cronies. But it was worth a shot: my assignment was to get Conifer back in business killing trees, after all.

"I'll make sure they understand." He grinned. "They're businessmen. I'm sure they'll want to be reasonable."

"You don't seem too upset by all this." He almost seemed pleased. That was beginning to annoy me.

"Why should I be upset?"

"Most people don't like losing."

He frowned. The 'L' word grated. "We're both pros, Paladin. I carried out my job just fine. Almost pulled off this operation without a hitch. It just turned out that one of my players was outmatched by someone on the other team."

"Hope the boys at Davis see it that way. Maybe they'll be hesitant to pay off the rest of the contract, now that they're not gonna get exclusive rights to the Oquala."

"Oh, they'll pay." The smile was back. "Companies don't stiff Darkmatter. That's really bad for business."

I took his point.

We stared at each other for awhile. Ending a meeting between killers without one of them dying is awkward.

"Now I'm gonna pick up this shotgun. Don't get cute."

"Don't worry. I think we've reached an understanding."

"Yeah." I squatted down carefully, grabbed it with my left hand, stood back up, Beretta still trained on him. Then I stuck the Beretta in the waistband of my trousers to get a good grip on the twelve-gauge, now pointed directly at his gut.

"Careful with that thing. It's loaded with double-ought buck." There was a catch in his voice.

"No problem." I pumped it until I'd ejected all the cartridges. His shoulders sagged with visible relief. "Now I'm gonna back out of here slowly. I'll leave the shotgun out back. Sit still for an hour."

"I can do that."

"Come after me, it'll be the last thing you do."

"I'm not going to come after you, Paladin. I've got a vested interest in you staying alive now."

"Sure." I eased backwards slowly, headed to the rear of the house.

"Just one more thing." I tensed. Maybe he was finally going to try something. No truce between professional murderers is really reliable.

"Yeah?" I eased my hand toward the Beretta.

"You're way too good to keep wasting your time with Uncle Sam. I could use a guy like you. Make it worth your while."

"I'll keep that in mind."

I backed out, left the shotgun by the door, and retreated fifty yards to the tree-line. After twenty minutes I decided he really wasn't coming out after me, put the Beretta on safe and made my way back to the F-150.

It's not like I'm completely sold on being a government droid. Critics who say most feds are blathering incompetents aren't that far from the truth. In fact, my feelings for Frank weren't that different from Alvarez's attitude about his boss. Having an "understanding," as Alvarez—or whatever his name really was—called it, with somebody on the outside who could use my services didn't seem like such a bad idea.

But I didn't sleep soundly that night. The only "understanding" I really trust is understanding that someone who might constitute a threat to my personal well-being is very dead. I could live with the chance I'd taken letting Alvarez walk away, but I reminded myself the whole drive back to the duplex that I damned well better plan on keeping my guard up for a long time.

Hell, who was I kidding? I never let my guard down anyway.

I made one last check of the e-mail site before hitting the road the next morning. I was looking forward to spending a few days on the road, in fact. So, of course, it was bad news.

Happy to hear your vacation was so much fun you've got souvenirs. Need you back here soonest. Contact in Portland can arrange shipment sensitive items and dispose of forest service gear. Will provide new docs and airline ticket. Contact instructions below.

Sorry to disappoint, but my job seems secure. Matter of fact, recent high-profile success in Oregon putting me on fast track to promotion. Thanks.

Take my word for it; you don't really want a new boss. Be careful what you wish for.

The contact instructions were a different motel and a new set of ridiculous verbal paroles. And shipping the Beretta Cheetah back to Frank wasn't what I'd had in mind. But he'd pass it on to me and probably verify that it was clean and untraceable. Certainly he'd have no objection to me wanting a weapon I could use on a job. Of course, after passing it through him, the EPA would have a record of it traced to me. That just meant I'd have to use another weapon if I ever decided to kill Frank. No problem there.

I'd earlier shoved all the Clayton Stillbridge gear—minus the .44, that is, and the ranger badge because I still had a use for it—into the shipping trunk and put it in the bed of the F-150 anyway, planning to dump it in a deep river somewhere on the drive back east. Now I'd just be handing it back to the .45-packing delivery dude. Admittedly, that would be a lot easier.

It was a sunny day, chilly but not freezing. Most of the snow had melted from the roads. I fired up the truck and left Ogloskie and it's significantly diminished population behind without bothering to say any goodbyes. No one there would miss me.

They'd miss Ruby, though. Eventually they'd wonder what had happened to her, contact authorities to start a search. What they found might even spark a few new stories and legends a lot more interesting than the myth of Ogloskie's ghost. Hell, maybe they'd even blame the bizarre deaths on the ghost of old Vladimir.

I wasn't so sure he hadn't been involved.

There was one more piece of business I wanted to attend to. It was personal. I drove around Prestonville until I found the Settler's Creek Medical Center, parked and went inside. I flashed the badge to the woman at the desk.

"You've got a patient here, Dewaldo Davis. I'd like to ask him a few questions."

"You're police?"

"Forest service." I hadn't given her too good a look at the badge, but some people can be pretty observant. "I just need to make out a report on his accident."

She typed something into her computer and studied the screen. "He had surgery late yesterday. He's probably still pretty sedated."

"Mind if I look in and see? I won't bother him if he's sleeping. I can always come back, but it's a long drive up from Ogloskie, and I'd like to get the report filed before the weekend. Forest Service likes us to be efficient."

"Well . . . " She wasn't sure.

"Besides, he's a friend of mine. I'd like to see how he's doing." Maybe appealing to her humanitarian side would be more effective than throwing my phony authority around.

"I guess that'll be okay, if you promise not to disturb him if he's sleeping."

"Wouldn't dream of it. I'm the one who patched him up and called the ambulance."

"All right." She smiled. I guess two weeks in the wilds hadn't destroyed my way with the ladies. "Just down the hall there. He's in room 37."

"Thanks so much." I smiled back at her. She wasn't bad looking, mid-thirties, trim, school-teacher glasses. Too bad I was on my way out of town.

The place was pretty quiet. I didn't have to run a gauntlet of nurses and doctors, just made my way down the corridor and let myself into his room. His leg was in a cast and elevated to provide traction, and an IV was attached, probably just providing fluids and sedation. Other than that, he looked a lot better than the last time I'd seen him. I pulled up a chair next to the bed and sat down, hoping my presence would rouse him. After a minute, his eyes fluttered open.

"How you doing, kid?"

"Clayton?"

"Yep. It's me."

"I'm in the hospital?"

"Settler's Creek Medical. Ambulance brought you here yesterday."

"Yeah, that's right. I remember." He was pretty doped up but his mind started clearing. "You dragged me back to Ogloskie. Saved my life."

"Just part of the job, kid." Somewhere in the Oquala, that grizzly was probably laughing again.

"Blue Feather's dead."

"You remember. That's good."

"Walker." He grimaced, whether in pain or grief I couldn't tell. "Walker killed him."

I stayed silent, letting it all come back to him.

"You told me Walker's dead." He closed his eyes, opened them again. "How'd that happen?"

"Well, kid, you're not gonna believe it"—I wasn't sure I did—"but the spirit of the Oquala appeared in the form of a big grizzly bear and took revenge for Blue Feather's murder."

He looked confused. Then he laughed and grimaced again. "Don't make jokes. It hurts when I move."

"Sorry."

"You know, I had the strangest dream out there."

"That doesn't surprise me. You were in shock most of the trip back." Not to mention the psychoactive drugs I'd been shooting into him.

"I guess so." He had a faraway look. "It was pretty vivid, though. Dreamed I woke up and you were talking to Vladimir Ogloskie."

"What was I saying to him?"

"He was telling you that the last Oquala Indian was dead, that he's free to stop haunting the forest. I guess that was Blue Feather, the last Oquala."

"Yeah, you were definitely out of your head." I didn't point out I'd had the same dream. Why feed a fantasy? "Besides, you don't really believe that old conman was an Indian, do you?"

"Why would he have lied about it? How was he going to con anybody out in the middle of the woods?"

"I don't know, maybe he was hiding from some victim he'd pissed off. Or maybe he was smarter than I'm giving him credit for. He was about to squeeze seventy-five grand out of Conifer, after all. Guess he didn't count on other companies using less subtle methods to remove obstacles."

"Yeah." He looked sad. Maybe he was remembering which company that was, the one run by his family. "So Walker's really dead."

"As a doornail, kid."

"Poor Ruby. She had a thing for him."

"Yeah, poor Ruby." I'd forgotten he didn't know about her. No one did, in fact. No one alive, anyway, except me. And when whatever local authority found her, they'd be looking for Dewaldo to ask him a lot of questions. Better to leave him in the dark and let him be surprised like everyone else.

"Who are you really, Clayton?"

"What do you mean?"

"You're not a forest ranger. You said you're not a cop. You obviously work for the government. So who are you?"

Death robed as justice, kid. Remember? "Ah, I'm just a civil servant. A fed. Came out here to look over the Oquala, write a natural resource report. Guess I just have a way of being in the wrong place at the wrong time."

"Sure. I didn't know federal resource engineers worked under cover."

"Guess that's a secret, too." As far as I knew, natural resource surveys might be classified. Just about everything the government does, it keeps secret. Keeps the public from figuring out what kind of government they have. "Speaking of keeping stuff to yourself, you might not want to mention what happened to Blue Feather to anyone."

"I can't just leave him up there. He should get a funeral."

"Oh, somebody'll find him eventually. And when they do, they'll find Walker." *And Ruby.* "You should plan on being somewhere else when that happens. Maybe back east with your family."

"What do I say if cops or somebody ask what happened to me?"

"Tell 'em you were out hiking with me and you fell off a cliff. That's what I told the EMTs."

"You're really not going to report Blue Feather's death? And Walker's?"

"Not to local authorities, kid. That's not my job."

"What are you going to tell them when they eventually find the bodies?"

"I won't be around any longer."

"What should I tell them about you?"

"Whatever you want to. They won't be able to track me down." I doubted anyone would try very hard, either. Cops lose interest real fast in people who just disappear. "But if you're smart, you'll tell anybody who asks that, as far as you know, I was just a ranger assigned here temporarily. You start telling stories about ghosts and government agents, cops are gonna figure you either cracked your head good or you're lying to cover something up."

"I guess you're right."

"And take my advice and get the hell out of here as soon as you're mobile."

"Okay." He sounded a little wistful. "There's really nothing to keep me hanging around here anymore."

"There's one more thing."

"Yeah?" He looked up at me with the saddest puppy eyes I've ever seen. I realized that Dewaldo is one of those lonely people who spend their whole lives looking for a friend or father figure. Now that Blue Feather was gone, he'd need a replacement. "Anything you want, Clayton. I owe you a lot."

"No you don't." He'd have to look elsewhere for a new pal and spiritual adviser. Even if I'd been available, I'm not exactly a good role model. "Besides, I just want to satisfy my curiosity about something."

"What?"

"I looked up your file."

"File? What file?"

"Everybody's in government databases, kid. Yours has an assault and battery conviction in it."

"Oh. Yeah, that. What about it?"

"I'm just wondering how a divinity student winds up assaulting someone." It really was just curiosity. I like to understand people I meet, even the ones I kill. It may be the one chink in my armor.

"Where'd you hear I studied theology?"

"Ruby told me."

He laughed, grimaced again. "That hurts. It's funny. She must have gotten that from Sven."

"Matter of fact, I think she said he's the one who told her."

"Big dumb Swede." He rolled his eyes. "First time I ate at his place, he asked me where I'm from. Told him my family lives in Georgia but I'd gone to college in

Cambridge, Massachusetts. So he makes a face and says 'Don't tell me. You one of those Harvard kids who studied Philosophy or Theology or something?' So I made up that Divinity degree stuff. Figured it'd make him happy, thinking he'd pegged me right."

I was impressed. That's the kind of thing I do. "So you lied. Good for you. What'd you study at Harvard?"

"I didn't go to Harvard. There are two schools in Cambridge. I went to M.I.T."

"You went to engineering school?" That surprised me.

"Only way my dad would pay for it."

"I'd have never taken you for an engineer, Dewaldo."

"I'm not. Engineering classes sucked. I cut most of them. Spent my time reading English lit, taking poetry classes."

"They teach poetry at M.I.T.?"

"It's a small department."

"Yeah, I guess so." But we'd gotten off the point. "So what about the assault conviction?"

"I was drunk. Beat up an English professor in a bar."

"An English professor?" That made me laugh. Again, it was something I could see myself doing. "You'll have to explain that one to me."

"I was minding my own business, reading Ezra Pound's *Cantos*."

"Ezra Pound?"

"The poet."

"Okay. At least now I know he wasn't the inventor of the pound cake."

"Very funny. Anyway, this prof comes by and asks me why I'm reading Nazi poetry."

"Ezra Pound was a Nazi?"

"No. He was a fascist."

"I thought Nazis were fascists."

"They were. But not all fascists were Nazis. Pound lived in Italy for awhile, admired Mussolini. But he wasn't a Nazi." He sounded disgusted.

"Gee, Dewaldo. That seems to me a mistake anybody could make. Hell, I've never even heard of Ezra Pound."

"Yeah, well you're not a professor of modern American poetry with a Ph.D. in English Literature. This guy was. He should have known better."

"So you beat up an M.I.T. faculty member because he insulted your favorite poet?"

"Yeah." He looked embarrassed. "Like I said, I was drunk. My family hired a big-shot lawyer who got me off with a suspended sentence. They kicked me out of M.I.T. though. Never got a degree. Dad made me go to one of those rehab clinics, too. Said I'm an alcoholic."

"And you believed him and stopped drinking." That was the saddest part of the story, I thought.

"Well, I have to admit, I tend to get belligerent when I drink. The psychologists at the rehab clinic said that's one of the first signs of alcoholism."

"What a load of crap." I despise psychologists; at least, I guess I would, if I ever met one. "One thing Blue Feather was right about. Booze doesn't make you kick somebody's ass. You do that because you're pissed off about something. Booze just stops you from keeping it bottled up."

"Okay. So what am I pissed off about that I won't admit to myself?"

"Probably the same thing every guy in the world is pissed off about. You're pissed because your dad's a jerk."

His face flushed. Maybe I was making him mad. Good. "Why would you say my dad's a jerk? You've never met him."

I met the professional killer his company hired. "No reason, kid. It's just, in my experience, most people are jerks, especially when they have kids."

"That's a depressing thing to say."

"Not at all. Just being realistic. So stop worrying about having an occasional beer. Let yourself get mad every once in awhile and you'll be fine. Or take up hunting. Killing animals is a great way to vent." I could have added that killing people is even better, but I didn't think someone who writes poetry is cut out for that kind of work.

"That'd make my dad happy. He's a big hunter. Thinks I'm a pansy 'cause I never wanted to shoot anything."

"So impress him for a change." And I'd almost forgotten the last thing I had to tell him. "By the way, I dropped your stuff off at your place before driving up here."

"How'd you get into my cabin?"

"Don't ask stupid questions. I dumped all your gear there, including that Colt Peacemaker you've been carrying. Where'd you pick up that relic? A garage sale?"

"It was my great-grandfather's. My dad gave it to me on my eighteenth birthday."

"You might want to get it framed and hang it on a wall someplace. You try to shoot it sometime, you're probably gonna lose a few fingers. Anyway, I left you a surprise."

"Really." His eyes lit up like a kid at Christmas. "What?"

"Blue Feather's M1. Something for you to remember the old con-artist by."

"The Garand?" He made a face. "I almost broke my thumb trying to load it."

"Yeah, it's a serious design flaw." I didn't mention that I was watching at the time. "Take it back to Georgia with you and learn how to load and shoot it. Could change your life."

He thought about it. "Okay. I will."

"Well, I gotta get going, kid." I stood up. "Been nice knowing you, Dewaldo."

"You, too, Clayton." At least he wasn't getting misty-eyed. "You ever find yourself in Macon, Georgia, look me up."

"Sorry, kid. Not gonna happen." At least, he'd better hope it didn't. Because if I ever looked him up, it would be because I'd realized letting him live had been a mistake. I walked out, through the corridor and exit, out to the F-150. I figured I could make Portland before sundown.

I'd had good reasons to let Alvarez and Dewaldo live. I didn't feel good about either decision, though. They'd both been involved in Davis Industries' anti-Conifer campaign; by all rights they were clients as much as Walker. One thought kept popping into my head as I drove through southwest Oregon that day.

Man, I hope I'm not getting soft.

Chapter XI
The Last Oquala

ARRIVING AT WASHINGTON DULLES early on Saturday morning after a red-eye flight from the West Coast with two layovers did not put me in a very good mood. I was already cranky about getting dragged back so fast. The verbal instructions I'd gotten from the Western Express guy still galled me.

"Frank said to hand you this envelope, give you this printout with your flight times and e-ticket number, and tell you to check your safe as soon as you get back." The envelope he handed me felt like it contained an ID and some credit cards. I shoved it in my pants pocket and looked at the itinerary.

"He wants me to go straight to my office when I get in on Sunday morning?"

"I just told you what he said. Me, I'd interpret it to mean go right there. But maybe you Washington types have a different conception of time than the rest of us. That's between you and him."

"Sorry. I forget you're just a delivery boy." I was hoping he'd take offense. Being called a "Washington type" pisses me off more than being referred to as an "agent." But he just laughed.

"Yeah, I'm not a big shot. Then again, I'm gonna sleep in late Sunday morning, maybe get up at noon and have a couple of beers. Enjoy opening your safe." We were talking in an even seedier motel room than our last meeting, his .45 again on the nightstand by the bed. A lot of low-class motels are going to lose customers if the government ever gets out of the spook business. "The room's paid for through Sunday. You can crash here and catch a cab to the airport. Give me the keys to your truck and I'll take care of it and your gear."

"Frank said you could ship some stuff to Washington for me."

"Sure. We're a shipping company. That's what we do." He rolled his eyes. "But whatever it is, it'll get there faster if you just take it on the plane with you."

"I know." I opened the knapsack I prefer as a carry-on and extracted the hideaway pouch I'd taken off Walker, dropping it on the bed. I took out the taser I'd retrieved from Walker's pack, too. That got a raised eyebrow from the delivery dude. Then I pulled out the Beretta Cheetah, spare magazines, and box of teflon-coated .38s and tossed those next to it. "But with all these new TSA regulations prohibiting toothpaste and mouthwash, I just don't know anymore what's allowed in my luggage and what's not."

He picked up the Beretta. "Cute. Don't see many .38s these days. Maybe I'll get myself one. If I decide to start carrying a purse."

"Well, it's a lot more subtle than that bazooka you tote around."

"Man, who wants a subtle gun? Defeats the purpose of carrying one." I could see his point. "Got an address to ship this stuff to?"

"Just ship it to Frank." I still had the two GPS units as well, but I figured I could stick those in my checked duffel, since they weren't lethal.

"Any message? He expecting this?"

"He's expecting it. But you can stick in a note that says the Beretta is a gift so he can play Russian roulette."

The Killer Trees 267

"You can't play Russian roulette with an automatic."
"I'm hoping he doesn't know that."

Being too cautious to take a cab straight to my apartment after arriving at Dulles as Philip Wepner, I caught a shuttle into Arlington, rode the Metro out to Fairfax, and grabbed a cab home from there, all of which made me even more tired and irritable. At least the weather wasn't too bad, cloudy and chilly but not raining. I'd had enough precipitation to last awhile. My mailbox was stuffed full with bills and junk mail—I never stop delivery when I'm away since I don't figure it's a good idea to put an announcement in a federal database that I'm away. I tossed it all on the kitchen table after dumping my bags in the living room, then grabbed my car keys. Might as well find out what miserable assignment couldn't have waited a few days.

At least the office was empty. I was in no mood to run into a curious colleague wondering where I'd been for two weeks. In fact, I'd half-planned to drive back from Oregon because I felt like taking some time to unwind. Shadow-boxing with a rival pro is a little more taxing than handling the usual losers I get assigned. I spun the dials on my safe, resolving to take care of whatever poor bastard turned out to be my next client as quickly as I could, then take a few days off whether Frank approved or not.

Inside was another envelope with *Richard* typed neatly on the front. I didn't even examine it for wires or other strange shapes. If Frank had called me back fast just to blow off my fingers with a letter bomb, I was tired enough to make it easy for him.

It was only the usual note, scrawled in his standard block letters.

Got a few things on my plate the next few days. Nothing pressing for you, so just do your paperwork and relax. Meet me for lunch Wednesday. Jersey Grill, Cleveland Park.

I stewed for a minute. What had he said in his last e-mail? *Work piling up, need you back soonest.* Son of a bitch. Then I laughed.

"Well, well, Frank. Are you developing a sense of humor?" So he'd finally jerked my chain. Maybe he wasn't a complete asshole.

I spent the rest of the day in the office typing up my report and accounting so it would be waiting for Frank's goon on Monday. Might as well get reimbursed as soon as possible. And the report was longer than most. I decided to give Frank enough detail to let him know I hadn't been screwing off, including an account of dragging Dewaldo to get medical treatment. I figured I'd been making my assignments look too easy. Maybe it was a good idea to let him appreciate how hard I really work.

I left out my parting conversation with Alvarez: I lied and said he'd lammed it before I got back from killing Walker. I left Karsten Felix Caruthers III out of the report, too. That was a lead I'd follow up personally when I got the chance. Alvarez had been right; I didn't want to risk tipping off the mole that I was onto him.

I didn't mention the grizzly or Vladimir Ogloskie's ghost, either. No point making Frank worry I was losing my mind.

Cleveland Park is an older, upscale neighborhood in DC surrounded by the Washington Zoo, the National Cathedral, American University and Rock Creek Park. I've never been to any of those places. The world I live and work in is enough of a zoo for me, and unlike everyone else in the Washington area, I'm not fascinated by pandas. Cathedrals don't interest me much, either, although if I ever decide to get religion, I don't think I'll go looking in a non-denominational one that advertises being open to "all faiths and perspectives." Tolerance isn't one of my strong points. I avoid universities, too, unless I've got a client who happens to be a student or faculty member at one. And Rock Creek Park is pretty much off-limits to anyone who's not a trendy jogger or serial killer. I don't fall into either of those categories—although some might argue about the latter.

I found the Jersey Grill and went in at exactly ten minutes before noon. I was hungry; spending the morning making sure I'm not being followed is a surefire way to work up an appetite. Bruce was hanging around outside as always, waiting until I showed up to pass the all clear to Frank. Hopefully his mood had improved since our last meeting.

The Jersey Grill wasn't what I was expecting—a sports bar with big screen TVs and jerseys of famous athletes hanging everywhere. It turned out to be a conservative, dimly lit seafood place that was trying to look like something out of the nineteenth century. My eyes took a moment to adjust when I went in.

"Do you have a reservation, sir?" A guy in a black suit with white shirt and black bow-tie was guarding the entrance. Frank had met me at enough restaurants to know I despise fancy places with tuxedoed staff. And he hadn't bothered to tell me whether he'd reserved a table. Maybe he was hoping I'd get pissed and beat somebody up.

"I'm meeting a business colleague here. I don't know if he made a reservation."

"What's the name?"

"Frank."

"Just Frank?"

"Yeah."

He looked at a list in a large, leather-bound book on a stand. "Sorry. No Frank on the list."

"That's too bad." Looking around the place, I got an inspiration. "Try Jack Ripper."

"Excuse me?" He scowled. "You're not serious."

"No Jack Ripper, either?"

"I'm afraid not." Now he was giving me one of those *we-are-not-amused* looks, which always make me want to give back an *I'm-not-fucking-impressed-by-you-either* fist to the jaw. "We are fully booked today."

I restrained the impulse to slug him. I had another idea. "How about Andy Jackson?"

He frowned. "No, that name is not here either."

"Maybe you're not looking for the right spelling." I took out my wallet. "It's with a J, as in J-A-C-K-S-O-N."

"Whatever are you talking about?" He looked up and rolled his eyes. I took out three twenties and set them on the reservation list in front of him.

"Andrew Jackson. Now you see it, right?"

He picked up the money. "Certainly, sir. My apologies. I'll have you shown to your table immediately."

"Thanks." I'd have preferred breaking his arm, but bribery is usually more effective at influencing people. And I didn't care. I'd just add an extra sixty bucks into my next expense report.

A tall, skinny kid in an ill-fitting tux led me to a table in the back and handed me a menu with a black-and-white photo of an attractive young woman who had obviously died a long time ago. It was a reproduction of an old poster. Emblazoned on the bottom was *The Jersey Lily*. At least I had an idea about the place's name at last.

"May I bring you a drink?" The kid had that bored look all waiters in pricey establishments seem to sport, the look that starts getting my blood up.

"What kind of beer you got?"

"It's a pretty long list. There are fifteen beers on draft." He glanced around, like he wanted to make sure no one was listening. "Honestly, if you like real bitter, English-style ale, just about any of them will do. I think most of them are made by the same brewery and they just give them different names for marketing purposes."

"I guess you don't have Bud or Miller on draft."

"I wish." He grinned. "Seems like every restaurant is trying to have the most exotic selection of microbrews and imports possible these days. Most people just want a cold beer like Budweiser. Hell, that's what I drink."

My blood pressure started to drop. This kid didn't seem all bad. "What's the closest thing you've got to Bud on draft?"

"Harp Lager, I guess. It's not bad. It's nine bucks a pint, though." He made a face. "Nine bucks for a beer. That's unbelievable, isn't it?"

"Par for the course these days. I'll have one of those."

He headed to the bar to get my beer. I looked over the menu, hoping to find something fried. I was disappointed. The kid came back with my glass of expensive suds.

"You recommend anything on the menu?"

"Well, the blackened salmon's pretty good. Comes with kinda chunky mashed potatoes that aren't bad." He made another face. "But they serve it with steamed broccoli and boiled carrots on the side."

"I'm not a big fan of those."

"Who is? Most people just push them out of the way and leave them on the plate. So you want to order the salmon?"

"Sure. Without the broccoli and carrots."

"Sorry. The chef's a real jerk. Went to some culinary school in California. I can tell him to hold the broccoli and carrots, but he'll just yell at me and put 'em on the plate anyway. Just push 'em off to the side."

I wondered if the chef was a classmate of Fred. Maybe his girl had dumped him, too, and he was taking it out on clients by trying to force them to eat vegetables no one likes. Fred was a drunk, but nobody complained about his cooking. Except Dewaldo, about the oatmeal.

"I'm meeting someone, so don't put my order in until you get his, too."

"Sure. I can do that."

"You worked here long?" I was getting curious. Honest waiters are rare.

"Three years. I go to American University part-time. Between this job and stocking shelves at the Safeway up the street, I almost make enough to cover my bills."

"If you don't mind my saying, you don't seem to like working here much."

He laughed. "There aren't a lot of job opportunities for guys working their way through college. Besides, this job's not so bad. I've been here long enough, the manager doesn't hassle me anymore. They have trouble keeping waiters."

"Why's that?"

"It's mostly businessmen meeting each other for lunch. They're lousy tippers." He caught himself. "No offense meant."

"Don't worry. I'm not a businessman."

"What do you do?"

"Civil servant. Federal government."

"Oh." It was a flat response.

"I guess they're lousy tippers too, huh?"

"Usually." He grinned again. "Don't sweat it. I'm not in this for the money. I work here because of all the great people I meet."

The place was starting to fill up. He went off to another table to take drink orders, leaving me to wonder what the hell was taking Frank so long. It was five past twelve. I'd give him another five minutes and then throw some money on the table and leave. You don't wait forever for a clandestine contact to show. If something's happened to them, it's best not to hang around to give someone the chance to make the same thing happen to you.

I was reaching for my wallet when Frank came through the foyer and headed to my table, Bruce following. They both sat down. This was a first. They looked irritated.

"I was about to give up on you, Frank. And you didn't warn me your date would be joining us."

"Asshole wouldn't let me in without a reservation." Bruce sounded pissed. "Wouldn't even let me in to drink at the bar. Said this isn't 'that kind of establishment.' What the fuck's that supposed to mean?"

"Calm down, Bruce." Frank glared at him. "You know better than to start arguing with civilians when you're on a job."

"I shoulda broke his fucking arm."

"That'd have impressed him." It was good to get a chance to needle Bruce again. "Think he'd have seated you before he called for medical attention or made you wait?"

"Fuck you, Paladin."

"Okay, both of you just stop." Frank decided to assert his authority, rein in his two goons. It was pretty funny, really. "We got a seat. Just order a drink and something to eat."

"How did you get in, Frank? You make a reservation here and didn't bother to tell me the name?"

"No. I thought this was some kind of sports bar and didn't think I'd need a reservation." So he'd made the same assumption about the name that I had. "I came in and found Bruce here arguing with the head waiter."

"Don't tell me. You told him you'd muzzle your attack dog if he'd let you in." Bruce growled at that, although I'm not sure he realized it.

"I explained that we were meeting a colleague and the head waiter asked if we were meeting Mr. Jackson. I said yes, figuring that would at least get us inside so we could see if you'd managed to get in somehow. And lo and behold, here you are, Mr. Jackson. Clever. Who's Jackson, anyway? You still using an alias? Those are supposed to be for assignments."

"Andrew Jackson. He was president a few years ago." He gave me a blank look. "His picture's on the twenty."

"Oh. That's how you got in." He glared at Bruce again. "Why didn't you think of that?"

"Just out of curiosity, Frank, how do you pick these restaurants?" I really was curious.

He looked back at me, suspicious. Maybe his method was classified above my clearance level. Hell, I'm not even sure what my clearance level is. "Well, since you ask, we've got a database of every restaurant in the Washington metropolitan area. There's this program we had a contractor develop that spits out a name every time I need one. It's got a sophisticated algorithm designed to make sure I don't fall into any regional patterns or restaurant types; makes every meeting location totally random."

"Wow. How many millions did that cost the taxpayer?"

"Five, I think." He'd picked up my menu and started perusing. Meaningful conversation stopped; his mind was on food.

The waiter came back to take their drink orders.

"Bring me a beer." Bruce obviously hadn't looked at the lengthy beer list on the menu.

"We've got fifteen on draft. Stouts, porters, IPAs." The waiter shot me a glance and winked, obviously aware that Bruce was having a bad day.

"Got anything that just tastes like beer?" I could see Bruce clenching his fist under the table. Whatever trouble he was having at home still hadn't cleared up, apparently.

"Just bring him one of these." I pointed to my glass. Diplomacy's not my strong suit. If Frank was going to keep relying on my tact to prevent Bruce from committing public mayhem at our meetings, there was an ugly scene in our future. "We've got similar tastes."

"You, sir?" The waiter looked at Frank. I braced myself for a long Q&A session about wines and beers. Frank knows nothing about either and often likes to display this fact.

"Iced tea."

That was a surprise. I waited for the kid to get out of earshot.

"Christ, Frank, you take the pledge?"

"I'm going home early this afternoon. Taking my wife out this evening to celebrate. I don't like to go home smelling like I've been drinking."

"Celebrate what? Your new promotion based on my work?"

"We closed on a new house yesterday. Moving in next week when we get back."

"Back from where?" Actually I was more interested in the new house. Frank moving up in the world might mean he'd come into some money. And someone in our office had recently been moonlighting, leaking my file to Darkmatter. I'd been right to omit that item from my report. Frank would be in a perfect position to knife me in the back for a little cash. It's not like I've ever really trusted him.

"West Virginia. We're spending the Thanksgiving weekend with my wife's family."

"Thanksgiving weekend?"

Frank looked up. It takes something to get his head out of a menu before he's ordered. "You are aware that tomorrow is Thanksgiving, aren't you?"

"Must have slipped my mind." Given that I go to my office pretty much when I feel like it, holiday schedules don't have a lot of meaning for me.

"You should think about settling down, Paladin, starting a family. Family's the most important thing." Frank stuck his nose back into his menu after serving up these words of wisdom. Apparently he'd forgotten his warning a few weeks back that wives are a "pain in the ass."

"Right. I need a wife nagging me about not being home enough. And I'm a great catch. Women are just lining up to marry guys like me." Who knows, maybe they are. Maybe assassins are at the top of every woman's dream-husband list. "How about you, Bruce? Got big holiday plans?"

"My mother-in-law's been staying at our place, so I'm spending Thanksgiving listening to her tell my wife how much better off she'd be if she'd married someone else."

"Oh." Something occurred to me. "How long's she been your houseguest?"

"Over a month." So that was the "trouble at home" Frank had mentioned   Bruce looked really miserable. "I think she's planning to stay through Christmas."

"Ouch."

The waiter returned to take their order. Frank had actually decided. It was a banner day for him, obviously.

"I'll have the trout almandine. What's that come with?"

"Mashed potatoes, broccoli, and steamed carrots."

"Can I get extra mashed potatoes instead of the broccoli and carrots?"

"Sorry, sir. No substitutions."

"Well, just leave them off, then."

"Can't do that, sir."

"Why not?"

"Don't ask, Frank." I wondered how often the waiter went through this with customers. Amazing, really, that the owners let the chef continue such a stupid policy. There were probably trash cans in the alley out back overflowing with discarded broccoli and carrots. Starving third-worlders would no doubt have been appalled. Then again, they probably don't like broccoli and steamed carrots any more than the rest of us. "Just push them to the side."

"Oh, all right."

"How about you sir?"

"Not hungry." Bruce was getting more and more sullen. "I'll just drink."

"Very good, sir." The waiter made a hasty exit. I didn't blame him. Bruce looked like a smoking volcano about to erupt.

"You not eating either, Paladin?" Passing on lunch is something Frank can't fathom.

"Already ordered."

"Oh. What're you getting?" How a government spook who supervises covert lethal activity can be so obsessed with food will always be a mystery to me.

"Blackened salmon. Waiter recommended it."

"Hey, that sounds good. Maybe I should change my order."

"I'll give you some of mine." I was hoping we could stop talking about holidays and seafood orders and get on with the business at hand.

"Great. Thanks." Things got quiet. Having Bruce at the table was turning out to be a real downer. Plus, I wasn't really sure how briefed-in he was about my work. I didn't feel all that comfortable discussing the details of a job in front of him. Frank apparently sensed that.

"Look, Bruce, I can manage without you the rest of the day. Why don't you take the afternoon off?"

"You sure?" He looked up like a kid who's been told he can leave the dinner table early and go play. "You don't want me to shadow you back to the office?"

"I'll risk it today. Why don't you just go home? Take your wife out to a movie or something. Everybody else in the federal government's getting early dismissal."

"Well, okay, if you're sure."

"I'll be fine. Don't worry. See you next week."

"Thanks, Frank. Have a nice time in West Virginia." His sour mood had vanished. He was almost whistling when he left.

"What the hell was that, Frank?" Security goons going erratic makes me nervous. "He's worse than last time. You think sending him home early to his wife and mother-in-law is gonna help? You might want to put someone on him to make sure he doesn't kill the two of them."

"Oh, he's not going home." Frank was looking thoughtful, like he was considering my suggestion to have Bruce watched. "He's got a girl on the side. I'm sure that's where he's headed. That's been the problem, I think. With his mother-in-law around, his wife's been keeping a tighter leash on him. He's getting tense, no chance to unwind." Apparently in Frank's world, the all-importance of family didn't stand in the way of a guy's basic need to relax periodically with a little infidelity.

"Well, I'm not real comfortable having him bird-dog our meetings while he's pissed off at the world."

"No, it's not at all conducive to clandestinity, is it? And he's usually so reliable. That mother-in-law is the problem. Wish there was some way to get her out of his life again."

"You could always arrange to have a bus run over her."

"Yes, that is what we do, isn't it." He was still looking thoughtful. I'd meant it as a joke. He'd obviously taken it as a serious suggestion.

"Frank, I was kidding."

"Oh." He gave me a nervous look, like a kid who's been caught ogling the cookie jar. "Of course. Me too."

"Right."

Our food arrived. As the waiter promised, the fish and mashed potatoes looked and smelled great. Both Frank and I shoved the broccoli and carrots to the side of the plate and dug in. Of course, Frank had to let me know how good his trout was while he was still chewing it.

"Have some salmon." I cut off a piece and slid it onto his plate. "It's good, too."

"Thanks. Sure you don't mind?"

"I've got more than enough."

"So," He was chewing salmon now, only spitting out a little. "I read your report. Nice work out there. The director is quite pleased."

"Director of what?"

"Our department, of course."

"Which is the EPA's department of . . . ?

"Oh, that's right. You're still not cleared for that." He shoveled some mashed potatoes into his mouth.

"Demarco was a real pro. His file's a foot thick, and that's just the part that's not restricted. Real feather in your cap, besting somebody with his experience and skill."

"Sometimes I get lucky."

"Don't be modest. You're getting a reputation as the department's go-to guy for sticky assignments like this one."

"Like I said, lucky me." I'd been hoping I'd seen the last of these figure-out-who-the-client-is nightmares and get back to straightforward jobs where I just get a name and address. "Maybe you should wait before you pat me on the back. When the local cops find all those bodies in the Oquala, they may not buy the convenient scenario I set up for them."

"That's not going to be a problem." Frank was beaming. "Getting that ranger killed was a stroke of genius, Paladin. Makes the whole thing a federal matter, her being a federal officer. US Marshalls will take control of the investigation, meaning we can dictate the findings."

"I didn't know the US Marshalls took orders from us."

"In a case like this, when we're working under high-level executive-branch authority, they do."

"I didn't arrange to get Ruby killed, either. She was too smart for her own good. Got suspicious of Treadman, stuck her nose in where it didn't belong, got greedy, and wound up in way over her head."

"Yes, too bad, really." It certainly wasn't affecting Frank's appetite. He continued to plow through his fish and potatoes. "But, you know, spilt milk and all that."

"You don't see me crying." I had to agree with him; regret's pretty useless. "Still, I can't say I'm happy about us getting dragged into what was just a corporate dispute."

"Neither am I." He shook his head slowly, scowling. "For what it's worth, the director called the CEO of Santomo personally with the news that their eco-terrorists turned out to be business rivals. The CEO was pretty chagrined. Said if he'd known it was just another corporation they'd have handled it without getting the government involved."

"Sure. Only go crying to Uncle Sam when it's scary environmental terrorists. When it's another corporation, I guess they prefer the free market. They'd have hired their own goons."

"Maybe not. Santomo's entered into negotiations with Davis Industries to sell them a piece of the Oquala contract."

"Nice." Corporations really do write the rules. Somebody has to, I guess. "Just a big misunderstanding. Nothing money can't fix. After all, a few dead Conifer employees can be replaced. Write the whole thing off as sunken costs. And there's plenty of trees to go around."

"Exactly." Frank put down his fork and took a big swig of iced tea. He seemed immensely satisfied. "There's one thing I'm not at all happy about, though. Honestly, you made an extremely bad decision on this job."

"Just one?"

"Hauling that hiking guide out of the woods was stupid. What were you thinking?"

I couldn't very well tell him the truth. "I don't know. I guess I figured three dead bodies were enough for one day's work."

"His body would have been easy to explain. You, on the other hand, dead of exposure out there; well, that would have had us scrambling back here. Losing a field operative is a big headache. I'd appreciate it if you don't get yourself killed trying to be a good Samaritan. That's not what we pay you for."

"I'll keep that in mind. Wouldn't want to cause you any grief."

He paused, looked me in the eye. I think he was trying to be sincere, not an easy thing for a spook. "I'm serious, Paladin. This work is risky enough without you taking crazy chances. Guys with your skills don't grow on trees."

It was almost touching, really, him trying to show real concern. I laughed.

"What's so funny?" He sounded irritated.

"Oh, nothing."

"I'm glad you find my advice so amusing." He didn't look glad.

"Don't worry, Frank, I'll try to be more careful. I appreciate your concern." Might as well let him think I bought his sincere routine. Spooks work so hard to manipulate people. Occasionally you have to let them think they're succeeding. "Got any more advice for me?"

"No." He resumed eating. The natural order of things had returned. "By the way, I had Bruce put Demarco's file in your safe. Read through it sometime. You might pick up a few tips. He knew his stuff."

"Will do." I could still hear Treadman/Demarco laughing it up after shooting Ruby. He was certainly somebody worth studying.

"What I don't understand, though, is how he wound up in our line of work." Frank put his fork down again, deep in thought. "There's an autobiographical essay he wrote at the academy in his file. He came from a long line of West Pointers, dating all the way back to the Civil War. Not just Demarcos, either. Claimed he was related to Pershing, William Donovan, Francis Lowry . . . "

"Who?" That got my attention.

"Francis Lowry. Cavalry officer who made a name for himself fighting Indians. Made it to Colonel before he was killed in the Spanish-American war. Demarco devoted a whole paragraph to him."

"Did he say how he was related to this Lowry?"

"One of his great-grandmothers was Lowry's daughter. She married Demarco's great grandfather shortly after he graduated from West Point. West Pointers are a pretty cliquish crowd." He signaled the waiter for the check. "Why the interest in Lowry?"

"Just curious. That hiking guide I saved was something of a local history buff. He told me the commander of the cavalry detachment that wiped out the local Indians in the 1880s was named Lowry."

"Probably the same one. Like I said, he was an Indian fighter. It's a small world."

"Yeah." And a pretty strange one at times. "Hell, Demarco didn't look like some blue blood to me. He probably made that entire biography up. For all we know, the whole file could be bogus. Federal agencies create fake histories for their goons all the time."

"We backstop covers for assignments. Nobody creates entire phony life histories like that. It's too much work." I was watching him closely while he talked. So he still didn't have a clue about Richard Paladin. "So who do you think he really was, then?"

"I don't know. Maybe he fell off one of those killer trees you mentioned earlier." And great-grandma was Lowry's adopted Indian princess. So Treadman/Demarco was maybe the last Oquala to walk the earth. I remembered my conversation with Ogloskie's ghost, involuntarily shook my head.

"You're looking a little tired, Paladin. Maybe you should take a few days off." The waiter had dropped off the check. Frank looked it over, did some mental calculations, pulled out his wallet and counted out the bill plus exactly fifteen percent. "Seriously, go find someplace to relax. Check in at the end of next week. Our clients can wait that long."

"I'm betting they'll be happy we're pushing back a few deadlines."

"Right."

"By the way, did you get that stuff I had your delivery boy ship back?"

"Not yet. What is it?"

"I took some phony papers off Demarco, extra IDs, credit cards. Figured they might raise a few questions when his body was found. I didn't realize we'd be sending federal rent-a-cops."

"I'll put them in his file. Should make a nice addition."

"I also shipped back the sidearm he was carrying."

"Why?" He looked puzzled. "You want me to run ballistics on it, check it against crime databases or something? You're not starting to take these cop covers I keep giving you seriously, are you?"

"It's a clean piece. Thought it might come in handy someday."

"Oh." The puzzled look vanished. "I'll have it checked out. If it's really clean, I'll have Bruce leave it in your safe."

"Thanks."

"I'd better get going. Don't want to keep the wife waiting." He stood up. "Well, have a nice Thanksgiving."

"Sure thing, Frank. You too. I'll hang out here, give you a chance to clear the area."

"Exactly." He started to leave, stopped, looked back at me. "Killer trees. I just got that. Like apple trees. Fell off a killer tree. Very amusing."

"I love to make you smile, Frank." Watching him walk out the door, I reflected on the fact that I'd enjoy wiping that smile off his face even more.

"Hope you enjoyed your lunch, sir." The kid had come back to collect the check.

"It was great. Hang on." I pulled out my wallet and tossed another twenty on the table. "You were right about government hacks being lousy tippers, too."

"Aw, I really wasn't complaining." He grinned. "But thanks."

"Don't mention it. What's your name, anyway?"

"Wesley."

"What're you studying up at that university?"

"Law and society." I must have made a face. "Hey, it's not that bad. Really, I just like good crime stories."

"You're not looking to become a cop or lawyer?"

"Well, I've thought about law school. But my grades aren't that good. Maybe I'll just try to hook on with a government agency."

I was thinking about Caruthers and unfinished business. I could drive down to Raleigh anytime and kill him, but I needed to find out who his source in my department was, which meant tailing him, collecting information on his routines, arranging a convenient time when I could sweat him without distractions. Going solo against an ex-spook in a complicated operation isn't smart, and I couldn't trust anyone I worked with.

"Interested in maybe making a little extra dough?"

He looked suspicious. "What you got in mind?"

"Don't worry, I'm not coming on to you." At least, not for sex. It's amazing how many guys assume you're gay when you start to make them an offer. "It's sorta national security work."

"What?" He laughed. "You want me to be a spy?"

"Not exactly. I need someone to help me watch somebody, make note of where they go, who they see, that sort of thing. It's more like being a cop on stakeout."

"Why would you think I know how to do stuff like that?"

"I'm sure you don't. I can show you." Random civilians are perfect for what I had in mind, like Alvarez using Dewaldo. They blend in better than trained spooks. And anybody can be taught the rudiments of surveillance. If he turned out to be a lousy student, I'd just drop him. "You seem like a kid with a good head on your shoulders. Tell you what, you spend a couple of weeks learning the ropes—I'm talking a couple hours a day, a few days a week—I'll pay you fifty bucks an hour. You decide it's not for you, we go our separate ways, no commitments. Except you're a few hundred bucks richer."

"I could use the money." So he was tempted.

"Write down your name and phone number. I'll call you in a couple of days, give you some instructions over the phone. Nothing illegal, don't worry. I'm betting you'll enjoy what I've got in mind." Of course, with Caruthers in North Carolina, getting this kid down there to watch him might not be feasible. But I could always have him tail Frank sometime.

"You really work for the government?"

"Absolutely, kid. And if you play ball, you may very well find yourself collecting a government paycheck someday, too." That was a lie, of course. I doubted Frank would hire someone on my recommendation.

"Why not? Sounds interesting. And like you said, if I don't like it, no commitments."

"My word on that." For whatever that's worth. He pulled out a pen and wrote his full name, Wesley Riley, and number on a napkin. I folded it up and put it in my pocket. "Be talking to you soon, kid."

"You gonna tell me your name?" He still looked a little suspicious.

"Sorry, almost slipped my mind." I stood up and extended my hand. "Millpond. Conrad Millpond."

"Nice to meet you, Mr. Millpond." We shook.

"Call me Conrad."

I spent the rest of the afternoon at the zoo. Okay, so I could give a shit about pandas and usually find zoos boring and smelly. But I had nothing better to do and actually had a hankering to stare at animals for awhile. Maybe the transition from wilderness to urban landscape had been too abrupt; I was having the land equivalent of the bends.

The Wednesday before Thanksgiving turned out to be a pretty quiet day at the Washington Zoo. There were no kids' groups, no busloads of tourists, just an occasional loner wandering among the exhibits—like me. I flattered myself, though, that I was the only killer ruminating about his last assignment.

Frank and our phantom director I'd never met might be pleased, but I was none too happy with the way things had gone in Oregon. Ruby and Blue Feather dead, Dewaldo lying crippled in a hospital, none of that had been necessary. I'd left the Army; I don't call in an airstrike to destroy an entire village because my client might be in one of the houses. I take pride in doing my work with some precision. In Oregon, I'd gotten sloppy.

I wasn't beating myself up, though. After all, the opposition had been a step ahead of me the whole way. Walker Treadman, Demarco, whoever the hell he'd been, had played with a stacked deck and I'd taken the pot anyway. That was something.

But I couldn't afford to get complacent, not with a rat in the basement leaking my assignments to Darkmatter goons and God knew who else. Caruthers didn't know it yet, but he was going to lead me to that rat. And then I'd take care of both of them. Hopefully the Riley kid would turn out to be a quick study—and maybe even a good clay pigeon. A plan was forming in my head.

I found myself leaning against the rail of a big outdoor display with rocks and bushes. An odd-looking black bear sat on one of the rocks, eating what looked like some kind of berry mush out of a bowl. I checked the sign along the fence; it said I was looking at an Andean Bear, also known as a Spectacled Bear. It was big, almost as big as the grizzly I'd gotten to know, but darker and shaggier. It wasn't paying any attention to me.

"Hey, hairy." Maybe I was going to talk to animals the rest of my life. It's a hard habit to break. "Met a cousin of yours recently."

It looked up at me, snorted.

"Yeah, he wasn't much of a conversationalist either."

Ruby popped into my head again. I'd been having trouble getting her out of my thoughts. Was I really getting that soft, pining after some dame I'd barely known, feeling bad because she'd gotten herself killed sticking her nose into my business?

"You know, hairy, she was right." The bear had gone back to its bowl of berry mush, ignoring me completely. "I'm wondering what I missed."

That was it. The long and short of it is that we're all just big, hairy primates. If we don't get our bowl of berry mush every day, we start to lose focus.

"Okay, Paladin. Time to get yourself laid again."

Life's pretty simple, really.

About the Author

DAVID E. MANUEL grew up in Houston, Texas and attended the University of Houston, receiving degrees in history and political science. After college, he worked for a few years in the corporate office of an offshore drilling company. In the mid-1980s he moved to the Washington, D.C. area and took a job with the U.S. Government, where he still works.

Made in the USA
Charleston, SC
05 December 2012